This captivating collection of short stories and visual art has something for everyone: a ghost, an unscrupulous businessman, a hot air balloon, murder, family, love...all set in and around Temecula, California. The anthology celebrates the unique character of the region; residents will recognize their hometown in charming detail, and readers from farther afield will want to visit. The original artwork that accompanies each story makes this collection a visual as well as literary delight.

— **Claudia Wair** writes literary and speculative short fiction. Her work has been nominated for the Pushcart Prize, Best Small Fictions, and Best Microfiction. She is also the author of *The MAP: A Ten-Minute-a-Day Journal.*

Finding a supportive in-person writer's group is a rarity, but when it happens, you get fascinating anthologies like Stay Awhile Longer. With stories for every mood and interest, you're transported to this lovely community and town of Temecula, CA without leaving your seat.

I want to visit the ghosts at Palomar Inn...and the 1909 restaurant... and Pennypickle's Workshop...and wine country...

— **Jennifer Worrell** is the author of *Edge of Sundown.*

Stay Awhile Longer

Longer: More Scenes from Temecula Valley

TVWI Book Two: Illustrated Short Stories

2

Cover art & design © 2024 by Ned Norman
Introduction © 2024 by Stacia Deutsch
Supervising Editor Trond E. Hildahl
Layout by Big Giant Media, Inc.

Published by TVWI
30732 Doral Ct
Temecula, CA 92592

First edition
Published in Temecula, CA (United States of America)
Published simultaneously worldwide

Identifiers:
ISBN: 979-8-9911302-2-6 (paperback 6x9)
ISBN: 979-8-9911302-3-3 (epub)

Disclaimer: The material in this book contains a mix of genres, language, and potentially triggering events.

TVWI is an imprint of
Temecula Valley Writers and Illustrators
"Creativity in Community"

This collection is dedicated to every creative —
well established, brand-new, or anywhere in-between —
that has ever toiled alone and longed for a community.

What you hold in your hands is tangible proof
that amazing things happen when we work together.

Table of Contents

Foreword

I WAS LONELY.

  As creatives, we tend to hole up in our caves, writing or putting the final touches on our art, or simply thinking. Being creative doesn't mean we don't need other people, it's just that we grow used to being alone.

  My husband and I moved to Temecula during the Pandemic so when I decided I wanted to get out of my cave, meeting people was difficult. I didn't know how to find a community.

  Then...one night...my Facebook Messenger buzzed. It was another writer in the Temecula Valley. She asked if we could have coffee. That meet-up with Felicia Horton turned into a small gathering of local writers. Gradually, artists joined us. Poets. Screenwriters. Over time, the coffees grew until we had too many people packed in the small café and needed more space.

  Someone from the group mentioned an anthology. Was it Trond Hildahl? Jeff Waddleton? Felicia, perhaps? I can't recall who lit the match, but once it sparked, the fire flamed bright. A small committee formed and we all began to ask the important questions: who, what, where, when, and most important of all — HOW?

  We met for pizza and by the time the last bits of crust were consumed, Kristen Trager, Rebecca Farnbach, Lori Carson, Tony Moramarco, and Veronika Childs had added their voices to shape the project into its current form.

Short stories are new territory for me. I've written longer children's books for years, had a few best sellers, but generally kept a distance from writing adult content. And yet, the instant the anthology was officially announced, the enthusiasm of the committee became contagious. Of course, I'd try my hand.

Tony brought the local artists aboard. We paired up the Valley's amazing talent: one writer with one illustrator. It was all so exciting that a commitment of one piece of art grew to two and the stories blossomed. Multi-talented artist and illustrator, Ned Norman, agreed to design the cover. We didn't even have to twist an arm to get Trond to take the entire project under his eagle editorial eye.

At the official "Temecula Valley Writers and Illustrators" 2023 holiday party, Jeff announced the anthology and outlined the theme: Stay Awhile: Scenes from Temecula Valley. So many writers asked to participate that once again, our group needed more space. Pages and pages of space!

From the sidelines, I watched the pairings turn in their amazing work, and wondered what kind of story should I contribute? I'd been writing mysteries for years. I'm quietly behind several Nancy Drew and Boxcar Children novels, so I decided to stick to the familiar genre, but longed to expand my vision in a new way. I signed up for a ghost tour of Old Town Temecula — and convinced some of other local talent to come along. To be honest, I don't know if ghosts exist or not. I'm admittedly a coward and would rather not find one. Until the night of the ghost tour, I'd never intentionally put myself in a possibly haunted space.

There were several ghosts reported lurking around the old Palomar Inn Hotel, including a "woman clad in black" who'd never had her story told. Her "name" felt inspiring. I'd found my angle. Looking back, perhaps I should have chosen a different entry to the broad theme of the anthology.

The committee had requested stories that linked to the richness of the Temecula Valley, but that was the only guideline. In these two volumes, you'll find wonderful tales, and amazing art that dives into the best of genre writing: horror, sci-fi, western, romance — whatever your taste, there's a story here for you.

Maybe I should have left the Woman in Black alone and followed author (committee member and editor) Kristen Tregar into a spiritual look at the Valley's deeply rooted equestrian community. Her story "Far From Here" is an intriguing twist on what you might think about destiny and soul mates. M.K. Warren's "The Journey" speaks of transformation and change. "The Rainbow Kid" by Brad Shaw Jr. adds yet another tone to the anthology with a captivating tale based on a historic unsolved crime.

Determination drove me, coupled with the drive to push past my own fears. There'd be no looking back, I was going to write about a local ghost! While walking around the inn with our guide, Dale Garcia, several narrative ideas flashed through my head. We used EMF sensors to search for ghostly energy. Some people in our group swore they saw orbs. No one saw the actual Woman in Black, though later, I wondered if I'd felt a hand on my back. Was it her? Or my husband messing around? I'd never know.

My story, a mystery about stolen gems and the reluctant captain who is tasked with the case, began to spill into consciousness as we left the inn, heading out to look for other ghosts down Front Street. It was there on the sidewalk, only a few steps away from the building, that I ran my tongue over the back of my teeth. I discovered an unexpected rough spot. I tried to ignore it, but found myself only half listening to Dale's next story about a murder and the ghost left behind. My brain was distracted with worry about my tooth. Finally, when we got in the car, I was able to look in the rearview mirror. Sure enough, the backside of my front tooth had completely broken off — something that I'd never experienced before. Never.

While I visited an emergency dentist, my mind flickered back to the Palomar Inn Hotel and the Woman in Black. Could it be that her story wasn't told because no one had dared to tell it? Could it be that she didn't want her tale told?

The dentist said the broken tooth could have been worse. He joked, without knowing about the ghost and the inn, that this was a "warning shot."

Perhaps? And yet, I mustered my courage and went back to the inn the following week with Ned Norman, the incredible artist who, in addition to designing the cover, would be creating illustrations for my anthology contribution. He was eager to hide clues, enhancing the mystery, in the artwork. This time, as we stood in the long, quiet hotel hallway, I know for certain that I felt a hand on my back, and unlike my husband, Ned is not the type to send my gutless, chicken-heart racing like that (or is he?).

I finished my story without further incident, and it's here for your review amongst the other wonderful contributions to this local anthology. Read the others first, then proceed to mine with caution. You've been warned.

Being part of this anthology has allowed me to stretch my writing style, to contribute to something lasting, and more — now that the Temecula Valley Writers and Illustrators is a formal organization, meeting regularly in the city space — I have met those creatives that I longed to find. I'm no longer lonely and my heart is full of gratitude.

Temecula is my home. The members of the **Temecula Valley Writers and Illustrators** are my inspiration. I am going to Stay Awhile.

Stacia Deutsch
Temecula, California
July 2024

"Meadow of Dreams"
Illustration by Kavitha Saminathan
Watercolor

Kavitha Saminathan

Kavitha is a self-taught, award-winning artist, driven by a lifelong passion for creativity. Having spent her childhood in India, she has always considered art to be an integral part of her life. In 2013, she discovered a profound love for painting and began an exploration of acrylics, creating Contemporary and Modern art with a focus on diverse textures. Recently, she has expanded into watercolors, embracing their deep therapeutic and calming qualities. Kavitha's work celebrates the joy of pursuing your passion and the fulfillment of sharing creativity with the world. Her works can be found in private collections around the globe.

THE GOLDEN TRIANGLE

Story by M. B. Bruce

Illustration by Amelia Kosmal
Digital

A STRONG GUST OF WIND slammed the office trailer's flimsy door wide open. The neat stacks of maps and property flyers on Connie Albright's improvised desk — an aluminum folding table mail-ordered from Montgomery Ward — fanned into chaos amid a swirl of dirt and debris. Amanda, her four-year-old, who a moment ago played quietly in the corner among a pile of Lincoln Logs, shrieked.

Connie lunged for the door and wrestled it shut. "It's okay — just the Santa Anas."

Amanda's face scrunched. "I hate Santnas!"

Despite her sour mood, Connie smiled at her daughter's adorable mispronunciation. "Me too, baby."

"Wanna go home," her daughter whined with a pouty face.

"We'll leave soon. Play with your toys until Mommy's done working, okay?"

"Okay," she echoed in a forlorn voice, then returned to the miniature red-brown logs and green roof slats.

Bittersweetness pressed against Connie's heart. Even-tempered and easygoing, Amanda was so like her father. There was a time, not so long ago, when the observation would have caused Connie unbearable grief. Now, she embraced her sadness as a testament to the love they'd shared. She only wished Kenny had lived long enough to meet his little girl.

Gathering up the papers scattered by the 'Devil Winds' as the locals so aptly called them, Connie glanced at the wall clock.

Half past three, and still no return call from Mr. Cordova.

He hadn't been overly thrilled with the offer received on his eighty-acre parcel. She could hardly blame him. Although all cash with a quick escrow, the buyer's offer was low; but with interest rates up over ten percent and the conflict in Vietnam dragging on, vacant land in the Temecula Valley just wasn't selling. Still, she'd hoped to hear back from him by now.

Caught between being perceived as pushy and a genuine concern that the buyer would withdraw their offer, Connie picked up the phone and dialed.

After the third ring, her seller answered; his deep voice pleasantly accented. "Buenos tardes."

"Hello Mr. Cordova. I hate to bother you, but—"

"Ahh, Connie! I was about to call you."

12

Her heart did a little flip. He sounded upbeat. A good sign.

"I've considered the offer and, after deducting all the costs involved plus your commission...I'm sorry, it's just not enough for me to be interested."

She closed her eyes and took a deep breath, trying to keep the disappointment out of her voice. "I understand."

"However, I have an idea. I own another property, five acres on Winchester Road just off the highway. If you're willing to take that in lieu of your commission, we have a deal."

"Gee, Mr. Cordova, I don't know...."

"Think it over and get back to me tomorrow. I'm in no hurry."

He may not be, but she certainly was. Connie had bills to pay and a little girl to feed and, for that, she needed money — not five acres of dirt and weeds in the middle of nowhere. "Okay...I'll think about it."

Replacing the receiver in the cradle, Connie leaned back in the folding chair and stared out the window. Billows of dust ghosted over the two-lane highway. Cars, in their haste to get to wherever they were going, whizzed on by. A tumbleweed blew across the parking lot, hit the rear bumper of her '71 Karmann Ghia, and broke apart.

Every weekend for the past six months she'd sat in this office trailer. And although sometimes people stopped on their way between here and there, a few even professing an interest in buying, no one ever did.

After Kenny was killed in action, Connie moved inland to Temecula because rent was cheaper than Oceanside. She got her real estate license in hopes of building a better life for her and her daughter. Struggling to launch a new career while living in a one-room flat behind a gas station and waiting tables to make ends meet, didn't exactly fit Connie's definition of success.

Pushing out of the chair, she knelt beside her daughter. "Time to go, baby."

Together, they put away the toys.

Maybe it was time to admit they had no future in California. At least in Nevada she had family willing to help. Her stomach churned at the thought. Not that she didn't love her parents, but she'd been on her own since eighteen. At twenty-three, she was too set-in-her-ways to retreat home.

Helping her daughter with her sneakers, Connie ushered her out the door and locked up. As they hurried down the metal steps, a gust buffeted the trailer. The warm wind carried the scent of sage and ragweed, making her eyes water. Her dark hair, charged with static electricity, rioted into a frizzy mess.

A pickup truck slowed and turned into the parking lot. One of those new, square body Chevys. Light blue, with white side panels. The driver, a sandy-haired man in his mid-to-late twenties, rolled down the window. "Excuse me, are you the real estate lady?"

Connie met his gaze over the roof of her car, assessing his inquisitive expression and polite smile. He didn't look like a serial killer. She raised her voice above the wind, "Yes. What can I do for you?"

"I inherited a piece of property from my grandmother,

somewhere around here. Been driving in circles trying to find it. I could use some help."

"Do you know what street it's on?"

He shook his head. "All I've got is a plat map, a legal description, and this." He held up an open Thomas Bros. map book.

Vacant land wasn't always easy to locate, but Connie had a knack for it. Once she situated her daughter in the passenger seat and closed the car door, she came around to the driver's side of the truck. "Let me have a look."

Through his open window, he passed her two loose sheets of paper. She laid them flat against the side of his truck, holding them down to keep the pages from flapping in the wind. By studying the plat map, and then the legal description, Connie had a pretty good idea where the property was located.

"The turnoff is just a couple of miles back up the highway. It's on an easement — that's probably why you're having trouble finding it. I'm heading that way. I could show you."

She handed back his paperwork and met his eyes.

Hazel, with flecks of green.

"If you're sure it's not too much trouble." His engaging smile came across as both shy and confident, transforming pleasant features into downright attractive.

She found herself smiling back. "No trouble."

"I'm sorry — where are my manners?" He stuck his hand out the open window. "I'm Aaron Temple."

"Connie." They shook. "Connie Albright."

* * *

By the time they reached the property, the sun hung low over the Santa Rosa Plateau. Connie pulled off alongside the dirt road. In her rearview mirror, she watched Mr. Temple do the same. As she got out, her daughter scooted across the seat toward the open door.

"Stay here, baby. I'll only be a minute."

"I wanna come, too," Amanda pleaded. "Please, Mommy?"

She'd always been a sucker for her daughter's big brown eyes. Besides, the poor kid had been cooped up all day. Now that the Santa Anas had calmed into an intermittent breeze, she didn't see any harm in letting her run around a bit.

"Alright. But don't wander off."

Beaming, Amanda scooched the rest of the way out of the car. Spotting an embankment, she scampered over to tromp footprints into the soft dirt.

"And watch for snakes," Connie called after her.

Aaron Temple stepped from his truck and walked toward her. Taller than she expected, he had to be every bit of six foot, and then some. By the way he carried himself — back straight, shoulders level — she suspected a military background. In a West Coast counter-culture dominated by bell bottoms and paisley shirts, his bootcut jeans and flannel button-down painted him a fashion rebel.

Keeping one eye on Amanda, she met him at the tail of her

car.

He nodded toward the vacant parcel of land on their side of the road. "This it?"

"Best I can tell. Of course, I'd recommend a surveyor mark the corners before you do any improvements."

Scanning the rolling terrain, he nodded, his expression thoughtful. "Not sure what I'm going to do with it. Whole thing came as a surprise. Didn't even know Grams owned property out here."

Not wanting to pry, she hadn't asked. But now, the moment seemed appropriate. "I'm sorry about your grandmother. Were the two of you close?"

He shook his head. "She moved to California when I was little. Once, maybe twice a year, we'd come to visit. I was on tour when I got word she'd passed."

His words confirmed her suspicion that he was a veteran. "Welcome home," she said softly, and meant it.

He held her gaze in silent appreciation. "Nice to hear somebody say that."

"Mommy, Mommy! Look what I found!" Amanda skipped up to them holding something shiny in her hands.

"What do you have there, baby?"

As Connie took the triangular-shaped object from her daughter, static electricity jolted her fingertips. Not enough to hurt, but it startled her. The flat, gold-toned compact was caked with dirt. Brushing it off, she pried open the lid. The mirror inside was so dirty she couldn't see her own reflection.

"Can I keep it, Mommy? Can I?"

"That's up to Mr. Temple. You found it on his property."

Unabashed, Amanda refocused her efforts. "Can I, Mr. Temple?"

His smile was immediate and without reservation. "Of course. Finder's keepers."

With a squeal of delight, Amanda reached for the filthy thing.

"Not so fast." Connie kept it out of range. "We don't know where it's been. Let me clean it up. And what do you say to Mr. Temple?"

Rocking toe to heel, Amanda batted her big browns at him. "Thank you, Mr. Temple."

"You're quite welcome."

"Now, go play. We'll be leaving in a few minutes."

Apparently satisfied, Amanda wandered away, all her attention trained on the ground in search of more treasures.

"She's a little charmer." He glanced Connie's way. "Bet she has her daddy wrapped around her finger."

His comment took Connie by surprise — though it shouldn't have. After all, she still wore her engagement ring; mostly to honor Kenny's memory, but also to dissuade men's unwanted attentions. To avoid complications, she usually allowed the assumption to stand. But with Aaron Temple, she didn't feel the need.

"Amanda's daddy didn't make it back." From the pained sympathy she saw in his eyes, Connie knew she needn't say more. "I — I need to go...but if you have questions about the market or decide to sell, I'll be in the sales office tomorrow at ten. It was nice meeting you, Mr. Temple."

"Please...call me Aaron." And then, as if realizing he might have overstepped, he stammered, "I mean, if you want to."

His uncertainty made her smile. "I'll keep that in mind."

As they parted ways, the sun finally surrendered to the horizon, the warm glow of late afternoon scoring the underbelly of distant coastal clouds. The winds had died down and shifted, cooler air off the ocean supplanting the hot breath of the Santa Anas. A soft breeze ruffled her hair as she opened the passenger door for Amanda.

Once settled in the driver's seat, Connie took a closer look at the grimy compact her daughter had found. It appeared quite old, the edges slightly worn, with a faded Faberge sticker on the back. She'd never seen one like it before. Where had it come from?

Amanda squirmed in her seat. "Can I have it now?"

"Let's see if I can get some of this dirt off."

Pulling a rag out of the glove box, she wiped the outside before opening it. A hazy film obscured her reflection. With the tip of the cloth, she rubbed the surface in repetitive, circular motions.

In her rearview, she watched Aaron Temple climb into his truck. Tall, good-looking, polite; he was the first man in a long while to pique her interest. Since her daughter was born, Connie hadn't dated much. Partly because, as a single mom, it was hard to find a decent guy; but mostly, she just hadn't felt ready to move on.

Although she barely knew Aaron, his sincere manner put her at ease.

Maybe she should give him a chance.

A glow flared from the compact in her hand. Startled, she jerked the cloth away. Glittering gold sparkles swirled on the mirrored surface. An image formed — not her reflection, but rather one of Aaron carrying Amanda on his shoulders, a stick of fluffy pink cotton candy in her hand. Both grinning, they headed toward a brightly lit Ferris wheel.

Connie gasped and dropped the compact into her lap. The lid snapped shut on impact, extinguishing the golden glow.

"Oooo, a light!" Amanda bounced in her seat. "Can I see?"

"Hold on, baby."

With trembling hands, Connie picked up the compact, reopened it, and stared at her reflection. The glow, the glittering swirl, the impossible images, were gone. "What in the world...?"

She closed the lid.

Opened it again.

When nothing happened, she snapped it shut.

In her driver's side mirror, she saw Aaron sitting in his truck, engine running, probably waiting for her to leave first — the gentlemanly thing to do. When she didn't, he pulled out and around, leaning over to roll down his passenger window.

"Everything okay?"

At a loss as to how to respond, she smiled at him like an idiot. She didn't dare tell him what she'd seen in the mirror. He'd think she was nuts. "Yes. Fine. Thanks." Laying the compact beside her on the seat, she waved goodbye and pulled away.

Aaron's truck fell in behind, following at a distance. When they reached the highway, she turned toward town, while he headed in the opposite direction. Idly, she wondered where he was going. She got the impression he wasn't from around here, but hadn't asked. Which meant, unless he made the effort, she'd probably never see him again.

Though it would be nice to find someone, she wasn't looking for a knight in shining armor to come to her rescue. She needed to make it on her own. Working two jobs while raising a child, Connie acknowledged she was under a lot of pressure. Was that what this was about? Some romanticized fantasy conjured by an over-stressed, overworked mind? By the time they reached town, she'd almost convinced herself that she had imagined the whole thing.

The click-snap of the compact's lid opening and closing caught Connie's attention. Lost in thought, she hadn't noticed her daughter pick it up off the seat.

"Mommy, how do I get the lights to work?"

So much for it having been her imagination.

* * *

After dropping Amanda off with the sitter, Connie headed to her second job. As she rushed in the back door, Tom Morganstern — chief cook and owner of the Rancho Café — scowled at her.

"You're late." He slid a plate of daily special onto the counter. "Third time this week."

Connie pulled her dark curls into a ponytail. "I know. Sorry."

"You're always 'sorry.'"

"Aww, lay off, Tommy." Madelaine, his wife, and the real boss of the place, swooped into the kitchen to pick up the order. "Can't you see the kid's doing the best she can?"

"And that's my problem, how?"

Madelaine rolled her eyes. "Don't listen to him. I never do."

Connie grimaced. She hated being the cause of an argument. Not that they needed an excuse. The middle-aged couple had been together since high school and, despite their constant bickering, neither one seemed to be going anywhere.

"Order up!" Tom bellowed in his gruff, could-have-been-a-drill-sergeant voice.

Connie tied on her apron and checked the pending order carousel. "Where do you need me?"

Madelaine tossed instructions over her shoulder as she headed toward the dining room. "Table three just got seated. Eight's ready for their bill."

Grabbing an order pad and pencil, Connie followed her out the swinging door.

It was shaping up to be another busy Saturday night.

* * *

A half hour before closing, the door chimed.

22

Connie sighed. If the late arrival wanted more than pie and coffee, she'd be late getting home. Which meant she'd have to give the babysitter a little extra...again.

The well-dressed couple hovering inside the doorway didn't look like the Rancho Café's usual customer base of locals, truckers, and tourists. The handsome man, trendy in a patterned satin shirt and tailored slacks, had a good ten years on the platinum blonde clinging to his arm. Her tight-fitting cashmere over flaring, rhinestone-studded bellbottoms clamored Hollywood chic. Amid the Café's décor of rusty farming implements, ceramic cows, and rooster art, they looked ridiculously out of place.

"Darling, isn't this just the quaintest?" The woman appeared genuinely enthralled. "We must do something like this — for the guest house, at least. What do you think?"

The man offered a non-committal grunt.

Connie greeted them with her best hostess smile. "Sit anywhere. We still have homemade peach cobbler and one slice of apple pie left. Coffee?"

"Not now, thank you," the man said as he waited for the woman to choose a table, then held the chair for her. "Perhaps after dinner."

So much for getting out of here on time.

Tom and Madelaine had gone home, leaving her and the relief cook, Sergio, to close. Once she took the couple's order, Connie called the babysitter, then claimed a stool in the kitchen for a much-needed break.

When she sat down, something hard gouged her skin. She

forgot she'd shoved the compact into her pants pocket before her shift began. After the weirdness this afternoon, she wasn't about to allow Amanda to play with it unsupervised.

Pulling the compact out, she turned the triangular case over in her hands. Looking for what exactly, she didn't know. Opening it only revealed her own weary reflection. No radiant glow. No sparkles. Just a plain old mirror. She tapped the surface with her fingernail, then searched around the edges for an on/off switch, a button, or some other way to activate the light show, but didn't find anything.

"Order up." Sergio grinned at her across the counter. "And turn the sign. Kitchen's closed."

"Whatever you say, Serg."

Hopping off the stool, Connie slid the compact back into her pocket. Dinner plates in hand, she headed for the dining room. As she approached the table, she overhead the couple talking.

"You heard him," the woman said. "He thinks Temecula has the perfect climate."

"Even if he's right, it will be years, maybe decades, before one could expect any significant return on investment."

"What do I care about 'return on investment?' I want what I want." Pouting prettily, the blonde looked at her companion from beneath unnaturally long lashes. "Besides, I think Ely's onto something. His vineyard is lovely, and I was quite impressed with our barrel tasting. For a first year's harvest, of course."

"Here you go." Connie set the plates down in front of them. "Can I get you anything else?"

24

"A crystal ball would be helpful," the man grumbled.

Connie blinked. The off-hand comment ignited a strange, and entirely improbable, thought. "Excuse me?"

"Don't mind my husband," the woman said. "He always gets this way when I'm about to spend a lot of money."

The man raised an eyebrow at his wife.

With a polite nod, Connie retreated. "Enjoy your meal."

After turning the door sign to 'closed', Connie hurried into the kitchen. She considered herself level-headed and practical, and here she was contemplating the possibility that the compact was some sort of mystical prognosticator.

Ducking into the storeroom, she pulled the compact out of her pocket, took a deep breath, and opened it.

Nothing happened.

She closed and opened it a couple more times.

Still nothing.

Frustrated, she frowned down at her reflection. There must be something she was missing. Some piece of this puzzle. Then she remembered; she'd been wiping the grime off the mirror while thinking about Aaron. Not just thinking about him — wondering if maybe she should give him a chance.

With the tail of her apron, she rubbed the mirrored surface in a circular pattern, like before. Only this time, instead of Aaron, she thought about the Hollywood couple and their conversation, wondering if the woman was right — if Temecula was a good place to grow wine grapes.

Light bloomed, the mirrored surface aswirl with glittering

sparkles. An image formed of a country road winding through rolling green hills. She recognized the terrain: Long Valley Road, renamed Rancho California recently by developers. As she watched, the image of the naturally verdant valley changed. Those same hills now covered with vineyards dotted by elegant estates, as far as the eye could see.

Gaping at the sweeping vista, Connie leaned against a stack of produce crates to steady herself, and whispered, "I'd call that a 'yes.'"

It made her wonder what the future held for Aaron's property.

The golden sparkles returned, momentarily obscuring the image before swirling into a new one of the unpaved easement road fronting the weed-covered hills of Aaron's parcel. A heartbeat later, the vision transformed into one of a wide, paved boulevard amid a tract of new homes.

If what the mirror showed was true....

Focusing her thoughts on Mr. Cordova's five acres on Winchester Road, she willed the mirror to show her what that property would look like in years to come.

Again, the surface glittered and swirled, revealing a vacant parcel of land just off the highway. As she watched, the image shifted into one of a massive shopping center. A dark-haired young woman — a familiar, jaunty bounce to her step — crossed the parking lot. She reminded Connie of...Amanda?

"Connie?" Sergio poked his head into the storeroom, a dishtowel in his hands.

She snapped the triangular lid shut.

"You alright?"

"Yeah. Fine." Pocketing the compact, she straightened away from the produce crate.

He studied her curiously, then bobbed his head, indicating the direction of the dining room. "I think they're ready for their bill."

Still trying to make sense of the situation, Connie tamped down her frazzled nerves and headed that way. She felt like she'd landed smack dab in the middle of a fairytale; the compact, a cross between a Magic Eight Ball and the Evil Queen's Mirror-on-the-Wall, with a pinch of Aladdin's Lamp thrown in. That was the best way she could think of to describe what was happening. As crazy as it sounded, she truly believed that the Golden Triangle was showing her the future of the Temecula Valley.

Tallying the bill, she met the couple at the register. "How was everything?"

"Good." The man pulled out a neatly folded wad of bills from his money clip. "You live in the area, don't you?" Without waiting for an answer, "What do you think about Temecula's investment potential?"

"I think" — Connie took a leap of faith and handed him her real estate card — "the future looks promising."

* * *

When Connie arrived at the land sales office the next

morning, the phone was already ringing. After rummaging frantically through her purse to find the keys, she had to jiggle the trailer door's deadbolt to get the lock to turn. Rushing in, she plopped hers and Amanda's lunch boxes on the aluminum folding table and lunged for the phone. "General Realty, Connie Albright speaking."

"Miss Albright? This is Sharon Nielsen. We met last night at the restaurant."

"Oh, yes, Mrs. Nielsen — good to hear from you." A jolt of excitement elevated Connie's voice. She sucked in a breath to calm herself before continuing. "Hope the drive back to Beverly Hills wasn't too terrible."

"Despite the traffic, we made it in record time."

Noticing her daughter still standing in the open doorway, Connie covered the receiver and whispered, "Amanda...come in and close the door."

Her daughter didn't do either of the things she was told. With the gold compact clutched in one hand, Amanda pointed out the door with the other. "Mommy, the man in the truck is here."

"So, you see, Connie," Mrs. Nielsen continued. "May I call you that?"

She uncovered the receiver — "Of course." — then covered it again.

Craning to look past her daughter, Connie spotted the blue and white Chevy in the parking lot. Her stomach did a little tilt-a-whirl. Switching the phone to her other ear, she smoothed her unruly curls away from her face.

The soft scrape of boots on the metal stairs and, a moment later, Aaron Temple filled the doorway. Seeing that she was on the phone, he hesitated.

She waved him in.

That's when she realized that the woman on the phone had continued talking. And Connie hadn't heard a word of it. "I'm sorry, Mrs. Nielsen. What were you saying?"

"I said that Barry and I plan to come out later this week to look at property."

She grabbed a pen and yellow legal pad. "Let me jot down the particulars of what you're looking for."

Five minutes later she had a firm appointment with the Nielsens and a list of their preferred criteria. She repeated everything back, just to make sure.

"I can tell you're thorough. My husband and I appreciate that quality in those with whom we choose to work." Although sweetly spoken, the implied expectation was clear.

"I won't disappoint you, Mrs. Nielsen. See you Thursday." Connie hung up, smiling, confident she'd be able to find the perfect property for them.

Looking up from her notes, she noticed Aaron smiling, too. Not at her. At Amanda. While she was on the phone, Aaron had hunkered down to her daughter's level. They appeared to be holding their own conversation.

"Sorry about that." She rose and came around her makeshift desk. "What can I do for you, Mr. Temple?"

"Aaron," he corrected as he straightened, meeting her eyes.

A pleasant tingle warmed her cheeks. "Okay...what can I do for you, Aaron?"

"I'm considering selling my grandmother's property. Thought I'd stop by to see what you think it's worth."

She didn't even hesitate. "I think it doesn't matter what it's worth, because it'll be worth a whole lot more in the future. I suggest you hold onto it."

His eyebrows rose. "You realize you're talking yourself out of a commission."

"For now." She bit her lower lip, trying to hide her secret smile. "But I have a hunch, when all's said and done, I'll do just fine."

Aaron held her gaze, his smile deepening. "I believe you will."

"Mommy, look what Mr. Temple gave me."

It took more effort than expected for Connie to tear away from his warm regard.

"What do you have there, baby?" She bent to see what her daughter had clutched in her little fist; two rectangular strips of thick paper — tickets, of some sort.

"The Farmer's Fair opened this weekend." Aaron cleared his throat. "I thought maybe the two of you would like to go."

"Can we, Mommy? Can we?" Amanda jumped up and down.

She took the tickets from her daughter. They were full access. Good any day.

Despite the obvious ploy, she had to give Aaron credit. By

including Amanda in his plans, he'd made it nearly impossible to turn down his invitation. Holding up the tickets, she cocked an eyebrow. "So? Where's yours?"

He pulled a third ticket from his breast pocket — his expression of shy confidence utterly disarming. "I was kind of hoping you'd ask."

Connie laughed.

"Can we go today, Mommy?" Amanda bounced on the balls of her feet. "Please? Can we?"

"I think it'll be okay to lock up early, this once." Tucking a wayward curl behind her ear, she glanced at Aaron. "After all, I am spending the day with a future client."

Eyes alight, he gestured over his shoulder. "Give me a minute to clear off the passenger seat."

"No rush. I need to make a call first, anyway." She couldn't wipe the grin off her face.

Neither could Aaron. "I'll be outside when you're ready." Then he was out the door and down the stairs.

"He's nice," Amanda announced, as if an unquestionable truth. "I like him."

"Me too, baby." More than she expected to like any man ever again. "Me too."

Retrieving the compact off the floor where her daughter had abandoned it in her excitement over the tickets, Connie studied the bizarre, mystical device, not entirely sure what she should do with it.

So far, the mirror had revealed the possibility of good things to come. But Connie suspected there was a danger in knowing too much about the future. For now, she knew enough to make, what she hoped, would prove to be the right decision.

Setting the Golden Triangle down on the aluminum table, she picked up the phone and dialed. While she waited, she spun the compact like a top, the surface glinting magically in the morning sunlight.

Through the office trailer window, she caught sight of Aaron. Finished with making room for them in the cab, he leaned up against the side of his truck to wait. For the first time in a long while, she felt like the heroine of her own storybook tale. One that promised a happy ending.

Her client answered; his accented voice, warm and friendly. "Buenos dias."

"Hello? Mr. Cordova? I thought about your offer" — she spun the compact again — "and I've decided to take you up on it."

Looked like she was going to stay awhile, after all.

Contributor Biographies

M. B. Bruce

Michelle's love affair with speculative fiction began between the pages of a hand-me-down copy of Frank Herbert's *Dune*. She's scripted commercials, music videos, and short and feature films. Her fantasy novel, *Minstrels' Daughter* took First Runner-Up in Mele Publishing's Starving Writers Reprieve. A believer in supporting fellow writers, she facilitates critique groups, speaks on panels, and hosts retreats. In her private life, she's an avid reader, roleplay enthusiast, and life-long skier. Writing under the name M. B. Bruce, she resides in Southern California with her husband, children, seven chickens, four goats, four cats, and one very spoiled rescue dog.

Amelia Kosmal

Amelia is a 19-year-old concept artist and entertainment design student. She integrates her passion for storytelling with art by crafting narrative-driven projects and illustrations. Currently pursuing her education at ArtCenter College of Design, she specializes in character and environment design. She is dedicated to refining her skills and expanding her creative vision with the goal of creating impactful stories that resonate with audiences in entertainment and beyond.

THE RAINBOW KID

Story by Brad Shaw Jr.

Illustration by Arman-Justin Solis
Digital

SIXTY MILES NORTH OF San Diego, the gorgeous green and amber rolling hills of the inland valleys are separated from the Pacific by the southernmost portion of the Santa Ana Mountains. Fortunately, enough moisture sneaks through the Rainbow Gap to keep the semiarid land from turning into a desert. Back in the day, relative newcomers and opportunistic European immigrants saw the engaging landscape as a pot of gold to be plundered. More in love with the riches the land provided than the land itself, these early settlers dug in for the long haul and for the most part their vision was realized. But as orchards, farms, and ranches grew it soon became apparent there was not enough water to go around. While the inland valleys were filled with numerous small creeks and dry riverbeds that became raging torrents flooding the land every few years, on average, there was not a sufficient and steady source of water, a basic requirement for the ranch owners and farmers. To remedy the situation, a few of the more well-to-do owners collaborated and acquired most of the land along the creeks and proceeded to build dams. This was good for the select few, but smaller land holders found themselves out of business or beholden to the newly formed water companies.

After a few plentiful years, and sitting on wads of cash, these same progressive citizens decided that a bank was what the community needed to continue its expansion. A fine concrete structure was erected and named the First National Bank. Soon thereafter, the wealthy ranchers and farmers who established the bank discovered lending money was almost as profitable, and a lot less work, than tending cattle or tilling the fields. All things considered, over the next couple of decades, businesses large and small that owed their success to the land managed to feed their families and keep shirts on their backs. Although, some better than others. Into this pleasant but not always egalitarian community, there occurred an unexpected disaster: the Great Depression.

Some small farmers and ranchers managed to keep their doors open but quite a few just slipped away into the night. The very large owners, the ones who directed and owned the bank and sat on the board of the water companies, held tight. They realized the Depression was a passing thing. It might take a while, years even, but it would eventually end. If a few of the smaller concerns failed, the bank directors would simply repossess their property and wait. The rich landowners did not see this behavior as immoral or view the small starving farmers as a menace. They didn't see them at all. In their minds, loss was part of the nature of things. Much like a calf that was doing poorly or an injured lamb, since only the strong and healthy survived, it only made good sense to put the weaker ones down.

In all fairness, some of the old guard was forced to cut back on buying a new piece of equipment or building a new addition to the homestead, but their kids still had food on the table and new shoes. It was a different story for the small landowners. Sitting on the outside, those without the sufficient financial resources had some hard decisions to make. Their future looked grim. Folks with growling stomachs and no prospects often made poor life choices. As a result, sometimes, a few legends were created.

* * *

The golden California sun floated casually above the swaying trees behind Mother's Café on Front Street. There wasn't much of a breeze and a tick away from nine o'clock in the morning the temperature was already hovering around ninety degrees. Denny Wheeler, an occasional ranch hand and still a youngster at nineteen, put in a grandiose appearance by locking up the brakes in the Model A and sliding to a stop with a flourish. The display was primarily for his girlfriend, Abigail Rainwater, who sat at one of the picnic tables adjacent to the café's parking lot. But on this warm August day, she was a little difficult to recognize as she wore a pair of men's denim dungarees and a checkered blue short-sleeve shirt. To top it off, Abby's silky blond hair was unceremoniously stuffed up into a green John Deere baseball cap. She could easily be mistaken for a boy. Although, a very pretty one.

Denny slid over to the passenger side of the Ford and gazed through the open window to have a better look at the lovely vision of Abby. She approached with both hands gripping an ancient carpet bag adorned with red and pink roses. It had been her grandmother's. Abby was packed and apparently eager to move on. This was going to be their big day.

"Where did you get the car?" she asked displaying a worrisome frown. "I saw one just like it cruising through town only a few days ago."

"Never you mind where I got the car," was his short response. "Are you ready to roll?" Denny didn't wait for her reply and pointed to the driver's seat. "You drive. You can throw your stuff in the back."

Abby grinned as she surveyed the shiny and almost new vehicle. She practically pranced around the bright yellow Ford. "Are you sure you want to go through with this?" she asked while tossing the bag behind the driver's seat.

Denny paused a moment to admire the gentle curve of Abby's apple cheeks and her long pale eye lashes. "Not sure we have any choice. How else are we going to get out of this crummy little town? Our parents have nothing, so we have nothing. They can barely afford to feed us." His words were harsh but true. It was 1930, jobs and cash were scarce, and nearly adult children still living at home were more of a bane than a joy.

"The whole thing seems risky to me," Abby responded, more in the form of a question than a statement.

"I know, but everything is risky these days," Denny answered. "I don't want to spend the rest of my life shoveling shit in Temecula. How about you? Want to change your mind?"

"No, I'm ready to leave. I just need to be wherever you are."

"Great, let's get this show on the road." His tone was euphoric.

"Okay Denny, but I hope you're right. It's not only your ass on the line if things go wrong." Abby flashed a quick smile as she fired up the Model A, stomped on the accelerator, and dumped the clutch spinning the rear tires.

It was a short ride and Denny lackadaisically scanned the smattering of buildings on the west side of the street. His eyes lingered on the Ramona Inn as he recalled a few happy, but rare, days rubbing elbows with the more affluent patrons and retirees inside the blind pig. Riverside County was mostly 'dry', but the Inn offered pool tables, card games, and more than a few illegal refreshments, all things Abby had made it clear she strongly disapproved of. With her nose in the air, Abby didn't slow down until they reached the First National Bank and she let the Ford roll to a quiet stop on the opposite side of the street from the large concrete structure.

The bank building itself had the appeal of a large gray

cement brick and gave the impression of permanence which stood out amongst the wood, used-brick, and flimsy solitary structures sporadically sprinkled up and down Front Street. At this stage in its life, Temecula was plain and functional without plan or organization. A simple irregular grid of paths, trails, and limited pavement, etched into the undulating landscape.

"Isn't that my grandpa's car?" Abby asked as she pointed at a large vehicle parked a few doors down from the bank.

"Yep," Denny replied, eyeing the big black-and-maroon Packard. He had met Marvin a few times at the blind pig, but they didn't mix socially.

"What's he doing down here?" There was a quaver in her voice.

"He's probably just shooting the shit with old Orville at the barbershop." Denny tried to sound confident.

"More than likely he's down at the blind pig having a beer," was her disgusted response. "Well, I don't care for that, and I don't like your foul language."

Taking his time, Denny reached under the seat and pulled the Peacemaker out from its hiding place and placed it in his lap.

"What is that?" she asked, sliding deep into the seat cushion as if she had seen the slithering snake from the Old Testament.

"It's my grand-dad's old hog-leg from the Spanish-American War."

"It looks like a cannon. What do you plan on doing with that god-awful thing?" Abby looked distressed.

"I need it for the holdup," was his simple reply.

42

"Why, are you planning on shooting somebody?"

"No, I wouldn't do that." Denny's reply was long and drawn out. "But nobody's going to do what I tell them if I don't have a gun. They'd just laugh at me."

"Good God Almighty," she whispered to herself.

* * *

Across the street, inside the bank, Ines Mason was busy filling her teller's cash drawer for the day while carrying on a conversation with Old Lady McCloud. The widow had no real business to carry out but stopped by every now and then for a little chit-chat with Ines. It was well known that Miss Mason was a practiced and excellent listener.

As was common, the bank cashier and only other employee, one Frederick "Freddy" Cowan, was sequestered in the vault indulging in a small sip from the silver hip flask that was embossed with his fathers' initials. The small sturdy flask also served an important and secondary function. Besides being his personal container of the precious and expensive firewater, it was the perfect door stop. Over the years the foundations of the building had settled, and the vault structure was no longer plumb. As a result, the heavy vault door would slowly swing closed of its own volition. After each of his regularly scheduled refreshment visits, Freddy made it a habit to place the flask in the door jamb to ensure the vault would not close and lock itself before returning to his desk.

It was during Freddy's usual morning eye opener that Denny entered the bank. In an effort to appear innocuous, Denny strolled over to the long oak counter facing the street and pretended to fill out a deposit slip. From the way he hunched over the counter furiously scribbling away, it was quite obvious Denny was annoyed by the presence of the old woman at the teller's window. He had counted on the bank being empty. But being a courteous young man, it seemed only right to let Old Lady McCloud finish her conversation. The small respite gave him the opportunity to stare out the window and across the street at sweet Abby sitting rigid in the Model A. He could clearly see her white knuckles locked on the steering wheel. She looked terrified as his own palms began to sweat.

Peeking around the old woman, it came to Denny's attention the teller was Ines Mason. Over the years they had never spoken much, but during high school he and Ines took the same school bus to Lake Elsinore for the two short years he bothered to attend. Small, pretty, and popular, the dark-haired girl had smiled at him once or twice before, and it was highly likely she would recognize him even now though he had grown some since those days. As an extra precaution, Denny extracted a red bandanna from his rear pocket and tied it over his face like one of the bad guys in a Hoot Gibson serial.

After Old Lady McCloud finally exited, Denny approached the teller's window. Since this was a small bank in a small town, there were no bars or glass at the window. He placed the paper bag and the revolver on the counter. "Put up your hands," he ordered.

Ines giggled. "Denny Wheeler, haven't seen you in years. What do you think you're up to? Are we playing some kind of game, or is this a joke?"

Denny was disappointed in her response. "Come on now, Ines. Don't give me any trouble." He picked up the gun and pointed it in her direction. "Let me in there, or I'll climb through this window." Observing her placid stare, Denny proceeded to do just that.

A slightly unsteady Freddy casually blundered into this scene, and before he could turn and run, Denny tossed him the paper bag. "Look you two," said Denny, "let's not make this any harder than it needs to be. I'll shoot if need be. Freddy, just put the cash in the bag, and I'll be on my way."

Without any argument, but with a look of dismay, Freddy turned and marched towards the vault. Denny gestured towards Ines with the gun. "You follow him. We'll all go together."

Ines frowned at Denny as she would to any naughty boy, and he was briefly startled by how short she had become over the years. The top of her head was barely even with his chin. After Freddy stuffed the bag with loose cash, he politely handed it over to Denny.

"You two just stay in the vault," Denny ordered and attempted to close the vault door in an effort to entrap the bank employees inside. Despite repeated attempts and a few choice curse words, the door refused to fully close. The silver flask had done its job. In the back corner of the vault, Freddy emitted a small snicker which brought him to Denny's attention. Denny wished he could shoot the smug cashier but only pointed the weapon in Freddy's general direction.

"Okay, to hell with it," Denny muttered. "You guys just stay in there. If you come out, I'll be waiting and I'll blow your ass off." Denny waved the weapon for emphasis then beat a hasty exit.

"What a maroon," said Freddy as he turned to face Ines. "I'm not waiting."

But Freddy did wait, and Ines had to cover her smile with her hands. "It's a shame," she said looking through the crack between the door jam and vault door. "He's such a good-looking fella."

Fulfilling her obligation, Abby started the car the moment Denny burst through the bank's front door. She had the engine wound up and shifter in first gear as he slipped into the passenger seat. "Go baby, go," Denny yelled.

After counting to ten, Freddy ran to his desk and grabbed an old thirty-two caliber automatic from the bottom drawer. Without breaking stride, he ran out into the middle of Front Street and fired several rounds at the receding getaway car. He could hear a few satisfying plinks as the bullets struck the back of the yellow Ford along with the sound of shattering glass. "Take that, asshole," he screamed.

A few doors north of the First National Bank, Marvin Rainwater was stretched out in a barber chair with a hot cloth draped across his face. He looked worse for wear after a night of drinking and desperately needed a shave, but the sound of

46

gunfire and someone screaming 'help' interrupted his otherwise peaceful morning. In his younger years he had been a well-known and trusted Deputy Marshall for Riverside County. In retirement he was still a respected member of the community if not a pillar of religious fervor. On reflex, Marvin shucked off the snow-white barber's cloth and ran outside to see Freddy Cowan standing the middle of the street waving a gun.

"What the hell are you doing Freddy?" Marvin yelled.

"It's the bank. We've been held up," was Freddy's mournful reply as he pointed northward towards Murrieta.

"How much did they get?" Marvin asked.

"Not much," Freddy gloated. "Just the loose cabbage. About two grand."

Without hesitation, Marvin ran to his Packard and made a quick U-turn in the center of Front Street and pulled up next to Freddy. "Give me that bean-shooter before you kill somebody," Marvin ordered.

"Aw, do I have to?" Freddy moaned.

"Give me the damn thing. I'll catch them. No car in the county can outrun my Packard." Marvin held out his hand and the cashier grudgingly handed over the weapon.

"And get out of the middle of the street," Marvin commanded as he blasted off in hot pursuit.

"Be careful," Freddy said to the exhaust fumes. "He's got an even bigger gun."

* * *

Three miles out of town, a steely-eyed Abby was focused on the road ahead when she heard Denny moan. "What's the matter?" she asked.

"I think you better pull over," said Denny.

"What? Why?" asked Abby.

"I think I've been shot."

"What do you mean, 'you think?'" Abby turned to see a pale Denny gaping at the copious amounts of blood running down his arm. "Oh Denny!" she cried as she maneuvered off the blacktop only to slide to a halt on the edge of an adjacent irrigation channel. "You're not gonna die, are you?"

"Don't know. Never been shot before."

"What do you want me to do?" she asked, barely able to get the words out.

Denny let out a long breath of consideration before answering. "You better take off. Head across the fields and circle back into town. Nobody has seen you. You'll be okay. Just get the hell away from here before you get arrested."

"What about you? I can't leave you here alone."

"Don't worry about me," was Denny's pitiful yet manly reply. "I'm probably done for. Just run, fast as you can." Almost as an afterthought, Denny leaned forward and extracted a twenty-dollar bill from the paper bag holding the stolen loot. He slipped off his father's ring and folded it inside the bill forming a tiny square about the size of a quarter and placed it in her shirt pocket. "Now go on. Get the hell out of here."

Abby jumped across the irrigation ditch snagging her shirt on the barbwire fence following the property line. Denny could hear it rip as she continued on her way. "Love you baby," he said softly as she left.

* * *

A few feet off the roadway with its tires almost in the ditch, the Model A sat at an angle to the highway with Denny slumped inside leaning against the passenger door grasping his left shoulder with his right hand. Blood was still seeping between his fingers and running down his sleeve. Alone and listening to the rustling of the oleanders on the other side of the road, Denny closed his eyes and waited. It shouldn't be long now. He tried not to panic as the Packard rolled to a stop behind him.

Marvin cautiously approached the driver's window with his hand on the butt of Freddy's automatic. He leaned over and peered inside.

"I think I'm a goner," said Denny as he continued to face the windshield. His head did not move and only his eyes tracked from the gun in Marvin's waistband to the green baseball hat bobbing through the recently plowed field just outside his window.

"Where's your chauffeur?" Marvin asked while scanning the immediate area around the vehicle.

"Ain't nobody else. There's just me."

Marvin glared at Denny as he examined the Ford's contents. Denny noted that Marvin paid particular attention to Abby's carpet bag resting behind the driver's seat. It was obvious they both knew who the bag belonged to.

"If there's no driver, why are you setting on that side of the car?" Marvin asked.

"It's more comfortable on this side, with my arm and all."

Marvin pointed to the open field, "Then who might that be in the green hat scampering across Wilson's potato field?"

"I haven't the faintest idea," Denny answered.

"Where's your weapon?" Marvin asked, changing the subject.

"In the floorboards under my feet."

Marvin's right hand did not leave Freddy's small automatic. "Slowly pick it up by the barrel and chuck it out the window." His voice was firm allowing no room for discussion. Moving like he was immersed in maple syrup, Denny did as he was told.

"I won't ask you where that Peacemaker came from, but did you plan on using it?" Marvin asked.

"Can't," Denny answered. "Ain't got no bullets."

"Right," said Marvin as he opened the car door and slid into the front driver's side seat. "Give me a look at that arm," he ordered, "and let's take off that shirt."

Denny grimaced with reluctance and significant pain but did as he was ordered and for the first time got a good look at the wound. There was a three-inch gash just below the shoulder.

"Looks like ole Freddy winged you, but I reckon you'll survive. Give me that bandanna you got draped around your neck." Marvin held out his hand.

50

Although his fingers didn't want to cooperate, Denny managed to untie the bandanna and handed it over. Marvin took the cloth and wrapped it tightly over the wound. He secured it with a square knot, a little extra tight to add emphasis.

"Where were you planning to go with my granddaughter?" Marvin asked.

"I don't know what you're talking about. Just trying to make my getaway. I needed to be somewhere that's not here."

"Save the horseshit," Marvin responded. "I need to know how Abby plays into this mess." Marvin could be quite imposing when the need arose.

Denny's false courage melted away. "I'm sorry Marvin, but I love her. We're just trying to get out of this place and start somewhere new with a little money in our pocket."

"Can't say as I blame you, but it doesn't appear you've made a great start." Marvin leaned back into the seat cushion as he spoke and calmly lit up a Camel. "What was the plan?"

"Neither of our families have any dough and neither does anyone else in this podunk town, except for the rich ranchers who own the bank. I thought maybe they wouldn't miss a small chunk of it."

"Well, there's the problem with your plan." Marvin's commentary didn't come across as particularly sympathetic. "The ranchers you're talking about aren't interested in sharing. They'd sooner hang any man who stole so much as a solitary dime from their bank."

"Do you think they'll let me go if I give the money back?"

"You know that's not going to happen," Marvin answered as Denny stared at the floorboards.

"What is gonna happen?" Denny asked.

Marvin leaned forward and picked up the bag of stolen cash, then turned to face Denny as he pulled a fat wallet from the back pocket of his jeans and extracted a wad of bills. "Tell you what. I'll take the stolen money back to the bank. Here's a couple hundred. Go catch Abby and get the hell away from here as fast as you can."

"Huh?" was Denny short response.

"You can drive, can't you?" Marvin asked.

Denny moved his wounded arm up and down. "Yeah, I think so. What about the cashier and Ines, the bank teller? They recognized me."

"You let me worry about them. I'll make sure they keep their traps shut. Maybe the council can give them some sort of medal for being so brave in the face of adversity. I'll tell the bank owners the bad guy got away but left the money bag behind as a gift."

"Will they believe that?" Denny asked.

"Probably not, but I can persuade them to let the matter drop. We go back awhile."

"Thanks Marvin," Denny was on the verge of tears and didn't know what else to say.

"Well, get your butt in gear and grab that girl while you've got the chance." Marvin exited the Model A then leaned in the front window so he could look Denny in the eye. "One other thing, son. Ditch the Ford. Half the state will be out looking for it."

In November, shortly after the start of the twenty-first century, in the house that his father built, Dennis "Bud" Wheeler Jr. poured himself a stiff drink as he gazed eastward at the rising sun. After a long night of waiting, he was taking a brief celebratory moment due to his election as the new mayor. He meandered out onto the veranda and let his eyes feast on the multicolored rooftops where only meadows and a few California Oaks had once grown. Easing into the chaise lounge, he wondered what his father and Old Man Rainwater would have thought. Not only about the election, but on how the city had grown. He grinned and speculated on what the citizenry would think about the son of a bank robber being elected as mayor. That is, if they had known. Bud was a firm believer in fairy tales. The image of the plaque on the side of the old bank building downtown came to mind.

The Rainbow Kid

On August 15, 1930, the notorious Rainbow Kid staged a daring daylight robbery of the First National Bank before escaping into the Anza Borrego with thousands of dollars belonging to the local citizens of Temecula Valley. The Kid was never captured, and his identity remains a mystery to this day.

It was quite a story and made him chuckle, but Bud had to

admit the tourists ate it up. Anyone who knew otherwise were mostly dead. The plaque had taught him one serious lesson: *Don't believe anything written on the wall of a bank.*

Bud had another sip of the soothing bourbon and as the warming effect of the alcohol spread throughout his body, he returned his gaze to the tile rooftops and patches of foliage encased in grids of gray concrete and sultry black asphalt. There were miles of the stuff displacing the once golden hills and dusty green Oaks of the arid valley. He speculated on whether this human world of traffic, tourists, and wineries was an improvement.

Contributor Biographies

Brad Shaw Jr.

Brad Shaw Jr. was born in Alton, Illinois but never really lived there. His father was an nomadic construction worker and they resided wherever the work took them. During his formative years Brad had taken up residence, however short, in almost every state in the USA. When he was a teenager, the family found themselves in Southern California and never left. In adulthood, his life has been a series of stages: boilermaker, college student, accountant, CPA, corporate controller, business owner, and finally a retiree. Brad took up writing as an enjoyable pastime.

Arman-Justin Solis

Arman-Justin Solis is a freelance 2D Artist and Animator whose love of comic strips and animation at an early age inspired him to seek out a career in the arts. He graduated from the Academy of Art University with a BFA in 2D Animation. His main comic inspirations include Calvin and Hobbes, The Far Side, and 1950s EC Horror Comics, while his film inspirations include Fantastic Mr. Fox, Cats Don't Dance, and Punch-Drunk Love. When he's not creating, he enjoys listening to his ever-growing record collection and playing retro video games.

THE MAN, THE MOUSE, AND THE BALLOON

Story by Pat Comerchero AKA
"Professor Phineas T. Pennypickle"

Illustrations by Amanda Le
India Ink

FIRST OF ALL, LET me start by saying that I didn't MEAN to crash the hot air balloon into the middle of the Workshop. It was definitely an accident. One which Beaker will never let me live down....

But wait! This isn't a very good beginning for a story, is it? Clearly you, Dear Reader, have no idea who I am or what I'm even talking about, so I guess I'll start over.

My name is Phineas T. Pennypickle. PhD. I love sunsets and

walking on the beach...NO NO NO!!! IGNORE THAT!!! START OVER!!! My name is Professor Phineas T. Pennypickle. I live in a crazy, cluttered, cozy home that doubles as a Workshop in the charming city of Temecula, California. I allow people to visit my Workshop because — well, I'm not entirely sure, exactly. Maybe because it's what my sister wanted. Anyway, did I mention that I am a scientist? And a time traveler? Uh...this is where it gets complicated. I have a time machine. But we'll get to that later.

I build lots of other interesting (some may call them wacky) inventions and naturally they are strewn about the Workshop as I am not the neatest, especially when I get totally embroiled in experimenting with stuff. (Everyone has their weaknesses.) The Workshop is not your typical — shall we say "home" — in that I've managed to clutter every room (Library, Music Room, Kitchen, Bathroom, etc.) with my contraptions, tunnels, secret passages, and illusions.

But I digress. We were talking about me, right? I'm not very comfortable talking about myself. My parents were Phillip, a clockmaker, and Philomena (Fee), a music teacher. They were killed in a tragic accident but we won't talk about that now because I don't know you well enough and it hurts to think about it. I have two siblings: an older sister, Phyllis, who is (was?) a musical prodigy, and our younger brother Fitzhugh, who is/was an arrogant blowhard. Okay, sorry. STRIKE THAT. Pretend you didn't see that about my brother and I didn't say it. I actually honestly don't know where either of them are right now, due to my impetuous brother's insistence upon using Phyllis as a guinea pig for HIS time (and supposedly "space") machine that had NO chance of working properly and now they're careening through the universe somewhere (hopefully NOT around any black hole event horizons) and hopefully Phyllis will come back because her son T2 (Templeton Torrance) ended up in MY care and that causes big problems with Beaker and OH MY GOSH I NEED TO TAKE A DEEP BREATH....

BREATHE!!!! One two three one two three one two three BREATHE!

Okay. Back in control. Not happy that my siblings contribute greatly to the anxiety I feel and my choice to become reclusive, but I guess families all can have issues, right? So let's get back to the story, shall we? Is there a story??? I'm not sure but let's keep going and see what happens.

My best friend and closest confidant is a field mouse named Beakerham Bettermouse IV. Yes, I'm sure you think that having an animal as a best friend is very strange and weird (Fitzhugh calls Beaker a "Lab Rat" which upsets him GREATLY) but we have some kind of psychic bond thing going on plus the little guy is a mathematical genius and my inventions wouldn't get off the ground (so to speak!) without him. (I'm not the greatest at math.)

So maybe back to the story of the hot air balloon?? Well, I was curious to see if I could potentially reach the highest theoretical maximum limit for a balloon (which as you know, is about 20 miles above the Earth's surface. Give or take.), when we happened to fly over Old Town Temecula. I spotted the Workshop! In my excitement, I leaned...well, truthfully more like climbed...waaay over the side of the basket. Beaker contends that the thin oxygen level when the balloon was around 10,000 feet gave me altitude sickness (in his exact words I was "air-deprived inebriated" and that was the kindest description of me that he spewed in his rage-filled rant about my foolishness). As I hovered in the void between the gondola (that's what a hot air balloon basket is called) and literal NOTHINGNESS, I dropped the statoscope and lunged at it, nearly causing what could have been a very fatal incident. You know that to keep the balloon at a steady altitude, bags of sand ballast have to be jettisoned (thrown overboard) to make up for gradual seeping of hydrogen gas from the envelope (the balloon part). Since there's a really delicate balance between venting the gas and throwing out ballast (which is what I was TRYING to do and I admit I am not the most delicate person in the world), the use of the sensitive barometric (pressure-controlled) statoscope is vital! Needless to say, dropping it wasn't a cool thing to do. Neither was trying to catch a rapidly falling, substantially heavy object while balancing with one foot on the basket and the rest of my body in the chilly thin air — we all remember my good friend Isaac Newton's experiments with gravity, and becoming a splat mark on the roof of my Workshop was not something I would have been thrilled about. But WOW!!! Did Beaker ever let me have it!! I think he was being far too dramatic to say I (we) could have been killed. Well...I guess we could have. If not from the crash (that was apparently inevitable), then perhaps from the frighteningly quick descent with me half (three-quarters? More??) out of the gondola, OR the hydrogen explosion WHICH

WAS NOT MY FAULT! Use your imagination, dear reader, and picture my lovely experimental hot air balloon crashing through the roof of my Workshop and coming to a not-so-subtle landing right in the Foyer. It was exhilarating to say the least but trust me, Beaker was NOT happy. Anyway, I removed the envelope to use for future experiments and patched up the roof and ceiling. Children who visit seem to like finding a hot air balloon gondola right in the middle of my Workshop. Bottom line though, Beaker is STILL in a snit about it even though I promised him multiple PB&J sandwiches shaped like his favorite math symbols. Now that I think about it, he wasn't too thrilled about my anti-gravity device either...(think I learned a terrifying hands-on physics lesson about gravity from hanging in thin air? Uh, yeah...yeah I did. Ha ha.)

Hmmm. Where was I? Did I mention that my all-time favorite human BFF is my best buddy Nicola Tesla? (I did mention I can time travel, didn't I?) We've been through LOTS of adventures together, especially at his lab in Colorado, and both Beaker's father (Beakerham Bettermouse III) and his grandfather (Beakerham Bettermouse II) were involved in our mishaps...uh, mischief...uh, let's refer to them as "experiments." It would take a whole BOOK to explain THOSE stories! Suffice it to say, a lot of the results of madcap schemes we indulged in have manifested themselves as "exhibits" in my Workshop.

I honestly don't know where I was going with all this and whether it tells you anything about me or lets you know things about me that I can't believe I told you, but it is what it is. Wait...

what was this "story" supposed to be all about, anyway???? Oh well.

The end for now.

PTP

Contributor Biographies

Pat Comerchero AKA "Professor Phineas T. Pennypickle"

Author Pat Comerchero is the Founder and Director of Pennypickle's Workshop, an award-winning children's science museum started in 2004 in Old Town Temecula, California. Writing under the pen name and using the voice of alter ego Professor Phineas T. Pennypickle (a time-traveling scientist whose Workshop allows children to discover science while playing with his wacky inventions), numerous littles and their grown-ups have been entertained by her quirky and amusing stories of the Professor's adventures.

Ms. Comerchero can be reached at Pennypickle's Workshop, 42081 Main Street, Temecula CA 92590; at 951-308-6376; or via www.pennypickles.org. Or, find her on Facebook and Instagram via @pennypicklesworkshop.

Amanda Le

Amanda Le is a Vietnamese-American artist local to Southern California. They identify as a nonbinary artist and as a bisexual, and are proud to represent LGBTQ+ artists in literature. They are a life-long lover of stories and art, and creates art that focuses on kindness and art as healing.

They earned a BA in Art and a Masters in Education from UC Irvine. Amanda designed a BIBA Award-winning book cover for the poetry anthology *A Burning Lake of Paper Suns* by Ellen Webre, and became a full-time book illustrator in 2023.

ANIMA NATION

Story by John Waddleton

Illustration by Shya
Digital

T RIP HUNTER STOOD ATOP a large boulder and registered the grand view without appreciating it. Positioned halfway up the hills that bounded the southwest end of the valley, he had a clear view of the expanse that spread before him. A lazy sun lingered on the eastern horizon, resting momentarily before rising to deliver a new day. Pink with anticipation, the pre-dawn sky spread its florid glow, brightening mist that clung to the valley floor. As Trip inhaled, he perceived the fragrance of damp sage mingled with the aroma of burning wood, but he could not appreciate it.

The smoke curled upward from his campfire, marking the spot where Trip spent the night. He had arrived the evening before, setting up camp at the mouth of a ravine where two meandering creeks joined to form the river he had followed since leaving the coast. A shallow pool sparkled at the intersection of the streams, its surface tickled in the afternoon by cool breezes that broke free of the ocean and rushed into the canyons, looking for a warm place to play. It had been an ideal place to stop for the night.

Watching the evidence of his campfire dissipate as it floated skyward, Trip climbed the hillside to familiarize himself with his surroundings. The rising smoke normally would have worried him, possibly alerting others to his presence, but here there would be no one to see it. Rational folks preferred the civilized coastal regions, where stifling inland heat did not present an existential threat. The valley, separated from the coast by twenty miles of hill country, was completely uninhabited. The animas that lingered here, and there were many, wouldn't care about the smoke.

Upon returning to camp, Trip found that the sage tea he left brewing had started to boil. He replaced the kettle with a skillet, waited for the pan to heat, and used it to warm beans and a dry tortilla. Pouring a steaming cup of tea, he enjoyed a simple breakfast before rinsing his plate in the river and kneeling to wash his face. Refreshed, Trip quenched the fire with leftover tea then stowed the gear on his packhorse.

As the sun climbed skyward, it busied itself chasing mist away from places it wasn't anchored by a foundation of cool water. Mist or not, Trip's path was clear. The patterns visible in the animas were unmistakable — J.M. Coopersson had passed this way no more than three days before.

Trip was certain of Coopersson's passage for the same reason he was unable to appreciate the sweeping vista of sunrise through the mist or the fresh smell of damp sage and wood smoke. Trip's world was forever dulled by the animas.

Sensing the animas was like looking through a window that wasn't there, at an object that didn't exist, but which nonetheless obscured the material world beyond.

In legends shared by his grandfather, Trip had learned that the animas were the collective residue of humanity, the ethereal aftertaste that lingered after most of mankind was swallowed whole. Individually, they were the manifestation of a life untethered when the body ceased to exist. To the approximately one billion living, breathing human beings that escaped extinction during that unprecedented event, the animas were nothing. To Trip and his forebears, they were everything — a distortion, a color, an energy, an essence, and a nuisance.

The animas were born during the cataclysmic whisper that had erased over seven billion bodies from the planet. It had happened in an instant, and no one had been able to identify the cause, though many tried. Some thought it was the anger of a petulant god; others believed it was a glitch in the simulation. Because the event had occurred around the time earth's population reached two to the power of thirty-three, some believed it was simply a hard reset programmed into the operating system, a calculation intended to conserve system resources — a sort of cosmic garbage collection routine. Almost eight hundred years after it happened, an agrarian philosopher had christened the event 'The Winnowing'. Trip often wondered whether he and everyone else currently on the planet were descended from the wheat or the chaff.

It didn't make any difference. Wheat or chaff, Trip had a bounty to collect.

Coopersson, the quarry, was an educationist — an academic — and not the typical lowlife scumbag Trip would normally hunt. The academic would not be skilled in obscuring tracks or evading pursuit — there would be no reason for that. And even if Coopersson had, for some reason, learned about the art of disappearing, it wouldn't change things. Trip didn't rely on normal means to stalk his prey. For him, the animas revealed the way.

They were hungry for human form. Like carp in a lake when food hits the surface, the animas churned in the presence of embodied humans. Tethered existentially to their point of severance, animas weakened with distance from that juncture. They interacted with each other like ripples from stones dropped into a pond. The diaphanous patterns they created were rendered atop reality, revealing things to Trip that couldn't otherwise be known. And to everyone else, they didn't exist.

His father had been absent, so Trip's grandfather shared the family lore, helping Trip understand his connection to the animas. And when the old man died, leaving Trip to fend for himself on the streets of Old Sandago, Trip put his skills to use as a thief. Later, he found a place in the Calimex militia, tracking deserters.

Trip considered his time in the militia a waste, not least because it had torn him from the arms of his first and only love. She'd been a friend, then a lover. He had dreamed of starting a family with her. But when he was finally free of the militia, she was gone. Why hadn't she waited?

He hadn't wanted to leave her, but what choice did he have? The law was clear regarding the penalty for dereliction of duty, and the militia was merciless in enforcing it. When the recruiters came for him, he went.

He bristled at memories of contrived confrontations and pointless brutality. In his opinion, the militias — all of them — were nothing more than institutionalized criminal gangs, each one zealously protecting its own interests at the expense of the others. Nonetheless, his time in the service had allowed him to hone his skill, to learn to read the animas with subtlety and precision. But most importantly, it allowed him to cultivate a reputation, and it was Trip's reputation that earned him the chance to chase Coopersson's bounty.

The bounty was all that mattered — it was all that ever mattered now. It drove Trip to do what he did, regardless of the human toll. Dead or alive, it made no difference. The animas were around to remind Trip what death looked like, so why not focus on the only thing in life that meant something? Money could buy food; it could buy companionship. Hell, it probably could buy happiness. But he'd never had enough to test the theory.

Coopersson's bounty was a big one — the biggest Trip had ever chased, by far. Maybe this time he would get the opportunity to learn what happiness was. He wondered if Coopersson would still be alive when he found out.

* * *

J.M. Coopersson — she had used only the initials since abandoning Old Sandago years ago — sought relief from the blazing midday sun by snugging up against the base of a large boulder. The narrow strip of shade bordering the rock offered respite from the extreme August temperatures. Later in the day, spirited ocean breezes would scamper up the river canyon to cool the inland valley, but for now, the sweltering heat was nearly unbearable. She wondered why she had forsaken the temperate climate back at the Institute.

Well, mostly it was about self-preservation.

She had only recently returned to Old Sandago. Her past in the region was...problematic...so she had forsaken the city and sought a new life in the Central Territories. Running from her past, yet not knowing in what direction her future lay, she had wandered aimlessly for a time. Eventually, J.M. had conned her way into the New Boulder Academy, first posing as a student, then gradually establishing a genuine reputation as a solid researcher and respected educationist. After a few years away from the coast, however, she was ready to return home. Taking advantage of her newly cultivated identity, J.M. had applied to the Carlsbad Coastal Institute and they had eagerly welcomed her as a new faculty member.

She had settled easily into the new environment, but it wasn't long before J.M. unwittingly became a thorn in the side of the Old Sandago governor, a powerful woman who had the reputation of not taking kindly to thorns. As the de facto commandant of the Calimex militia, the Governor — who preferred to be called la Jefa — was in a position to act upon her whims with devastating force. And currently, the full strength of la Jefa's power was focused on J.M. — simply because J.M. had uncovered an inconvenient legend deep within the Institute's archives.

That was how J.M. found herself staving off sunstroke in the shade of a giant rock in an infernal valley far from home. Damn la Jefa and her thirst for power.

Despite some minor personnel clashes at the Institute, she had enjoyed being home. Now she was on the run — again — forced to abandon Old Sandago this time because la Jefa coveted power and wealth.

J.M. was a Paleoethnotist, dammit. It was her job to study pre-cultures and their mythology, and to learn how their lives may have foreshadowed, or even caused, the Winnowing. She had made her unwanted and attention-grabbing discovery while investigating the role of certain pre-cultures that thrived in the region north of Old Sandago. It was ridiculous to think some long-forgotten legend of buried treasure would have anything to do with the sudden loss of seven billion lives, and therefore the legend was of no interest to J.M. It probably wasn't even true — most legends weren't. Unfortunately, J.M. had learned the hard way that la Jefa disagreed. The Governor considered any fortune, legendary or otherwise, that was not under her personal control to be a significant threat to her power. No one could be allowed that kind of wealth except la Jefa herself. Because of the Governor's paranoia, the Calimex militia was ordered to arrest J.M. Coopersson.

J.M. learned of the warrant almost as soon as it was issued. Despite her new role as an educationist, she had grown up on the streets. Her hardscrabble youth in the dark corners of Old Sandago left her with friends that would alert her to such danger before the militia could act. Even so, by the time her contacts relayed their warning, J.M. was already prepared to disappear. For reasons she didn't understand, she always knew when it was time to leave. So, she had collected her meager belongings, stolen the documents relating to the ridiculous legend, and made it her goal to bring la Jefa's darkest fear to life.

Now, as she sat in the shadow of the large chunk of granite, those warning signals sounded again, stronger than ever. J.M. had grown more sensitive since she broke free of the river canyon and descended into the huge inland valley for the first time. It was something about the land, particularly where the two creeks joined. There was an essence there — a vortex of spiritualism that J.M. didn't understand but which touched her strongly and heightened her sensitivity.

She knew she would need to leave soon — somebody was

coming for her, although this time it felt different, maybe not as threatening. The sensation had been growing for days, ever since she entered the valley. It didn't come as a surprise that someone might be after her, but she'd hoped to lose them when she turned inland. She'd taken precautions, and the sense that told her when to leave also usually guided her escape. Maybe one more day, then she must leave.

The legend that guided J.M.'s path, the same one that brought such existential fear to la Jefa, told of vast wealth that lay somewhere in the valley. She was close to the legend's source; her senses told her so. J.M. hadn't believed it at first, but each day she spent in the valley increased her certainty that the treasure was near. There was something here. Something she needed to find.

Today, J.M. would return to the valley floor and explore the ruins she had identified from the top of the mountain called Wexéwxi Pu'éska. The boulder under which she sheltered represented the halfway point on her descent from the summit. She had spent the night on the mountain, staring up at the heavens and contemplating the legend that drew her to the valley. The Pechanga, a pre-culture that preceded others in the area by more than ten thousand years — had deemed the mountain a sacred place, and J.M. was inclined to agree. Her senses had come alive on the mountaintop. She had felt a connection like never before, to this life and to everything beyond.

The ruins below had been hidden before her ascent, but now they called out to her, a siren song leading her to...what?

Fortune? Retribution? She didn't know, but she was certain it was what she had been seeking.

J.M. knew there must be many ruins in the valley. Before the Winnowing, the area had been densely populated, and legend said dwellings spread as far as the eye could see. But the passing of a thousand years since the event had allowed nature sufficient time to reclaim her empire, except for the ruins that were beckoning so urgently to J.M.

She dared to wait no longer. J.M. abandoned her perch under the boulder and hurried to meet her destiny.

* * *

Trip was hot on Coopersson's trail, following the path revealed in the animas' frenzy. The ascent ahead was steep, but the trail was obvious. He had climbed a significant portion of the rocky slope when he paused to catch his breath. Surveying the valley below, Trip was bewildered by what he saw.

Intermingled with mankind, the animas were always in turmoil, but the valley was empty, abandoned long ago and showing no evidence of human discord. Here, the animas' invisible presence glimmered like a vast inland sea, stolid and languorous under the doldrums of human absence. The animas were at rest, at peace. Trip skirted an epiphany — is this what heaven is like?

He considered that for a moment, wondering where the thought had originated. But something else tugged at the edge of his senses. Near the southern end of the valley, directly below where he stood now, there was an unfamiliar pattern. A void — like an island in the ocean of animas that inundated the area. And the animas that serenely encircled the void seemed to be held at bay by something unusual, stronger, and more ancient. If circumstances had been different, Trip might have been tempted to investigate. But he had no time for that now; it was the bounty that mattered, and it was almost within his grasp. It was then that he hesitated.

The compulsion wrought by the animas, the one he was following inexorably to his quarry, was abruptly...different. He felt disoriented — physically and spiritually. Suddenly, he sensed the path he followed had reversed. Coopersson must have doubled back, trying to throw Trip off. No...it was more than that. There was a temporal inflection of some sort. The path had changed and so had the time frame. Trip could read that Coopersson must have come this way for some reason, traveled further along, and then returned along the same path later, the second time with an increased sense of...what? Urgency? Determination? He wasn't sure.

Regardless, it was the same mix of feelings that propelled Trip as he circled back to follow Coopersson's lead.

* * *

J.M.'s descent into the valley seemed to have passed in an instant. It felt as if, for the first time in her life, she knew she was on the right path. As if something that could see where she needed to go had taken hold and was pulling her toward her destination. It was an unprecedented sensation — for most of J.M.'s life she had lived with uncertainty. From her misspent youth in Sandago to her aimless meanderings in the CT, J.M. had never known where she was heading. Only that she must get away from where she was.

Now, she found herself wandering alone among the ruins. Her guiding presence had evaporated, leaving her to uncover the final truth on her own. That was probably for the best — the sensation of being propelled by an unseen force was both thrilling and frightening. She would no doubt be better off on her own. She always was.

The clear outline of the ruins had been obvious from the mountain, but as she neared they had dissolved into piles of crumbling concrete and rusted steel, most of them hidden by overgrowth. Sage and other chaparral natives had invaded the area, staking claim to the rubbish and hastening its disintegration. Here and there, the remnants formed the clear outline of a structure, drawing J.M.'s attention and piquing her interest. This had to be the place the legend described.

In the ancient manuscript J.M. had liberated from the Institute's archives, the area was described as a cultural gathering place, a destination that attracted pilgrims from afar who came to test their fortune in games of chance. Some would leave with riches; most would leave with less than they brought. But the pilgrims always came, and the center amassed great wealth, which it guarded carefully. It was said that only certain senior officiants knew the secrets of accessing the treasure. When the Winnowing happened, those that held the secrets were lost.

J.M. doubted that such a formidable treasure could ever be completely forsaken or forgotten. But many things were lost during the chaos born by the Winnowing. Civilization was one of them; certainly, a sizable local fortune might also disappear.

She walked to an opening in the largest decaying structure and looked inside. The wild plants that covered the surface spread into the dark interior, making the only visual difference one of illumination. Using a handlumen from her pack, she looked around the darkened space. It was larger than it appeared from the outside, and, to her surprise, some signs of civilization remained. A handful of columns struggled valiantly to uphold a decaying roof that was invisible from the outside, hidden by sage, windblown sand, and its own decay. Faded tiles covered the ground that hadn't already been reclaimed by nature.

It's real. The treasure is real! It was more than she had expected to find. Carefully adjusting the bag slung over her shoulder, J.M. walked with purpose into the darkness. Maybe she would make la Jefa regret issuing that arrest warrant after all.

* * *

Trip had followed the trail cautiously, taking an hour to reach the valley floor. Coopersson may be an educationist, but that didn't mean he could neglect his normal precautions. People on the run often resorted to desperate measures they might not normally consider. Besides, trails painted by the animas did not grow cold quickly. Coopersson's trail was still plenty warm when Trip approached an area that appeared to be some kind of ruins.

Crossing the creek that separated the mountains from the valley, he approached the ruins from the southwest. Across the wide-open space before him, the area appeared to be nothing more than an overgrown collection of ceremonial mounds. The hillocks provided ample cover for anyone hoping to evade capture, but they also offered several locations from where the potential captor could be shot. Even educationists had been known to carry weapons upon occasion.

West of his current position lay the void in the anima ocean he had noticed earlier, and at its center grew an enormous tree. It drew Trip's attention, almost convincing him to abandon his quarry and go there instead. But he didn't — the bounty was the reason Trip was here, not a search for some mystical revelation. Maybe he would come back and investigate someday.

Waiting patiently near the creek, he read the animas for indications of human presence. Except for the trail leading into the center of the mounds, there was nothing. His sidearm drawn, Trip moved forward carefully.

He was more than halfway to the ruins when he heard a blast from inside the area. Fighting the instinct to dive for cover, he sprinted toward the ruins. He knew the person he sought was alone — the animas told him that — and the explosion sounded as if it originated from within one of the mounds. He covered the remaining distance in time to see dust settling in a nearby opening.

Dammit! Coopersson's worth more to me alive than dead. I hope he didn't just blow himself up! Trip had come too far to lose the bounty now, dead or alive.

He ducked into the dusty entrance with his weapon drawn. As the air cleared, Trip saw a figure stagger from a doorway near the edge of his vision. The animas in the vicinity writhed in agony as they fought to merge with the injured woman. Trip knew from the patterns that it was Coopersson.

A woman! Why didn't the Governor tell me?

Stumbling, Coopersson landed against a wall and crumbled to the floor. She mumbled incoherently as Trip approached.

"…nothing but little, round…tokens…." She stared blankly at Trip from a face he suddenly recognized.

No! He kneeled desperately to tend to her wounds. I will not lose her — not again!

* * *

The sound of bacon sizzling over an open campfire wriggled its way into J.M.'s mind before consciousness did. She was dreaming of a morning long ago, the first morning she had awakened in the arms of the childhood friend who had later become her lover. Together, they had spent the night wrapped in each other's embrace, the two of them, alone on the beach, both hoping it was the first moment in an eternity. Later they cooked breakfast over an open fire, the bacon sizzling in an uncovered pan as it did now, just at the edge of her consciousness.

J.M. awoke with a start, disappointed the dream had ended. What had resurrected that long dead memory? The last thing she remembered was ...an explosion, immediate pain, then disappointment. Stumbling down a long dark corridor, a doorway. A man? Looking down at her and holding a weapon. Then, nothing.

"You know, I'm going to lose a fortune because of you."

She recoiled from the sound of his deep voice, then relaxed slightly. It was somehow familiar. Her senses, which should have been screaming at her to escape, weren't. Her vision was hazy as she stared through eyes that refused to focus. She must have taken quite a beating from him.

"What happened? What have you done to me?" J.M. tried to repress a rising panic. The man, standing above her, smiled.

"I didn't do anything. You were hit by debris when you blew that vault looking for your treasure. You were a bloody mess when I found you."

That voice! J.M. was certain she knew it, but she couldn't place it, and her vision still wasn't cooperating. She blinked. "Where are we?"

"Close to the ruins. I brought you here — to this giant oak tree. It's not far from where I found you, but there's something here that I haven't felt in a long time — peace." Trip kneeled. "I wanted to share it with you. To explore that feeling together."

What an unexpected thing for him to say. She continued to

84

search his face, hoping her vision would clear.

"What did you mean when you said you were losing a fortune because of me?"

"The bounty. I can't possibly collect it now. Too many memories...." He laughed gently.

J.M. stared at him as her vision finally cleared, focusing across time onto a face she had no hope of seeing again. The face in her dream of the beach — had it escaped her fantasy and become real?

"Hector? It can't be...is it you?"

"I go by Trip now." His smile was warm, but his voice, the one she knew so well, held a touch of remorse. "It's good to see you again, Mary, I almost didn't recognize you when you stumbled out of that doorway in the ruins. It's been a long time. Too long."

"Trip? I don't understand." Confused, J.M. sat up. She wanted to stand, to go to him, but sudden vertigo kept her rooted in place.

"Sure. Hector Henri Hunter. They called me 'Triple H.' It got shortened to Trip." He ducked his head and touched the brim of his hat, as if meeting her for the first time.

"I...I don't believe this. I thought I'd never see you again. When the recruiters took you away...I don't know, it felt like betrayal." She felt tears welling in her eyes.

"I had no choice, Mary. Everyone must do their time. It's not like I wanted to leave."

"But I never heard from you."

Trip shrugged. "It wasn't allowed. I looked for you when I got out. But you were gone. Nobody knew where. And by that time, your trail was so cold. I couldn't find you, and my reputation for tracking is...well — known." He paused. "You changed your name."

"Yeah — I had to. You probably remember neither of us were upstanding citizens back in the day. But you should've recognized my new name." A smile played at the corner of her mouth.

"What do you mean?"

"Well, Coopersson was my mom's name. But I didn't talk about her very much, so I can't blame you for not remembering. But J.M. — don't you recall?"

"I guess not." Trip scratched his jaw.

"You teased me when we were little. I could never remember my middle name. It was difficult to say and hard to spell, so I just forgot about it. You thought it was so funny. You said you'd always call me 'Just Mary'.'

They both laughed out loud, remembering happier times that felt much too distant. Trip sat down next to her, cross-legged, with his hands in his lap. "I missed you, Mary. I searched for you. For a long time. And when I finally found you, after following a trail I didn't even know was yours, you were lying covered in your own blood. I was afraid I might lose you all over again."

"I missed you too." Mary leaned into him, letting her gaze encompass the ancient oak.

"I know this place. I've seen pictures at the Institute." Mary admired the massive tree, its huge branches arching wide and falling back to the ground, supporting itself in its old age.

This is Wi'áasal — the Great Oak. It's holy ground for the Pechanga — the people who originally built these ruins. Wuyóot — legend says he's leader of their First People — died and was cremated on Pu'éska mountain. Right up there." Mary pointed in the direction from which she'd approached the ruins.

"The First People collected his remains and brought them here. The oak grew from where his ashes were spread. Wuyóot prophesied that its acorns would feed generations of his descendants." She fell silent, thinking about the legend that brought her to the valley. "This tree was ancient when its story was first told. I can't believe it's still here today. There must be magic here."

Trip gazed up at the tree, the boughs draping over them, offering a haven they both needed. "I don't know if it's magic, Mary, but I know there's something special about this place." His voice resonated with certainty, and Mary took comfort in it.

Mary sighed. "I came here seeking treasure, following a path to retribution. But that path led only to worthless piles of decorated plastic." She paused, thinking.

"But here I am, now, with you. And I think maybe I have found treasure. It's this valley, this place. And you. I found you again." Staring into his eyes, she looked for a sign that he felt the same way.

Trip nodded. "I didn't expect this when la Jefa offered me your bounty, but…I don't want to go back to Old Sandago. There's nothing for me there. I think this valley is a place where both of us could start over. Together." He picked something out of the dirt and held it up for her to see. "We have acorns! And there's plenty of wildlife. We wouldn't starve."

Just Mary laughed. "And there's plenty of space to raise a family...." A mischievous grin brightened her face.

Trip simply smiled. "Yeah. I think we should stay awhile."

Contributor Biographies

John Waddleton

John Waddleton is halfway through writing his first novel, and he has a handful of short stories to his credit. John is working toward the day his name will be listed amongst the literary greats, and not just because they all lived on the same planet.

Shya

I am a seventeen-year-old artist who has cultivated a lifelong passion for drawing. Over the past four years, I have been actively involved in the Bigfoot Graphics program, dedicating myself to honing my skills and gaining valuable experience in the creative field. I love creating fantastical pieces of art and am currently striving for a career as an illustrator or graphic designer.

GHOST HUNTING FOR LOVE

Story by Theresa Halvorsen

Illustration by Barbara C. Nelson
Oil

I STUCK MY HANDS INTO the pockets of my jeans, a cold wind biting through my clothes and tugging on my hair. So much for the thirty minutes I'd spend curling, straightening, and scrunching my blonde hair, so it framed my face perfectly. But maybe it wouldn't matter.

God, what was I thinking, dating again? I hated this feeling of uncertainty and anxiety. How would the date go? Would we hit it off or would the conversation be forced — the evening ending in an awkward handshake and lies to text each other later?

But I was lonely and my best friend, Becca, had dared me to go out on a date. In exchange, she'd be buying drinks next

Saturday night at the Apparition Room in Old Town Temecula, and those drinks were expensive. It was worth it. I could put up with an awkward date for a few hours if necessary.

Assuming he showed, of course. I resisted the urge to check my phone and re-read the text message from my potential date, Xander. I was on time, and at the correct location — 6:00 p.m. at Temecula's Vail Ranch Headquarters. I kicked at a weed and looked toward the mountains surrounding Temecula. The sun was setting, painting the sky with oranges, pinks, and purples in another spectacular Southern California sunset. Tonight the fog from the coast was cresting over the mountains, adding textures of lavenders and apricots to the sky. Normally, I loved it...when it was warm or from the comfort of my house, where I had a space heater. The freezing wind chilling me to my core was taking the appreciation out of the experience.

I gave in and glanced at my phone. 6:02, no text messages. He wasn't that late. I was being ridiculous. I hadn't dated much since my divorce, and using a dating app was definitely a new thing. But I'd chatted with Xander a fair amount over text and even had a few phone calls before agreeing to an in-person date. We'd seemed fairly compatible — and he was funny. I was a sucker for someone who made me laugh.

I looked at my phone again. 6:03. No Xander and no one walking in from the parking lot that met his description. Had he really stood me up? If he had, I was still going to insist Becca buy me the drinks. Probably tonight.

Tucking the phone back into a pocket, I looked around. I

lived in the northern part of Temecula, off Winchester Road, and didn't come down to the southern part of Temecula often. And I'd never been to Vail Ranch Headquarters before. Sandwiched between Kohls and a strip mall was a small cluster of old-looking buildings offering mom-and-pop shops and restaurants with lots of outdoor dining. Between all of them sat a stage and grassy area, with picnic tables, perfect for farmer's markets and craft shows. Today there were a few people wandering between the buildings, but almost no one sat outside in the frigid wind. Someone had painted an odd mural of cowboys onto the outside of the Kohls building. I frowned. Why would someone put that there?

And more importantly, why was I even here?

Xander hadn't told me what we were doing tonight — just to meet him at the front of Vail Ranch for our date. I was starving and hoped we were going to eat; the restaurants looked like a fun mix of sandwiches, pizza, and salads. If he didn't show up soon, I'd meander over to the restaurants and see what their menus looked like. With a large glass of wine, I texted Becca about how I was never going to date again.

A small group was gathering at one of the picnic benches, clustered around a gentleman wearing cowboy boots and a hat and holding an old-fashioned lantern with a flickering candle inside. I watched one group, a family with two teenagers, count out money and pass it to him. In exchange, he gave them something out of the blue Walmart bag at his feet. One of the teenager's voices carried to me on the wind, "...so fucking cool! I can't wait."

"Language," the mom intoned, like she said it two hundred times a day. Remembering stories from my friends with teenagers, I realized she probably did. I snickered a little.

6:05. Still no Xander. I resisted the urge to huff and stomp a foot. While not a total control freak, I didn't like it when people were late. It made me feel like I wasn't a priority, that my time didn't matter to them.

And it left a nasty taste in my mouth for a first date.

Another couple joined the cowboy guy. Same transaction happened — they passed him money, and he passed them something out of his bag. He looked like he was going to do some sort of history reenactment — oh no. Oh hell no.

"Hi — Calla?" a voice asked behind me.

I turned around. This had to be Xander. He looked like his picture — reasonably good looking, with blue-black hair brushing the collar of his jacket, tanned skin, full lips, and emerald eyes. He wore jeans, a black hoodie, and a Pearl Jam beanie.

I was definitely overdressed for this date in my designer jeans, heeled boots, and poufy turquoise blouse.

"Xander?" I asked.

He nodded and held out a hand. "It's good to meet you."

"You too."

We shook, then stood around awkwardly while I waited for him to say something. Or tell me what we were going to do, for crying out loud. Hopefully, it involved warmth and food; I was starting to shiver.

96

"I like your beanie," I said in desperation. "You a fan of Pearl Jam?" Maybe that's what we were going to do, see some local retro band.

"Yeah," Xander said, stuffing his hands into his pockets. "I go see them when they come around. They put on a great show."

"I haven't been to a concert in years," I said.

"They put on a great show," he said again.

I nodded, but he didn't say anything else. Well, this was horribly uncomfortable. Where was the nice guy I'd chatted with that had a giant shepherd named Max, and had all the jokes about his co-workers? This was not the Xander that made me laugh so hard I'd spit water across my kitchen. Maybe I should pretend to take an emergency phone call and just leave.

And never date again.

"Well, I guess we'll head over," he said, pointing. I turned. Yep, he was pointing at the cowboy and the group clustered around him. Of course he was. This night couldn't get any worse.

* * *

I clutched at the odd device the cowboy — David — had given me. He'd told us it was an EMF reader designed to let us know when ghosts were present. We were to hold it and call out if the numbers increased on the electronic screen. Because naturally, this date wasn't just a history lecture. It was a ghost hunt AND history lecture.

First dates shouldn't be this — they should be coffee or

drinks with maybe a meal. At a place where we could chat and flirt and laugh. We couldn't even talk to each other because it would be rude to interrupt David's lecture. I should've realized this was a huge mistake when Xander hadn't told me what we were doing and to just meet at Vail Ranch Headquarters. And when I'd asked him what to wear, he'd only said nothing fancy.

For a first date. That should've been the red flag.

In Xander's defense, after I'd stumbled in my heels on the dirt path, he'd apologized for being so vague. "I thought I'd surprise you and that it would be fun," he'd said. "You said you like watching ghost movies and this would be something more than just going to a boring meal and making uncomfortable conversation. You know, we could talk afterwards about what we learned over a drink, or coffee or...."

Xander's neck flushed with embarrassment. He had tried. And we had discussed ghosts and ghost movies, but ghost movies weren't...real. Real ghost stories, like the ones you'd find at a ghost hunt, were usually pretty boring. Tales about footsteps and shadows told fifth-hand just weren't all that interesting. There were always logical explanations. And Hollywood could do their Hollywoodness to make ghost movies interesting.

But he'd tried to find something I'd enjoy, and that had to count. "I mean we could go somewhere else," he'd said. "Dinner or...wherever you want."

"Let's try this." Then I'd leaned up and brushed a kiss along his cheek. I could play along, and this would give us something interesting to chat about if there was a second date. And he'd given me his Pearl Jam beanie to keep my ears warm and offered his hoodie, though all he wore was a t-shirt (Dave Mathew's Band) underneath. He smelled like soap and gardening dirt, and was a good height for me in my heels. I could handle this for an hour.

David walked us over to the coffee-and-ice cream store. Someone had enclosed a window and staged a bedroom to show how people in Temecula used to live a hundred or so years ago. It was spartan, with just an iron bed, a wooden chair, and a beat-up trunk with a pitcher on it. A small rag doll sat on the bed. David launched into a lecture about what the building had started as; the Wolf Store owned by Louis Wolf. The building next door, now a series of restaurants, had been his house. Apparently, Temecula had been like the wild west, which explained David's costume, with actual cowboys, farmers, and laborers.

David beckoned us to step closer together and pulled a small tape recorder out of his pocket. "This is a very haunted area. There are reports of shadowy figures seen late at night by the security guards. They go to chase them away and the shadows disappear before their eyes. The stores report sounds of people knocking, doors opening and closing, and even voices when there's no one else around. And objects in this window tend to move. See that doll?"

I peered into the window at the rag doll. She seemed pretty normal, though creepy in that way old dolls looked.

His voice dropped. "Sometimes she's on the bed, sometimes she's against the wall on the floor, and sometimes she's in the chair."

While I knew, I KNEW there was a simple explanation, such as the staff in the store moving the doll to mess with people like David, goosebumps still popped out on my arms. I didn't believe in ghosts, but this guy was good. He'd conjured up images of security guards doing rounds, seeing shadows turning past corners that disappeared in a puff of fog.

One of the teenagers, a girl with short spiky hair, let out a nervous giggle and moved closer to her mom. The mom noticed and touched her daughter's arm. The other teenager, a boy wearing a puffy jacket, pulled out his EMF reader and held it against the window, the numbers shifting but not spiking.

"Before this was built up," David continued. "I got to do a ghost hunt here and recorded the following EVPs. EVP stands for Electronic Voice Phenomenon. That basically means a voice was recorded that we didn't hear at the time of recording and can't explain." The group stepped closer, and my foot hit a small hole, making me stumble. Xander grabbed my arm and steadied me.

"Thanks," I said with a small smile. It was silly, but my nerves were jangling, like they did before going on a roller coaster or giving a presentation at work. I was grateful for Xander's presence and warmth.

"You'll hear my voice asking a question. Listen for what comes afterwards." David pushed a button on the tape recorder.

"Can you hear my voice?" asked a male voice in the background. "If so, can you let us know you're here?"

There was a soft sound in the background. Almost like a

radio announcer or a voice carried by the wind. Xander gasped and clutched at my arm.

David turned off the tape recorder. "Did you hear that?"

The male teenager nodded enthusiastically, while the rest of us shook our heads or frowned.

"Let's do it again," David said, rewinding and hitting play again. We listened to the recording several times.

"I think I hear a woman saying, 'the train is here,'" the boy said.

"Yes!" David said. "I hear the word train, too. Anyone else?"

"Pain?" one half of the couple said. "Pain is here?"

"No one would say that," his partner, a blonde with her hair tied back in a tight ponytail, snapped.

"Maybe she's seeing the doctor," he responded. "Or she hurt herself and she's explaining where to someone."

"Could be," David said.

The girl crept closer to her mom, so close the mom put her arm around her. "I don't like this," the teenager whispered.

"Nothing is going to happen," the mom said. "But do you want to wait in the car?"

"No," she whispered. "But I'm getting the heebie-jeebies." She glanced down at her EMF reader. "The numbers are really high."

As one, we all pulled out our devices. The readouts showed 20s to 30s depending on who was holding it. Xander's hand found mine, and he enclosed his fingers tightly around me. Was he just using the ghosts as an excuse to touch me, or was he as nervous as I was?

"You might be a sensitive," David told the teenager. "Hold them up. Let's see if anyone else picks up anything."

As directed, we held the EMF meters up in the air, moving them around like we were looking for a phone signal back when cell phones had first come out. Suddenly, the numbers dropped back down to zero.

My stomach lurched. Had something been here? Or was it just some odd electrical Wi-Fi thing?

"Whatever was here has left," David proclaimed. "That's pretty common. Ghosts tend to suck up all the energy from an area, do an action, and then disappear back to wherever they hang out. Anyone sensing anything?"

My teeth were chattering, and my legs were wobbly, but was it ghostly or was the icy wind just getting worse? I was going to go with the wind.

"Anything?" I whispered to Xander.

He shook his head, but he was shivering as much as I was. I stepped closer and hooked my arm through his, glad I hadn't taken his hoodie. I leaned up to whisper, my lips brushing his ear. "Do you believe in ghosts? I've never asked."

His eyes were wide, but not with attraction or the beginnings of lust as I'd intended. They were wide with fear.

"I didn't. But—"

"I want to show you all where Louis Wolf used to live," David interrupted, leading us into a patio area with picnic benches and high-top tables. "This is now The Cookhouse with four restaurants, a bar and a small kitschy store. The food is pretty good here. But we're not here to eat, though I'll give you a coupon once we're done."

Xander was shaking so badly, I thought he might fall. I held onto his arm tighter, pressing my body against his. Normally I wouldn't be this forward on a first date, but Xander seemed like he needed the physical contact.

But David didn't seem to notice, continuing his lecture. "There's lots of activity in this building. The owner of the store has reported something knocking over their items at night. Once they'd put up little Christmas trees covered with ornaments they were selling." David's voice dropped. "The owner reported that one morning they came in and someone or something had removed all the ornaments, placing them in a heap on one of the restaurant tables." The others exclaimed, but I saw sweat beading on Xander's forehead despite the cold.

"Are you getting sick?" I asked.

"I'm okay," he said. "I just didn't think…are you having fun?"

"I am, surprisingly. But if you're not feeling good—"

"No, I'm okay," he said. "If you're liking it; let's keep going. I don't want to ruin our date."

"Guests and the restaurant staff often see Louis Wolf's ghost here," David continued. "He appears as either as a gentleman in old clothing — a white shirt with a heavy jacket over the top, or as a shadowy male shape. There are reports in the men's bathroom of seeing a dark figure in the mirror and when men turn around," David pointed toward the bathroom, "There's no one there."

Xander's hand clenched mine again, damp to the touch. Maybe he had hyperhidrosis. I hoped he didn't have COVID or the flu. Okay, it was time to call it and turn in our EMF meters, whether or not the tour was over. Maybe we could get a cup of coffee at the ice cream place and talk more if Xander felt up to it. I waited for a break in David's lecturing.

But David kept talking, barely drawing in a breath between stories. "The most well-known story is about two lost boys, before this area was renovated." The guide flicked at the brim of his hat. "They'd come here because they were dared by some kids at their school."

Though I needed to get Xander inside, I couldn't help stepping closer, trying to hear every word.

"The older teenager left the younger one hiding against the barn to play a joke on him. The youngster got super scared but didn't know where his brother had gone. He ran around from building to building, not finding him, crying. That's when he heard a voice tell him, 'Shhh...it'll be okay.' The voice surprised him, especially since it didn't seem to come from anywhere, but the boy felt so safe he stopped crying. So he waited, against the east wall of the barn, not moving until his brother came back for him."

"That's really sweet," the mom said, rubbing her pale daughter's back. Her other teenager was rapt though, absorbing every word.

"The story's not done," David said, dropping his voice again and making us all crowd closer. Everyone except Xander. He stepped away and my hand fell away from his. "When the older boy came back, something tripped him, and he went sprawling at the younger boy's feet with a broken wrist. The thought is that the ghost, Wolf, punished him for leaving his brother behind."

"No way," the son whispered.

"Let's head over to the barn — there's lots of sounds of footsteps and knocking on the walls there," David said. "There was a haunted house held there, one Halloween, and there were reports of screams coming from it, after they'd shut everything down. They even turned the power off, and the screams continued. I have another recording of an EVP I'd like to share with you."

Behind me, I heard footsteps running away. Heart in my throat — could it be a ghost? — I turned and saw Xander sprinting toward the parking lot. Open-mouthed, I watched him jump into the driver's seat of a Jeep and peel out of the lot.

He'd left me. This tour was his idea, and he'd left me!

What the hell? Everyone in the tour stared at me, the ghost forgotten, pity clear on their faces.

Seriously? He'd gotten so scared by a couple of ghost stories that he'd abandoned me?

An hour later, I opened the door to my house and tossed the drive-thru food onto my kitchen table. After this crazy night, nothing had sounded better than a greasy burger and fries. Unless it was a greasy burger and fries with wine. I'd left the tour soon after Xander had. David had been very charming and offered to let me come back to his tour free of charge. I'd refused, hurrying to my car, away from their pity as quickly as I could. In the parking lot, I'd texted Becca and gotten an explosion of "screw hims!" in return.

But I hadn't heard anything from Xander. He hadn't messaged me to apologize or anything. What a jerk. Taking a big bite of my burger, I deleted the dating app from my phone. Dating wasn't worth this amount of drama. The fridge clicked, and I jumped, still a bit spooked by the stories David had shared.

My phone buzzed. "Hey girl," I answered.

"Are you home yet?" I could hear Becca's kids in the background, shouting about some sort of video game.

"Yep." I took a big guzzle from my wine glass.

"So, he invited you to a ghost hunt, without telling you what it was, then got so scared he ditched you?" she summarized.

"Pretty much."

"Girl, I'm having a glass of wine for you. What an ass! I can't believe he just left you."

I swiped a fry through ketchup and munched. The combination of white wine and ketchuped fries shouldn't have worked, but was actually pretty awesome. More awesome than my date, at least.

"Have you called him?"

"No!" I said. "Don't be ridiculous. And I deleted the dating app. About to delete the texts and his number."

"Hang on," Becca said. "I mean, maybe there's a reason he got so scared."

I refilled my wine glass. "Yeah, he's a jerk," I said, taking a long gulp.

"Tell me his name again," Becca said. "I'm going to look him up."

"I already did that; nothing came up." But I gave her his full name and even his phone number for good measure. "He's just some guy who works in finance and likes 90s rock. I found his LinkedIn, and some pictures on his Instagram from a concert he went to a few years ago. He's so vanilla he got scared at a ghost hunt." My wine glass was empty again. I should stop — my head was getting fuzzy — but I poured another half glass, anyway. It wasn't every day I got abandoned after a first date.

I could hear Becca's fingers tapping on the keyboard. "So... ummmm...tell me his name again."

"Just stop," I slurred slightly. "It doesn't matter. I'm going to put on an old movie, finish my wine and go to bed."

"Calla...." her voice was different, flat, without any of the playful girl banter. I heard her lick her lips. "The only Xander Shaw I can find in this area died about two years ago. Car accident. On the way to San Diego State for a Pearl Jam concert. His dog Max died too."

"Oh, shut up," I said, though the Pearl Jam and dog reference added a frightening level of realism. The wine in my stomach lurched. "Don't mess with me. How would a ghost use a dating app? And a cell phone?"

"I'm not messing with you." Becca's voice was a little shaken. "I swear I'm not."

"I saw him get into his Jeep and drive away," I said, rubbing away goosebumps on my arms. I stood and double-checked to make sure all the doors were locked. "There's all these texts from him. Ghosts can't do that."

"I know," Becca said. "I can't explain it. Want me to come over? Do you want to come over here?"

"No. You're just messing with me. We both have work tomorrow. And this isn't real. I'm sure there was just another Xander Shaw or reports got confused or...." I pulled the blinds shut, finishing my wine, then poured a bit more into my glass.

"Okay," Becca said. "I love you. Be careful. And call if you need anything. I'll check on you in the morning."

"You're being ridiculous," I said.

"Look it up yourself, then. I'm not screwing around here."

"I'm not going to. Night. Love you too."

Draining my wine, my head swam. I looked over at my closed laptop, sitting on the kitchen table, mocking me. Should I do a search for Xander? Or I could call him; confirm I hadn't gone out on a date with a ghost — which, of course, I hadn't — but that would be absurd.

My hands moved of their own violation, pulling the laptop over. I opened the cover, a search engine popping up on the screen immediately, taunting me.

I should go to bed. I'd had too much wine after an enormous disappointment. Becca was just messing with me, which she'd done before. In the morning, things would seem better. More clear. I was letting Becca and David's ghost stories mess with my head.

I laid my fingers across the keyboard and, cursing myself for being an idiot, began to type.

Contributor Biographies

Theresa Halvorsen

Theresa Halvorsen is an overly caffeinated YouTuber, editor, and author of non-fiction and speculative fiction works, including *Warehouse Dreams*, *Lost Aboard*, and *River City Widows*. She lives in San Diego, is a host for the popular YouTube channel Semi-Sages of the Pages, and is the owner and Chief Editor at No Bad Books. Find her on Threads, TikTok, and Facebook.

Barbara C. Nelson

Barbara C. Nelson has a dedicated career in art: 30 years as an art teacher, many years as an architectural illustrator, and since retirement, as a plein air and portrait painter. Barbara has trained with many renowned artists and is a signature member of the Western Colorado Watercolor Society. She has been a recipient of many awards including Best of Show, first and second place at the wonderful Ralph Love Plein Air competition in Temecula over the years. Examples of Barbara's work can be seen on the website BryantMNelson.com.

STAY AWHILE, STAY WITH ME

Story by Suzanne Y. Saunders

Illustration by Sabin R. Flores
Gouache & Watercolor

G OLDEN-RED LEAVES BLOW ACROSS the sidewalk of the Temecula Valley College campus as the cool autumn air chills Brandon and Karina's faces. Walking to the parking lot, they hold hands, trying to keep warm. Karina picks up the pace and releases Brandon's hand.

"Hey, why'd you do that?" he asks.

She heads to the car. "It's cold, and you gotta get to your dad's shop."

"Slow down. Don't be in such a rush," he says, trying to catch up to her.

"I'm not the one always in a rush. You are!"

Brandon opens the car door for her, and she gets in.

"Let's go," she says.

He starts the car, concerned by her behavior.

"Aren't you going to ask me if we can get coffee like we always do?"

She looks at him, annoyed. "No."

The car motor rumbles as the heater slowly kicks in.

"Your car is always so cold," she says.

He wonders if his plan to surprise her with a night out will fail. "Let's get some coffee."

She tilts her head back. "I told you I don't want to get coffee." She looks at him, "And, I said it for a reason." She looks out the window. "The last time I held you up from getting to your dad's shop, you got irritated with me. I'm not letting that happen again."

"Let's get coffee anyway," he says as he drives up to the little coffee shop near the campus. He parks the car. Karina stays silent.

"You wanna go in?" he asks.

"I'll stay in the car," she says.

Brandon orders the coffee extra sweet in a big to-go cup. He explains to the barista that his girlfriend waits in the car, mad at him. The barista wishes him luck.

When he gets back in the car, he hands Karina her coffee, "This will make you feel better."

She looks at it and cracks a smile, "I think it might." She takes a sip. Her eyes open wide with approval, "It's sweeter than usual. I like it."

"Good, because you need to be warmed up."

"Hey," she says, defensively.

"Well, to be honest, you're a little icy right now," he says.

She smiles, aware of her behavior, "I hope I'm not holding you up from getting back to your dad's shop."

"No, I'm off tonight. Anyways, I've got a surprise for you."

"Oh, yeah?" She looks around. "Is the surprise here?"

"No, I have to drive you to it."

"So, it's a place? Where is it?"

He smiles, "It's a place that has rows and rows of corn stalks."

She laughs, "Where? Iowa?

"No, think closer to home."

"Oh, um...."

He adds, "You pass it every day to work."

"Rows and rows of corn stalks? I don't know."

"You can't give up that easily. Really think. Whenever we pass it, you say how you love the place."

Her eyes open wide, "Oh, then, I know where you're talking about...the big feed store on the corner of Butterfield Stage and Temecula Parkway!"

"That's it!"

"Really? We're gonna do the corn maze? This evening?"

"Yeah, we still have some daylight left. I decided we're gonna do it this year. I'll take my allergy pills and keep my inhaler on me, and we'll go through it. I think taking our public speaking class has upped my confidence."

"Brandon, I'm so proud of you. I know it's tough with your allergies. I like the outdoors and I know it's a little hard for you to go to some of the places I like, but I'm happy you want to go. You want to go, right?"

"I do because I'm making some changes...big changes, and you're a part of it," he declares.

"Wow, thanks. I'm excited, so we better go if we want to get there before the sun goes down."

"Yeah, so let's roll."

As Brandon drives, Karina shares her excitement, "I know you know this, but I'm so excited about going to the feed store. When I was little, I'd buy horse books there and daydream about having one."

"At least you get to see horses when you go to your riding lesson."

"I know. They're so beautiful. Once I'm done with college, I hope to buy a horse," she glows.

"There's a lot we can do once we're both done with college."

"Yeah, I suppose there is. We still have three more years 'til we're done."

"I know, but our situation may change sooner than you think."

"Really? Why?"

"Because things may change," he offers.

Karina looks out the window, "We're almost to the corn maze!"

116

Brandon parks the car in an open field, which during the rest of the year grows crops, but now is full of cars. They get out to walk to the festival entrance.

"I haven't been here in ages," Karina says. She looks at the stacks of straw with pumpkins everywhere and a scarecrow here and there.

"Sorry, that's probably my fault."

"Don't think that way."

They walk through the dirt parking lot, making their shoes dusty.

"Well, it is. Any time you suggested it, I dismissed it because of my allergies."

"You can't help that," Karina assures.

"But, I can because I've decided I'm getting allergy shots. I'm scheduled to begin treatment in a week."

"Wow. You didn't tell me."

"I wanted to surprise you. Coming to the fall festival corn maze is the beginning of me making changes...for the better."

They approach the entrance.

"Let's see the draft horses and the goats first," she squeals.

Brandon stops. "Of course." He pats his jacket pocket. "Got my inhaler."

She smiles. "Did you take an allergy pill?"

"Yep, at the coffee shop."

Enthusiastically, she declares "Then, let's go!"

"I'm right behind you."

Making their way to the goat pen, designed like a mini red

barn, they see goats of all sizes and colors: cream, beige, black, white, and brown. The goats clamor around Karina and Brandon, searching for food. Karina pulls feed pellets out of her pocket and feeds them. They climb onto her legs, reaching for her hand full of pellets. She laughs and falls to her knees as the goats swarm her like bees to honey. Karina's face lights up. Pulling more feed pellets out of her pockets, she says, "They're so cute. One day, I'll have one, or two, or maybe more." She laughs.

"They are cute," agrees Brandon.

They give the goats the last of the feed pellets, say their good-byes, and eagerly make their way to the horses. When they reach the corral, they see three golden-red horses.

"They're big," Brandon says.

"And, beautiful," adds Karina.

"Yeah, that too."

"Can you imagine having such a magnificent animal?" she says dreamily.

"Can you imagine the feed bill?"

Karina laughs, "Who cares! As long as they're mine to admire."

Karina reaches into the corral to touch the nose of one of the horses. "I swear, her nose feels like velvet." The horse steps closer to Karina. "I think she wants me to pet her." Karina places her hand on the horse's forehead and gently pats it. Stroking the horse, she says to the horse, "You're such a good girl. If you were mine, I'd name you Emaline, and call you Emy for short."

Brandon looks at the sky. "Sorry to say, but I think we better go if we want to get through the corn maze before dark."

"Of course," agrees Karina. She looks at the horse, "Bye, Emaline."

Brandon takes Karina's hand, "Let's go this way."

Making their way through the various booths set up at the festival, they pass food vendors, and fall craft displays. Finally, they reach the entrance to the corn maze with its big archway and pictures of corn painted on it.

Brandon looks at the seven-foot corn stalks, "We could easily get lost in here."

"I know. That's what makes it exciting," says Karina. "There's the box with the pamphlets. We have to read questions and answer them to guide our way through the maze." She looks in the box. "Let's pick this one." She opens it. "Oooooh. It has questions about the stars. I can't believe we're gonna do this. We'll be in here for an hour, so...you sure you're ready?"

"I'm all in," he declares.

"Okay, here's the first question," she begins, "If the sun rises in the East, which direction does it set?"

"The West. That was easy," says Brandon.

"Okay, if we answered 'the west' then we go this way to signpost Two."

"You lead the way."

"Next question, 'What's the difference between a star and a planet?'"

"I got this," he says. "A star, like the sun, is made of gases and fire."

"Yeah, and planets aren't on fire," she adds. "Since we gave that as our answer, we go this way to signpost Three."

"We got this. We'll be out of here in no time."

They continue through the maze, answering questions about stars, constellations, and the universe. As they walk, they talk about their future.

Thinking out loud, Karina says, "I wonder what the stars have in mind for us?"

"What do you mean?"

"You know, sayings like 'It's in the stars' and 'When stars align.'"

"Oh, yeah, I bet the stars have a plan."

"I wish I knew the plan. What do you want to do when you finish college? Do you think you'll continue working in your dad's shop or do something else?"

Brandon considers her question, "I'm lucky to have my dad's shop as an option. I like running the machines to make banners and prints on t-shirts, but I think the store can offer more."

"Like what?"

"I think we really need to branch out on our promotional items. We can do everything. That's why I'm majoring in marketing because I want to know all aspects of marketing and promotion."

"I bet your dad will go with it."

"I hope so."

A thought occurs to Karina, "This maze is a lot like life — trying to find your way to a destination."

"Yeah."

"It's the whole thing of trying to pick a path...you know...like with college." She looks at the path in front of them and at the tall corn stalks that hide what's ahead.

"I thought you had your plan for college," says Brandon.

With reluctance, Karina explains, "I have my plan, but my friends all disagree with me."

"Really? Why?"

"They think I should go to school out of state, like to Arizona."

Brandon's face shows concern, "But, we have extension classes here in the area. And, there are universities within driving distance."

"That's what I've told them. But, they say I should live the full college experience."

Brandon's distress comes through when he says, "And, do what? Get drunk at parties? Date a bunch of frat guys?"

"I guess," she sighs. "But, I don't want that."

"You have to decide what you want. If you leave for college that could...that could...." He stops mid-sentence.

"That could what? What are you saying?"

"That could be it for us. That could end us."

Raising her eyebrows and her voice, Karina says, "I don't want that to happen."

"Neither do I," says Brandon.

Stopping at the next signpost, Karina reads the next question. "Here's the question: How many solstices does the Earth have?"

Brandon thinks aloud, "Is it two or four?"

"I think it's only two," she laughs. "We have four seasons, but I think a solstice happens twice a year. Maybe in June and December." She looks at the answer. "Yep, two a year. It says the Earth tilts a different direction with each solstice." Thinking more deeply about their dilemma, she adds "I wish we had a guidebook for making life's decisions."

"You can probably buy one if you want one, but I think we can make our own decisions."

She agrees, "I think we can. For now, we just have one more signpost to show us the way out."

"Yep, it should be coming up if we're on track," says Brandon. "We better find it quick because we're losing sunlight."

"We'll find it," she assures.

"I see it," he says.

Making their way down the last path of the corn maze, they see the exit. As they stand at the exit, Brandon says "We're here! Our final destination!"

"We did it! You did it! And, your allergies didn't bother at all."

Brandon takes her hand and stands with Karina before stepping through the exit of the maze.

Karina says, "This is it. Now, I'm sad we're done."

"Me, too," he says. "It was fun. I didn't realize what I was missing."

"Yeah, it's a great place. Kind of magical in a way."

"True! When you're in the maze, you feel like you're lost in no-where-land."

She laughs, "I know. It takes you somewhere else."

Facing Karina, Brandon says, "Let's stand right here for a moment."

"Sure," she agrees.

He releases his hand from hers and puts both his hands behind his back and smirks.

"What are you doing?" she asks.

"You have to figure it out," he teases.

"You're holding something behind your back."

"Maybe."

She grabs at his hands. "Did you buy me something in the store?

He backs away, laughing, "No." He backs away more so that she can't reach it. Tripping over a corn stalk, he falls backwards into the maze. A box drops out of his hand. He gets up. "I lost the box!"

"But you just had it!"

He holds his hands up, "It's gone." He rushes into the corn stalks. "I gotta find it."

"It's got to be here," says Karina, trying to help.

"And, we're losing sunlight."

Searching frantically, they feel hopeless. It's nowhere to be found. In frustration, they sit down and look at each other. "It's lost forever," says Brandon.

"I hope it wasn't expensive."

"It's not about the money. It's about what it meant." He adds, "I hope we're not lost forever."

"Don't say that."

"We better stand up, so we don't look strange sitting here," he says as he helps her up.

An older couple walks by them. "Hey," says the man. "Did you just drop that box?" The man points to it.

On the ground, under a stalk, sits the box.

Both Brandon and Karina's eyes open wide. "Yes!" says Brandon. "We did. Thanks!"

"Have a good day," says the man as the couple walk on.

"We were sitting on it," she laughs. "It was right here all along."

Brandon holds it in his hands, "Now, we have the box."

Karina smiles, "We have the box. So, what's in the box?"

"To find out, you have to answer three questions."

"Okay, I'm ready," she says.

"Question number one: What's your favorite thing to do?"

"Hang out with you."

He raises his eyebrows, "Good answer."

"Now, question number two: Where's your favorite place to live?"

"Easy, here in Temecula," she smiles.

"Another good answer," he says. "Okay, now for question number three: Where do you see yourself in five years?"

Her face becomes serious. "Oh, wow, now I really have to think, but I have an answer. I see myself done with school — working as a vet tech — and, I see myself—" She stops and looks at him. "I see myself with you."

He furrows his brows to tease her, and then smiles big. "That's the best answer!!"

"So, do I get to see what's in the box?"

"Yeah." He holds it up high so she has to reach for it. When she does, he hugs her, then hands it to her, "Be warned. You open it at your own risk."

"I'll take that risk."

She looks at the top of the box. It has a note written on it.

Gazing at him curiously, she asks, "What's this? It says, 'I promise to....'"

"You have to open it."

"Okay." She opens it slowly. Inside, she sees a slim silver ring with a small sapphire.

"Brandon, it's a ring. Is this a—?"

He interrupts, "It's a promise ring."

"A 'promise' ring?"

"Yeah, it's a promise ring. It means I promise to ask you to marry you when you're ready."

She hugs him. "I promise to let you ask me when I'm ready."

"I'm so glad you accepted the ring."

"I love it. Can I wear it?"

"Of course, it's yours."

Brandon looks up at the autumn sky to assess the remaining sunlight.

Karina looks at him. "It's not only your promise to me, it's mine to you, too."

"I like that."

"Look at that beautiful fall sunset," she says.

"It is, but it's getting dark, so I better get you home," he says as he puts his arm around her.

"I know it's getting dark, but can we just stay awhile, until the sun fully sinks into the hills. I never get tired of looking at the plateau range. I would stay right here, forever, if I could — with you — in this place I love," Karina says.

"Me, too."

Karina thinks for a moment, "You know what I'll always remember about this evening?"

"What? The ring?" he asks.

"No, that we made a commitment to stay with each other."

Brandon smiles at Karina. She wraps her arms around him. They watch the golden-red sunset light up the sky above the Temecula Valley hills.

Contributor Biographies

Suzanne Y. Saunders

Suzanne Y. Saunders writes novels, plays, and more recently screenplays that she hopes will be produced someday. Her stories and scripts uplift and inspire her audience to take on the challenges of life, encouraging them to always move forward. In addition to writing, she teaches college students at Mt. San Jacinto College and rides horses. Her education includes an M.A. in Literature and Writing Studies and a screenplay writing certificate from UCLA.

Sabin R. Flores

Sabin R Flores is a multi-medium artist who takes inspiration from various sources. They grew up aspiring to work in the animation industry and learned a lot about the technical aspect of cartoons. They furthered their education by attending online art school classes taught by the masters in the field. Although they specialize in drawing they have also recently experimented with traditional painting and crocheting.

THE PRECARIOUS CITY

Story by Jeff Comerchero & E.J. Radford

Illustration by Charlie Schimmel
Digital

PART 1

DECEMBER 1, 1989: THE City of Temecula was born. The question of cityhood was on the ballot asking the residents if they wanted the 26 square miles of unincorporated Iand on which they lived, formerly known as Rancho California, to self-govern and become a new city. Fully 88% voted yes, and Temecula, with its 26,000 people, was off and running.

Twenty-five years earlier, in the small midwestern township of Spartan Missouri, Michael Trenwell was born. Spartan's population was under 2,000, and it was the last place you would expect a future business mogul to be born and raised. Michael was a good student, but a quality education was hard to come by in that tiny one-room schoolhouse. The advantage, though, was if you had a brain, it was easy to rise to the head of the class. If you were a mischievous troublemaker, everyone in town knew your name. Everyone in Spartan knew the name Michael Trenwell, and not always because they admired him.

Others did take note of his academic prowess and at the age of 18, Trenwell won a scholarship to a mid-level Southern California university. His grades were good enough, in part because he was always open to plagiarizing the work of others, and in 1986, at the age of 22 and with a degree in business in his attaché case, he set off to make his fortune. Michael started up his 1972 Volkswagen Beetle and headed south from Los Angeles with no destination in his thoughts. He took the inland route on the mostly completed Interstate 15 and, almost out of gas, he got off at the Rancho California Road exit. He didn't know what it was, maybe a wealth of opportunity, but he liked what he saw and decided to stay for a while. What he couldn't know at that time was "a while" was the rest of his life.

Trenwell was right about seeing opportunity. He learned that the Rancho California area had a master plan to grow rapidly, and all he could see was acre upon acre of vacant land. Others might have simply seen a lot of nothing, but not Michael. He saw dollar signs.

Just a few years later, many of the 26,000 residents of what was called Rancho California were getting disgruntled over the fact that their governing body was 30 miles north, in the City of

Riverside. Decisions that could have a profound effect on them were being made by people who in most cases had never even set foot in the area these thousands of people called home. Housing tract after housing tract were being approved and built and the local residents had no say in how their now rapidly growing community was developing.

One person taking advantage of those easy land development approvals was young Mike Trenwell. It made no difference to him that, as a result of the rapid, dynamic growth, the roads were insufficient, as were parks, libraries, medical facilities, and the other amenities that would create a reason for people to want to live there.

He had one objective and no scruples. Any avenue he could find to put money in his bank accounts, he took. If that meant shady, sometimes illegal tactics, Michael didn't really care. He started by falsifying information on a loan application and borrowed $150,000 to purchase 20 acres. He over-inflated the value of the property, and with the local loan officers handling so many transactions at that time, they skipped the time and expense of having an appraisal done.

Michael was smooth and convincing. The purchase price of the 40 acres was $100,000, and he used the balance of the money to plan homes on the property. That would obtaining the simple zoning approvals from the County Planning Commission. With the approvals to build 120 homes on the property and values rising, he was able to sell them to a homebuilding company for $12,000 "a door" or a total of $1,440,000. He was becoming something dangerous to the young community, a greedy developer with a bankroll.

Michael Trenwell was well on his way. With no shortage of either raw land or local opportunity, he duplicated his business model several times over the next 30 years and became one of the wealthiest people in what was now the City of Temecula. He was ruthless. He continued to borrow or steal, cheating many along the way. As his wealth grew, so did his list of enemies — a list that included most of the City's elected leaders.

The residents' desire for local control in that 1989 election worked out as they had hoped. They elected a City Council who proved to be caring, business-minded and with a goal of making Temecula the finest city in California. Over the next 30 years, peace, harmony, and a great deal of progress was the order of the day. The new city became a very desirable place to live and as a result, it became one of the fastest-growing cities in the nation. By 2018, the population was over 100,000. The early city leaders formulated and implemented a plan that not only made Temecula a great place to live, but it also became the economic and political powerhouse of the region.

Trenwell, now in his 50s and driving as hard as ever, had a personal balance sheet that pegged his net worth at more than $200,000,000. It would have been substantially higher were it not for the property settlements and alimony in favor of his four ex-wives and the amounts he was forced to pay to others as a result of the sixteen lawsuits that were ruled against him. He had two children, one from each of his first two wives. The older child,

Alicia, inherited most of her father's traits. She was brilliant and had a business mind that surpassed even that of her dad. She also possessed the meanness and shadiness that had marked Michael's life. Alicia's brother, Kyle, three years younger, was the antithesis of his sister. He was intelligent enough, but also mild-mannered and ethical. Dear old Dad had no plans to slow down or retire anytime soon, but eventually his two kids would take over the business, and the chaos that would be created was beyond Michael's comprehension.

Part 2

In 2018, the city was 30 years old and, while it was still running smoothly, cracks started to develop at the top. With retirements and some new faces on the City Council, the feeling of Camelot that existed previously was all but disappearing. Politics started rearing its ugly head in a manner that mirrored the national rancor between those who were left-leaning and the emergence of a hardline conservative movement that had its roots in religion. This dynamic, having begun with the city council election of 2020, then found its way to the local school boards starting in 2022. It was an ultra-conservative national movement fueled by Bible-thumping zealots. They started by rewriting history, removing anything from school textbooks that wasn't to their liking. Then they banned books they felt were outside of their Christian principles. Eventually they tried to ostracize any group who looked different or didn't believe as they did. It became a lesson in how to turn a city that was once the envy of much of the nation into a place where its residents couldn't wait to leave.

Developer Michael Trenwell didn't care much about local politics, but when property values plummeted and his real estate business began to dry up, he was forced to take notice. He anticipated running his company for at least another 20 years. Unfortunately, stress took its toll and in 2023 he had a debilitating massive stroke. He could no longer function on his own, and it took a conservator to implement the company's succession plan. That plan gave siblings Alicia and Kyle each 50% ownership and shared management of Trenwell Development Inc.

Throughout the last several years, the company had branched out into more than just real estate development. Anything in which its founder saw potential profit was fair game. This included a string of not-always permitted massage parlors, backroom gambling establishments and a stable of prostitutes. By the time cannabis was legalized in California, Trenwell already had a monopoly in both its growing and distribution. He seemed hell bent on turning this once beautiful city, a city that he himself built so much of, into the scourge of Riverside County. It should have been up to the leadership of the city to stop him, but with their own political infighting and agendas, little relevant work was getting done. It was ironic that the newly elected officials were consumed by banning books, rather than trying to limit what Trenwell was doing.

By 2026, the senior city staff, once the bastion of dedication and efficiency, was decimated. These were very talented people who would be in high demand in any other city. Until now, they chose to remain in Temecula because they took pride in the city they helped create. With weak and divided elected leadership, that pride was rapidly waning. They no longer had a desire to deal with the crap, so either they retired or left the area for other jobs. Contrary to what most people believe, although the city council sets policy, it's the senior staff that makes everything work.

In addition to the internal struggles of Temecula, the State of California was acting as if its primary objective was to eliminate local control of cities. The problems started in 2012, when Governor Jerry Brown decided that the Redevelopment Agency Program was a detriment to the state. In February of that year, he forced all cities and counties to terminate the program. It had provided valuable funding for many beneficial projects, especially in growing cities like Temecula.

The program had been innovative, yet simple. The local Redevelopment Agency would identify their vacant properties and work with local businesses to plan and build something, most importantly "affordable housing." The property taxes on vacant land were very low. So, as an example, a private business comes in and, with the City's help, builds an affordable housing complex. The property, now fully improved, has a much higher tax rate paid by the private company. The difference in the property tax rates was called "Tax Increment" and the city got to keep it all instead of it going into the State's coffers as all other property taxes did. The city then used that tax increment to assist in the building of additional projects that were beneficial to its residents. Over the years, the Redevelopment Agencies played a significant role in the successful growth of cities like Temecula. Then, just like that, it was gone.

The Federal government didn't help either, constantly taking away local dollars or cutting grants drastically. If they didn't cut funds altogether, the Feds put so many strings and restricted uses on the money that cities couldn't use it.

It took several years but eventually the City of Temecula lost its way. With political instability and gradually reduced financial resources, the city started on a downward spiral that would take many years to reverse. Some cities never recovered. The residents became disillusioned and apathetic, making it easier for the extremists to get elected. By 2032, they had full control of the city. Their goal then became to do away with the constitutional protections mandating the separation of church and state and combine them both in a devout Christian enclave. They insisted that they only had to answer to God and not the people. Rather than making the important decisions from the city council dais, they started preaching their gospel from their individual pulpits. Temecula became a full-blown theocracy.

Part 3

Almost unnoticed through all the turmoil was that Michael Trenwell, the wealthiest, but most despised man in Temecula, died in 2034. Although his earlier stroke destroyed most of his ability to move or communicate, as long as he was alive his presence was felt — particularly by his children. Only Alicia, Kyle, and Mr. Trenwell's caregiver, Marie Gardner, attended the funeral. Marie Gardner had begun caring for him at the tender age of 20 and proved to be so valuable that they couldn't do without her. The old man needed constant supervision and care, and his children wanted no part of it. Marie seemed simply to appear. No one knew much about her or her past, but what the family did know, they liked. They sensed a certain air about Marie that contradicted her place. Nothing they could quantify, just a feeling.

The Trenwell children were now 41 and 38 years old. They had both spent the last sixteen years working at The Trenwell Development Company. After their father's stroke, they each held the title of "Co-CEO" with joint decision-making authority. Neither could move without the other. Considering that they were total opposites and rarely agreed on even a restaurant for dinner, running the company became a near impossibility. The business became paralyzed by indecision, and it seemed that everything drove a wedge between them. They almost came to blows over what to do with Marie Gardner now that she no longer had a job. Kyle, recognizing her value, wanted to keep her on and find an appropriate place for her within the company. The size of Trenwell Development had shrunk substantially during the last decade, but they still had assets that needed to be managed. Alicia came to despise Marie, if only because Kyle liked her. The truth is that Kyle, who had been consumed by the family business, had fallen in love with her.

With their father gone and the new regime at City Hall, sustaining the company became harder and harder. Although there were a few income-producing assets, most of the properties still owned were raw land that they hoped to sell when the market was ripe. Given the downhill spiral the city was on and its effect on property values, they had to acknowledge that the market might not ripen for a while.

Although the new city council majority was elected by the people, the voters never saw who they REALLY were until after the election. The candidates, and the religious forces behind them, were quite adept at campaigning by telling the residents only what they wanted to hear. In political races the accepted wisdom is that you choose three buzz phases and repeat them repeatedly until the public believes them. In most cases, particularly in local elections, those three statements were well intended promises. But in the campaign of 2032, it was anything but that. The three candidates who would eventually comprise the new majority, used every trick imaginable to convince the voters that their election was critical to the welfare of the city. Their mantra became 1) we will drastically reduce or abolish all your taxes, 2) we will establish a minimum wage of $45 an hour for all workers within the city limits and, 3) we will ensure that everyone over the age of eighteen would have a local job so no one would have to commute outside of Temecula. They would have said they would eliminate traffic too, a perennial issue, but flying air taxis were gaining favor nationally and were starting to

140

gain a foothold in Temecula as well.

Although these hollow promises were impossible to achieve, they resonated with the voters. They even defeated a 70-year-old, very popular incumbent by accusing him of being a septuagenarian. Most people thought that meant he was a sex addict, and they wanted him booted out of office. Another incumbent council member lost all his support when the three extremists called a press conference advising the world that they didn't want to run a negative campaign and said there was no truth to the rumor that Council Member Stanton was a child molester. The extremists won easily and the road to city oblivion began.

With all the negatives piling up and working against them, Alicia and Kyle Trenwell were at a crossroads. Kyle, ever the optimist, wanted to persevere and look for creative ways to keep the company alive. He had grown tired of his sister's attempt to demoralize him by questioning his every decision and generally exerting undue pressure on him. Alicia, on the other hand, felt it was time for her to move on, possibly to another city or region and do something totally different. Although the company itself was not doing well, both owners were astute enough to have built their personal fortunes through all the good years. Considering that Kyle was optimistic, and Alicia disgruntled, it seemed to be a good time for them to discuss a mutual agreement under which Kyle Trenwell would become the sole owner of Trenwell Development Inc.

The negotiations were contentious. Although the discussions

centered around money, that wasn't the reason for the hostility. They were sister and brother, but they really didn't like one another. If there was a hint that one of them would be perceived as the winner and one the loser, they would never come to an agreement. The trick was for Alicia to believe that what she was getting was more than half what the business was worth and for Kyle to at least feel that he was paying no more than fair market value. They arrived at a price of 8.25 million dollars for Alicia's half. That was high, but Kyle's net worth could support it. He would have to liquidate some personal assets to raise all the money. It was important for him to be free of his antagonistic sister, so he agreed and was happy.

Unbeknown to Alicia, Kyle and Marie Chandler had started dating after Mr. Trenwell passed away. On the evening after the deal with Alicia was agreed to but not yet consummated, Kyle and Marie were having dinner and discussing this new business arrangement. Casually over an after-dinner aperitif, Marie began to reveal herself.

"I want to be your new partner!"

Kyle wasn't sure he heard right. While she had taken care of his father, they paid her a very modest sum plus room and board. Now she was talking about putting several million dollars into a business venture. Kyle always felt Marie had a good head on her shoulders, but now he was questioning whether or not she had lost her sanity. "Marie, do you mean you want to put in a few thousand dollars?"

Marie seemed a bit offended. "No, silly. A partner is a

partner. I want to buy the half you're buying from Alicia!"

"You do realize, Marie, that I just committed to pay more than eight million dollars for that half, don't you?"

"I do," she answered. And those were the same two words she was hoping they would say in a different context. What she didn't know was that Kyle was wishing for the same thing.

Marie was good at creating the impression that she was a hard-working girl who didn't make much money — just adequate to fill her limited needs. She was only twenty when she began taking care of Mr. Trenwell, so she really didn't know much of a world beyond the family home. What Marie kept hidden was the fact that she was a "trust-fund" baby. And a large trust fund it was. The family wealth came from her great-grandfather. He was born in 1889 in a small town in Massachusetts. In 1911, after three years of working at a law firm, he was admitted to the California Bar. As a young lawyer he became enamored with criminal trials, especially murder trials. He bought a ranch that he called "Rancho del Paisano" on the south side of what is now Temecula, and it was there that he wrote many of the novels published during his lifetime.

In 1933, Uncle Erle, as he was known to those close to him, penned his first novel about a Los Angeles area attorney who mostly accepted offbeat murder cases. The character would often use courtroom theatrics and won virtually all his cases, while also exposing the real murderer. Erle Stanley Gardner wrote more than 80 Perry Mason books that were read all over the world. His works were also turned into a television series that ran from 1957 to 1966. He died in 1970, and generations after him benefited from the financial rewards that his prolific career created. His great-granddaughter Marie was a very wealthy woman. Although her name was Gardner, that's not an unusual name, and no one made the connection.

Just an ounce of alcohol was enough for Marie to tell Kyle of her family history. "I really can afford to be your partner. Why don't you just let me buy out Alicia for the same $8,250,000?"

Kyle, trying to get over his shock at what he just heard, thought for a moment. He concluded that Alicia would never knowingly sell half the company to her father's caregiver, but this might be the opening he'd been waiting for. He poured himself another drink, summoned all his courage and said, "Marie, you've absolutely floored me with this revelation. I just don't know what to say, other than I would love to have you for a partner in business...and in life. Marie, will you do me the honor of becoming my wife?"

With tears streaming down her cheeks, she said yes.

Kyle knew that Alicia wouldn't sell to Marie, but nothing prevented him from doing so. Thirty days later, the deal between the siblings was complete, and the next day Kyle sold half the company to Marie. It became a moot point when on September 3, 2034, after a beautiful ceremony on the Great Oak Ranch, formally Rancho del Paisano, Marie Gardner became Mrs. Kyle Trenwell. California is a community property state, so by law Marie would have owned half the business anyway. The irony is that without her offer to purchase, who knows if Kyle would have ever gotten up the nerve to ask for her hand.

With Alicia out of the picture and Marie sharing his life, Kyle jumped back into the business looking for ways to generate revenue. Although he had serious issues with the way the city was being run, he heartily agreed with the city council shutting down the company's massage parlors, strip clubs and gambling halls. The only remaining segments of the company were the land development business and the cannabis empire. Since no one wanted to live in Temecula anymore, the real estate market had totally stagnated. The Trenwells took a hard look at their assets to determine what they might be able to leverage. It wasn't about money — they had all they needed — but rather it was about preserving a legacy.

They wanted to start a family. Realizing they were getting older, they didn't want to wait.

"How about you and I going on nice vacation for a few weeks, then getting serious about a baby?" Kyle asked.

Marie liked the idea and said, "I'd love to go to New York for the Christmas season."

They arranged their flights and hotels. Marie said she always wanted to stay at the Plaza Hotel, so Kyle booked it. He also made a few dinner reservations and bought tickets to a handful of Broadway shows. Off they went.

They went to several shows and rediscovered that there was little that was original on the stage anymore; rather, it was almost exclusively either revivals or storylines that came from other sources. On the evening after one such show, they were having dinner at the iconic Tavern on the Green restaurant in the middle of snow-covered Central Park. The show they saw the night before was a stage version of the 1957 Agatha Christie movie, "Witness for the Prosecution".

As Marie and Kyle discussed the play and how much they enjoyed it, Marie said, "Agatha Christie's work always makes me think of my great-grandfather's Perry Mason novels. In many ways the plot lines are similar".

That statement hit Kyle over the head like a sledgehammer. In assessing their assets, they never thought about the fact that Marie, as Erle Stanley Gardner's only heir, now owned the rights to all his books.

On February 10, 2037, the first of what was to be fifty Perry Mason plays opened at the Old Town Temecula Theater to rave reviews. The venue, which was originally opened in 2004 as a small community theater, was enlarged in 2028 and now could accommodate up to 1200 patrons. On this night, there was a body in every seat. There were few people left who remembered that the famous author made his home in Temecula, but with the publicity surrounding what the Trenwells were doing, new generations of residents were exposed to the history of Rancho del Paisano and its famous resident. Sales of the more than 80 books in the Perry Mason series were revived after many years of inactivity.

After the success of the Temecula opening, the other Perry Mason plays opened all over the country. By 2041, there was a different Perry Mason play running in 50 different cities. The idea was to have a play run for 90 days, then rotate to another city. It would take more than twelve years, but eventually, all the plays ran in every city, for three months at a time. It was an entirely new concept in live theater and the public couldn't get enough of it. It did several things for the Trenwell family. It created a huge revenue stream that resulted in tremendous generational wealth. By the time their third child was born in 2044, they knew that someday their kids would be managing a juggernaut. It also allowed them to liquidate Trenwell Development Inc., shut it down, and erase the negative reputation their father had created.

The extremists who had been elected to the city council managed to convince the voters in 2036 that they deserved to be re-elected. But after eight years of their control and the city moving steadily downhill, the public — at least those who hadn't yet moved away — clearly saw that the decline and the negative leadership were tied to each other. The elections of 2040 produced a stunning turnaround, and the council once again had a majority that cared about the welfare of its constituents. At first the changes were slow to develop, but over the next decade, Temecula regained its position amongst the best places to live in California. High quality senior staff once again started to find Temecula a great place to work. The city also annexed all the surrounding land it could for the purpose of designing and building the kind of world-class facilities that normally would be found in much larger cities around the world.

In addition to being caring and compassionate, the new city leaders were intelligent and highly diverse. Each could work with the others without regard to race, religion, or lifestyle. The order that replaced the chaos was a beautiful thing to see.

The new leaders knew that if they wanted great new facilities, they would have to find a way to finance them. In a quirk of fate, a retired financial whiz who happened to be the former Chief Financial Officer for Trenwell Development was brought on as a consultant to help them set up a strategy. He devised a program through which they could sell "revenue bonds," build a stadium and an arena, then use the proceeds from ticket sales to service the debt. In essence, they found a creative and legal way to duplicate the Redevelopment Agency program that California's governor had shut down so many years before. The idea was brilliant, and it worked perfectly.

Paying homage to its more recent local history, the "Trenwell Sports Complex" opened on June 24, 2048. The first football game played in the stadium pitted the Temecula University Vintners against the San Diego State Aztecs. The honor of the traditional coin toss was given to Alicia Trenwell, who came back from her home in North Carolina for the event. She hadn't aged well, and the difference between she and Kyle was stark. They hadn't seen each other in more than 15 years. They hugged at midfield, then went their separate ways. It was as if they were two old prizefighters returning to their respective corners. Two years later, Alicia died. She had all the money she could need, yet she died a poor and empty soul.

The locals lost the game, but the winners were the citizens of Temecula, as it should be. In 2055, in a significant coup, Temecula

148

landed a major league baseball expansion team. In 2058, the Los Angeles Lakers moved their operation to Temecula. The team had only one request. Their opening game at the new Kobe Bryant Arena, was, of course, was a sellout. Everyone thought that was as good as it could get...that is, until the Summer Olympics of 2064.

Contributor Biographies

Jeff Comerchero & E.J. Radford

Comerchero and Radford are the authors of their transformative story, *The Old Man and the Queer*. The book details their unique and beautiful friendship. It follows them from the impossible to the incredible.

Jeff Comerchero, at 77, is the retired mayor of the City of Temecula and CEO of a major real estate development company. He lives with his wife of 40 years, with their 2 sons and 2 granddaughters nearby.

E.J. Radford, 26, is a Master Barber, owning a shop in Temecula. They identify as non-binary, trans-masculine. Triumphing over a challenging youth of being wrongly gendered and misunderstood, they live with their wife and young daughter.

Charlie Schimmel

Charlie is a San Diego-born artist who specializes in traditional and digital illustration. He has a history in graphic design as well, from creating logo designs for the US military to local museums. Style inspiration for him comes from various forms of animation and pop culture art. He hopes to work his way up to a career at Sony Studios.

Hollywood
&
Vines

Murder Noir

HOLLYWOOD & VINES: MURDER NOIR

Story by George Stez

Illustration by Erin Warren
Digital

P ETER GALLO PERUSED THE menu. "The filet medallions sound good," he said to June, his wife of 20 years.

"When haven't you ordered that?" she quipped.

"It goes so well with the Pinot Noir here," Gallo replied.

Gallo and June were enjoying Sunday brunch at the Hollywood & Vines, in the middle of Temecula's wine country. They had been going twice monthly since moving to the city a year before. They discovered Temecula, north of San Diego and southeast of Los Angeles, when they celebrated their wedding anniversary a few years back. Looking for a getaway, the wine country seemed like the perfect spot. When Gallo retired as a detective lieutenant after 25 years with the LAPD, they opted to trade big-city life for more tranquil environs.

June didn't understand ordering one's entree based on the wine. Usually, it was the other way around. But he loved his Pinot...maybe sometimes a little too much. June told him she could live with that if that were his worst vice. They were happily married. She met Gallo — which is what he preferred being called — when he ended up in the hospital, grazed by a bullet. She was his attending nurse, and it was love at first sight.

They placed their order and took in the view from the outdoor terrace. The grapes had been long picked from the last harvest, and vines with spent branches waited patiently for their winter pruning.

"Hello, Gallo, June. I'm glad to see you again," said owner Max Green, who had meandered over to their table. Max looked trim and fit for a man in his mid-60s. The couple had gotten to know him months before. Max was an interesting sort. When they first met, he conceded that he didn't know how to make wine; Max spent most of his life producing B-grade films. He was tired of moviemaking and wanted to try wine-making instead. "Money isn't a problem," he told them, "because my father was the once-famous child actor Guy Green, who later became a successful producer."

"Gallo, could you join me inside for a few minutes? There's something I need to speak with you about," Max asked, looking flustered.

"I'd be happy to," Gallo responded.

154

"June, I won't keep him long," Max promised. "I saw you didn't order dessert. I hope you don't mind, but I asked Chef Pierre to make your favorite crème brulée while you wait. On the house, of course." June nodded approval.

Gallo followed Max to his office and was offered a seat at the desk. As Gallo moved close to the desk, he couldn't help but notice a strong floral scent, as if someone had mistaken perfume for furniture polish.

"I have a proposition for you, Gallo. I need your help." Max took three Temecula postcards from his jacket pocket and laid them on his desk.

All three read the same thing.

"You've taken something from me. Now it's my turn."

The text letters were glued to the paper and clearly came from different sources — magazines, newspapers, and flyers.

Gallo studied the postcards. "It looks pretty cliché, Max. Any idea what this is about?"

"I don't know, but I do have an idea. Next week, I'll be hosting a 'Murder Noir Night' and I plan to set a trap. I'm hoping that maybe you'll help me solve the mystery. I've invited all the suspects. And, before you ask, yes, it's an interactive murder mystery dinner. But I have no plans to fall victim to murder," Max chuckled nervously. "I just need to figure out who hates me enough to threaten me."

"How do you plan that?"

"My method will be quite unorthodox. But I have a thick skin," Max boasted. "I've invited my closest competitors under the ruse of the dinner theatre."

"But why would your competitors want to come?" Gallo asked.

"Because I've also told them I'll be announcing my expansion plans for the winery. If the dinner theatre doesn't pique their interest, my announcement will."

"How do I fit in?" Gallo asked.

"I'm bringing this up because I'm hoping you'll attend. And June, of course. I can make it worth your while with some vintage Pinot I have stashed away in the cellar."

"The wine won't be necessary, Max. I'd be willing to help, but have you considered calling the Sheriff's office?"

"They'll just tell me the threat is too vague. It's probably someone whom I've angered and just wants to scare me, blah, blah, blah." He handed Gallo an invitation, which read "Murder Mystery Dinner, Hollywood & Vines, 1940s themed, black tie. Saturday, Jan. 20. Dinner to be followed by a special presentation on winery expansion."

Gallo wasn't sure he wanted to get involved, much less bring June into it. He thought he'd left his crime-solving days behind. But the threat could be real. "Let me speak with June about it."

"I'd appreciate it," Max said. When the two shook hands, Gallo could feel the sweat in Max's grip.

Gallo returned to the table and leaned down to kiss June on the cheek. "Thanks for waiting, honey. How was dessert?"

"It was amazing, but what did Max want?" June asked with more than a hint of curiosity.

Gallo looked around to ensure no one was in earshot.

He handed her the invitation. "Max is hosting a Murder Noir dinner next weekend, and he wants us to come."

"And...?" she said, dragging a three-letter word into a sentence.

"He wants me to keep an eye on things. He received some threatening postcards, and he's worried there may be trouble."

"So, are you thinking we'll go?" she asked as her eyes widened in interest.

"I'm not sure," Gallo replied. "For one thing, I don't know that I want to play Cops and Robbers anymore. And second, what if something...goes wrong? I wouldn't want you in the middle of it."

"I'm up for it if you are, Detective Lieutenant Gallo," she said. "Just let me know ASAP. I'll need to go shopping to fit the theme," she added playfully.

They headed home, west on Rancho California Road, passing wineries on both sides. Many of them shared a Southern California Spanish-style design; others reflected Italian and other European styles. The one that stood out from the others was the Hollywood & Vines, a huge stone edifice with distinctly etched blocks. It reminded Gallo of Frank Lloyd Wright's Ennis House of the 1920s, used in the film "House on Haunted Hill." To say this winery was an anachronism to the feel of the wine country was an understatement.

* * *

"You look really handsome in black tie, honey," said June as she appraised him from head to toe.

He struck a pose, eliciting a laugh from June. "Don't get too excited; it's just a rental," he quipped.

"Maybe we should go formal more often," said June, who put her arms around him. Her hand clipped a bulge around his belt. "Do you really have to bring your gun?" she asked.

"Let's just say it's for insurance," he responded.

Gallo was taller than most, at six-foot-two, and even though his black hair was sporting some gray these days, June often told him he wore it well. One thing Gallo knew she loved about him was that he wasn't a typical city cop. He wasn't all football and sports bars; he was well-read and cultured. He thought that attracted her to him when she could have had her pick.

Gallo knew June also appreciated that he was a good listener and didn't forget things. This, he had told her when they started dating, was a benefit of his "superpower" — eidetic memory. Gallo could remember every detail of an image, even after viewing it for only a few seconds. This went beyond photographic memory; it included other sensory aspects, like smell or taste. This rare gift had always given him an edge at crime scenes.

"How do I look?" June asked. While usually this was a trap, Gallo took one look at her, and "Amazing" was the first word that came out. June had curled her dark locks to make her hair look shorter to fit the Noir style. She wore red lipstick. Around her neck was a long strand of pearls, which belonged to her late grandmother. The pearls hung down into the V-neck of her shimmering gown, which ended at her T-strap high heels.

"I won't ask you how much you spent, but it was worth it," he said with a grin.

They left for the winery. The sun was setting. There wasn't any traffic, other than cars leaving the wine country. Most of the tasting rooms were shutting down, though several of the wineries now had restaurants serving a wide range of cuisine created by renowned chefs. Temecula had undoubtedly come of age as a resort destination.

Gallo turned left at the sign for Hollywood & Vines. The sign was hard to miss, made up of letters mimicking those of the world-famous Hollywood sign and flanked by movie-premiere spotlights. Spot-lit palms flanked the long, ascending driveway. The parking lot had fewer than a dozen cars. The restaurant was closed tonight because of Max's private event.

The main winery building was lit by ground-level flood lights that gave the façade an eerie glow and highlighted the etched designs of the gray stone blocks. The typical evening breeze gave life to the shadows of the plants that danced between the lights and the edifice.

"This building takes on a whole different look at night. Are you thinking what I'm thinking?" June asked.

"Something out of a Roger Corman film?" Gallo fired back. He and June shared a love of Vincent Price horror films from the early '60s.

"Close. I was thinking Film Noir," June responded. "Certainly fits the theme."

They made their way to the main entrance. They were greeted by a man and woman dressed in character: one a butler with tailcoat, bow tie, and gloves; the other a maid in a black dress to the knees and white ruffled apron, and starched hat.

"Welcome, sir and madam, to the Hollywood & Vines," said the butler.

"Thank you," said Gallo. He looked around. A few couples had already arrived. Gallo and June gladly accepted glasses of wine from a server as he passed by. Gallo took the first sip. Ah, the Pinot!

Max was standing before a wall of photos that made up the shrine to his family history in Hollywood. He wore a sharp navy-blue tuxedo with felt lapels and a matching bow tie. There were pictures of his father with Cecil B. DeMille, Douglas Fairbanks, and Greta Garbo. The largest photo was of his father with a dozen film stars in front of the historic Brown Derby restaurant in Hollywood, just steps from the famous intersection of Hollywood & Vine. This, Max said, was where deals and careers were made in old Hollywood.

"My father spent a lot of time there hobnobbing with the Hollywood elite," Max said with an air of pride. "Please make it a point to see the bottle of Pinot Noir Charlie Chaplin gifted to my father, the Domaine de la Romanée-Conti Grand Cru 1945. A similar bottle recently sold at auction for nearly half a million dollars."

The tour ended before Max reached a large easel covered

with a white sheet. Pointing to the easel, he said, "This will be for later."

Max approached with his wife, Lydia, a beautiful platinum blonde wearing a sequined dark gray gown with white crosses and gloves to her elbows to match. Around her neck was a long double strand of large, high-luster pearls. Her earrings were large silver crosses, matching the pattern on her gown and bedazzled with diamonds. Gallo estimated she was ten years younger than Max.

"Lydia, I'd like you to meet Gallo and his wife, June. They're faithful patrons."

Lydia set her eyes on Gallo. "Is that your first name or your last?" Lydia asked.

"My last," Gallo responded. He could see Lydia was enjoying herself.

"Let me guess: Is your first name Ernest, or perhaps…Julio?" she asked with more than a hint of sarcasm.

"Just Gallo will do," he said with a forced smile as though he hadn't heard that one before.

Gallo could sense Lydia was getting bored with him when she turned to June and gave her the once over. "That's a pretty dress, dear. I love your pearls. They look so…antique," she said backhandedly.

"Well, thank you, Lydia. The nice thing about antiques is that they tell stories and have a character that money just can't buy," June retorted with a smile of satisfaction.

"It was nice to meet you finally, Lydia," Gallo said as he

quickly took June by the hand to escape toward another couple.

"Ernest or Julio," June mimicked with well-deserved sarcasm.

Gallo and June then headed for the appetizer table, where they met Mark Jones and his partner, Greg Salter, the owners of Walker Bros. winery, and Jonas and Elena Bowman of Sunset Vineyards.

Gallo and June went for some more wine, where they met Joe and Isabella Bonetti of Vino Bella. Joe said they had opened their winery around the same time as Hollywood & Vines. "Since then, we've been close competitors," Joe said.

"Very close," Isabella piped in. Joe looked at her disapprovingly. They were both in their 50s. Joe was on the shorter side, but muscles protruded from the arms and chest of his tuxedo. Joe and Isabella excused themselves.

"He looks like he works out," Gallo observed, feigning a slight tone of jealousy.

"Isabella's a natural beauty," June added. "There definitely was some friction between those two." Gallo knew that when June had a "feeling" about something, she usually was right.

"Did you smell her perfume?" Gallo asked. "It had a familiar scent."

"I think it was Frederic Malle Portrait of a Lady...it's, like, $400 a bottle," June said.

"How do you know that?"

"My friend Liz wears it. It's heavenly, but I can't bring myself to spend that much on perfume."

162

"I appreciate that," Gallo mused.

The guests sat around a long table, set with fine china and Deco silver utensils. Everyone began perusing the set menu options for the evening.

Lydia spoke out. "As you can see, Max insisted we offer a Cobb salad as an appetizer, if for no other reason than it's what the Brown Derby became famous for, invented by restaurant owner Robert Howard Cobb himself in 1937." Lydia pronounced it as though it were a public service announcement.

"Who knew?" Gallo quipped to June. He noticed the guests looking around and smiling at one another, as though sharing an inside joke.

"Max does lay the Hollywood thing kind of thick," June whispered.

"That, he does," Gallo agreed.

The rest of the dinner included a choice of meat, fowl, seafood, and a side of small talk. Gallo thought it odd that a room full of vintners didn't want to talk wine.

"Are you seeing what I'm seeing?" asked June.

"You mean Max and Isabella are trading furtive glances across the table?"

"Exactly."

"You missed your calling, dear. You'd make a great detective," Gallo said, leaning over to kiss her.

"You know," Gallo said, "I think I just figured out where I smelled that perfume before. It was in Max's office. I remembered it smelled like someone spilled perfume over his desk."

"And you just remembered that?" she asked, tilting her head to one side.

"Remember my eidetic memory?"

"So, maybe Max and Isabella are involved?"

"It's plausible."

Once dinner and dessert were over, the tables were cleared. Just then, a spotlight lit up the front of the room where Max stood.

"Ladies and gentlemen, I hope you enjoyed your meal. Let's get started with tonight's entertainment...." his voice trailed off as the lights flickered and the room went dark. There was a thunk. One of the guests shrieked while others talked loudly among themselves.

The lights flickered back on after about eight seconds. To Max's right lay the body of a man. A knife protruded from his chest. A steak knife? Gallo observed that blood had soaked the white tuxedo shirt. As the group quieted down from the sudden jolt, Gallo could see the "victim" was a dummy but looked realistic. "It resembles Max," he told June.

Max rejoined Lydia at the table.

"Again, welcome to the entertainment," Max announced. "This won't be like other murder mystery dinners. We'll dispense with the fictitious names and the script. We all know one another here. What we will figure out this evening is who killed the victim. And if you haven't noticed, the victim looks a lot like me. I'm sure Detective Lieutenant Gallo here has already figured that out," he said pointing to Gallo.

All eyes turned to Gallo in surprise, who simply clarified,

"RETIRED Detective Lieutenant Gallo."

"Nevertheless," Max said, "this should be an enlightening evening. I'm the victim, and you are all the suspects, and you get to play yourselves."

"This is sounding better all the time," Joe Bonetti intoned sarcastically. "Why don't we skip this charade and you tell us why you really wanted us here...to rub our noses in your expansion plans? That's what we all want to hear."

"Patience, patience, Joe," Max responded. "The detective will pose questions to each of you. At the end of the evening, you will need to guess who killed...me, so to speak."

While Gallo knew Max needed his help, he was caught off guard at the surprise introduction. But thinking quickly, he proceeded with the mock interrogation. "Why don't we start with the Bowmans?" Gallo suggested. "With the winery next door, you've probably known the victim...um, Max...the longest. Would you say you've had a good relationship with him?"

The Bowmans looked at each other hesitantly. Jonas took the initiative to speak. "When Max first bought the property, he came over and introduced himself. He seemed nice enough. He told us he was from Hollywood and planned to theme his property around that to help bring in customers."

"Did you have any issues with him?"

"Well, no, we didn't see him until after the construction was well underway."

"And then what?" Gallo asked.

"Elena and I were upset at how his winery turned out. We

had no idea the property would look like THIS," he shouted, waving his arms. I mean, take a look around. We have a Country European-style winery, and he comes in and builds a mausoleum next door. It detracts from our charm."

"Did you say anything to Max after that?"

"We just told him how disappointed we were. What else could we do?"

"Thank you, Jonas."

June nudged Gallo with her knee. He glanced at her. She motioned for him to look at Max, who was again making eyes with Isabella Bonetti. Meanwhile, Joe got up in a huff and left the table. Gallo noticed the furious expression on his face.

"How about you, Mark, and Greg? Did you have any issues with Max?" Gallo asked.

Mark responded. "We bought Walker Bros. at about the time Max finished building his winery. We learned during the escrow process that Max approached a number of our employees, including our head vintner, and—"

"—poached our employees," Greg interjected. "In addition to dealing with the transfer of ownership, we also had to find key personnel to make up for the ones he stole from us."

"That must have put you in a difficult situation," Gallo said. "Did you speak with him about it?"

"I did," Greg said. "We ran into him at a Chamber event, and I let him have a piece of my mind."

"And how did he respond?

"He said, 'It's just business. Your employees wanted more

money, and I was able to give it to them.'"

"Thanks, gentlemen," Gallo said.

Just then, Joe returned to the table. He was carrying something bulky under his coat, but Gallo couldn't tell what it was.

"Just in time," Gallo said to Joe. "How about you, Joe and Isabella? What kind of relationship have you had with Max?"

Joe sat down and responded, "We opened at about the same time. We were friends with Max and Lydia. But then something changed. Max managed to undercut our price. Whether it was the wine tastings or special events — and even the cost of certain wines, he always seemed to be a step ahead."

"Did you confront Max about that?"

"I was feeling that something wasn't right. I figured it was time to meet with him and sort things out," Joe said. "I came to the winery to speak to him one evening, and I found him in his office...with Isabella. And they were doing more than talking."

"You cheating bastard," Lydia yelled at Max, dousing him with her glass of wine and running out of the room.

"That's not what was going on," Max protested.

"Like hell, it wasn't," Joe shouted. "I'm not blind. You took advantage of our friendship. You went after our business, and then you took away my wife!"

Isabella looked at Joe, tears running down her face. "Please don't do this now."

"Max can have you," he said angrily to Isabella. He then turned to Max, "You hear that, Max? You can have her. She's like one of your sour wines."

Joe stood up and pulled a bottle out from under his coat. "But I now have something that you want. Something you hold more precious than anything. Your damn bottle of half-million-dollar Pinot Noir!"

Max looked with horror at Joe clutching the bottle.

"How did you break into the wine safe, Joe?"

"I made my fortune in security technology. Who do you think made the software for your wine safe? Or is that the ONE thing my wife didn't share with you?"

"You son-of-a-bitch! Give it back to me," Max growled, glaring at Joe.

Joe looked at his wife, who gazed at him with her mouth agape. He held onto the bottle and ran out the side door toward the vineyard.

Murmurs filled the room as the other guests turned to one another.

"Damn it! This is going to get ugly," cursed Gallo. "Stay here and call 911," he said to June urgently. He ran out the door after Joe, who was going deeper into the vineyard.

"Joe, stop!" Gallo yelled as loudly as he could into the breeze. He lost track of him. He continued through the vineyard, trying not to trip in the light, sandy loam. To his rear, Gallo heard the muffled sound of Max yelling. The shadows from the spotlit vines grew more animated as the light breeze transformed into a gust.

"You won't get away with this," Max shouted as he drew closer to Joe.

168

Gallo saw Joe about 100 feet away and a few rows across and started closing in on him. Since Max was nearing Joe's left, Gallo planned to go further down the vineyard and surprise him from the right.

Joe stopped to catch his breath, clutching the wine bottle in his left hand. Gallo traversed the rows by squeezing under the wire that supported the horizontal branches of the grapevines.

Gallo considered drawing his gun but thought he could subdue Joe without it. He jumped out from the shadows of the vines and leaped toward Joe, who moved out of the way just in time, leaving Gallo to land in the dirt.

As Gallo got up, Joe threw his weight into a punch that landed on the side of Gallo's face.

Gallo then lunged at Joe when he felt a sharp jab in his gut. Reaching down, he felt warm blood trickling onto his hand. He looked at Joe, who was holding a steak knife in his right hand, tipped red with blood. Gallo crouched down to the ground from the pain. A steak knife? He considered the irony.

Joe looked down at Gallo. "I didn't want to hurt you. You should have stayed out of it." He climbed through the vines and disappeared.

Gallo could hear Max approaching and yelled, "Max, watch out, he has a knife."

Gallo tried to get up but felt queasy. Finally managing to stand, he could hear Max and Joe arguing.

"Just give me the bottle, and we'll talk things over," Max pleaded.

"There's nothing to talk over. You stole my wife. I let you know I'd take something of yours. Something you value more than anything else," Joe yelled.

Gallo could see the shadows of the two men as they grappled in front of a spotlight. Their shadows were surreal, elongated against a stone wall. It looked like Max was wrestling Joe for either the bottle or the knife.

The wind picked up. Gallo could hear several voices approaching from the restaurant. The vineyard was a cacophony of shadows and sounds. He found the strength to draw his gun and headed for Max and Joe.

Suddenly, one of the shadows grew taller as he lifted what looked like the bottle and swung it down on Max's head. Gallo could hear a clunk as the bottle hit its mark.

Gallo approached Joe and trained his gun on him. Joe stood shaking, as if in shock, over Max's blood-soaked and lifeless body. He let go of the bottle, the prized Domaine de la Romanée-Conti Grand Cru 1945.

* * *

Six months later, Gallo's wounds were healing well. He and June were eating brunch on the patio at the Hollywood & Vines on a typical warm summer day.

"I'm glad Lydia decided to reopen the winery," Gallo said.

"It was either that or sell," June guessed. "But can she keep it going?"

"Max wasn't involved in the wine-making part of the business anyway, so the quality of the wine isn't likely to change," Gallo said. "The marketing spin, I'm not so sure about. With Max gone, so goes the link to old Hollywood. And it's likely the expansion plans for the winery are off. The only silver lining, Lydia had confided, was that with all the publicity, reservations for the restaurant and tasting room have never been higher."

June asked, "What happened to the bottle of Domaine de la—"

"—Domaine de la Romanée-Conti Grand Cru 1945," Gallo helped.

"Yes, that one."

"It's being held as evidence until the end of Joe's murder trial. Lydia said she then plans to sell it at auction to pay off a backlog of bills," Gallo said.

"I take it the label survived the, uh, tussle?" June asked, clearly avoiding a term like bludgeoning.

"The label was bloodied, but the bottle has quite a story, like an antique," Gallo added with a wink.

"So, other than what happened, are you enjoying your retirement, Gallo? Getting bored yet?"

"A little. I must admit, the murder noir made me miss the job a bit. While I can do without the physical aspect of law enforcement, I did enjoy playing detective again."

"Nothing says you have to stop that," June said with a mischievous grin.

"Are you thinking what I'm thinking?" asked Gallo, taking a

long sip and savoring his favorite Pinot Noir.

Contributor Biographies

George Stez

George Stez is a writer who blends his journalism background with a passion for World War 2 era European history. When he's not penning historical fiction, he dabbles in short stories in various genres, including noir mystery. He lives with his family in the Temecula Valley.

Erin Warren

I have always enjoyed making art. I went to Cal State Fullerton and earned my Bachelor of Fine Arts in 2021. I have had my art shown at shows in Temecula and I have also written and illustrated my own comic series called "Trudge." I love making both fantasy and horror inspired art. Lately I have been doing realistic pet portraits and working at a vet hospital. Though art hasn't ever become a career for me, it continues to make me happy.

QUANTUM HEARTS: A LOVE BEYOND TIME

Story by Veronika Childs

Illustration by Mya Hill
Digital

D R. JADE CARDEA PACED around the large workstation on the observation deck of the research vessel Endeavor, shooting yet another impatient glance at her wrist cuff.

"You're being ridiculous. It's been less than a minute," she mumbled under her breath. Exhausted, her shoulders ached with tension.

As the progress bar inched across the display, Jade envisioned the download streaming into the ship's processor from the relay station on Verdantis 9. In her mind, the encrypted data stream morphed into a series of complex expressions, numbers, and symbols. Her opus, the defining formula for her emerging theory on Quantum Convergence, flowed through her thoughts like electric blue characters dancing through the infinite cosmos, only to crumble before her eyes.

"It's no use," she sighed.

It had been months since Admiral Fidus had recruited Jade for this assignment, and she still didn't have concrete answers to explain what was causing the spatial anomalies appearing throughout CITADEL space. She needed more data.

Suddenly struck by inspiration, she paused to manipulate the three-dimensional representation of Lumina projected above the smooth surface of the display table. Using hand gestures, she rotated the white dwarf on its axis, studying the diagram carefully.

"You know, the real thing is right behind you."

Jade jumped. Lost in thought, she hadn't heard her life mate and soul partner, Captain Aeron Custos, walk up behind her.

"You scared me!" Jade exclaimed, twisting to punch him playfully on the shoulder.

Aeron laughed. "But, you knew I was here."

"I know." Jade grinned. "I just didn't know you were there."

"I'm sorry I startled you. I guess I'll just have to make it up to you." With a twinkle in his eye, Aeron twirled his index finger.

Understanding his meaning, Jade grinned and turned to face away from him.

"Serenity subroutine, engage!" Aeron ordered with feigned seriousness, directing her towards the view of Lumina, the dying star they were observing from their cloaked cruiser.

"Aye, aye, Captain," she teased, her voice laced with a hint of mischief. The warmth of Aeron's touch seeped through the layers of her uniform as he kneaded the knots out of her shoulders. For a moment, the progress bar and its exasperating lack of progress faded away.

"How do you always know just what I need?" Jade asked with a soft sigh.

"Because I love you." Aeron leaned in to kiss the nape of her neck, igniting a spark within her.

The lingering charge from their exchange hung in the air as a stray thought danced at the edge of Jade's consciousness. Despite her effort, it pulled her attention from the present moment to the series of green symbols streaming across the ANI display at her wrist.

"I think 'Annie' can manage without you for a bit," Aeron chuckled, playfully covering the display with one hand, while wrapping the other around her waist. "You need to take a break."

Jade looked up, catching a glimpse of him in her peripheral vision. Their spirited banter had been a constant of their relationship since their days at the Academy. He had always teased her about cheating on him with her 'girlfriend' ANI, the AI-Assisted Advance Neural Interface. Jade had playfully and provocatively addressed Aeron as 'Captain' whenever they were alone, long before he was a commissioned officer. But this time, instead of reveling in their shared jokes, Jade thought she noticed a flicker of concern in his expression.

"I know, but I can't shake this feeling of unease," Jade

admitted, her brow furrowed in thought. "It's like there's something right in front of me, but I just can't see...." Her voice trailed off as her mind conjured the images and tables of data she had compiled.

"Where did you go?" Aeron whispered.

Jade shook her head, trying to break free from her thoughts. "Sorry. But you know this is important."

"Yes, the potential catastrophic unraveling of space and time is important, to say the least. But who's going to save the universe when you work yourself to death?" Aeron gave her a loving squeeze. "If you can't relax, then I'll have to find another way to help you decompress." He purred into her ear, eliciting a low sigh of contentment as his powerful arms pulled her closer. The scent of his cologne, an intoxicating mix of sandalwood and spice, drew Jade in until her body melted into him. It had been far too long.

"My stars, I've missed you." Jade sighed, tilting her head back to rest against his chest. "It feels like we've hardly had any alone time lately." On their next inhale, in perfect harmony, their bodies moved as one, and she could feel the beating of his heart echoed through her own.

Beyond the transparent observation panels, Lumina loomed large in the foreground, its intense gravitational pull distorting the space around it as its surface shimmered with a faint, ethereal light. In the distance, Steller Cometra, the comet they had been expecting, came into view — a faint glimmer against the backdrop of stars. Its icy nucleus trailed a luminous tail that stretched out behind it, catching the light of distant suns and ensnaring her thoughts.

"According to my sources in the Counsel, this download will include the historical observations from the Outer Expanse. I will finally be able to prove Quantum Convergence," Jade said, her voice brimming with excitement.

"I know you will." He gave her a reassuring squeeze, then continued, "I have full confidence in you. But you know as well as I do, the file migration won't conclude for a while, and ANI can conduct a preliminary analysis without input from you. You need to let your mind rest, have a few bites to eat, and get your blood circulating."

"But what if I missed some—"

"I wonder what I could do to help you let go of all that worry." He winked. "That brain of yours works too hard."

Resting his nose on the nape of her neck, Aeron inhaled deeply, his energy caressing every inch of her skin, sending tantalizing goosebumps across her body. Pinching the fabric at her waist, he turned her gently to face him.

"The rest of you needs to relax too," he added with a downward glance and a raised brow. "And if I can't get you to sit down and join me for a bite, maybe there is something else I can do to entice you to relax."

Jade leaned in, trembling with anticipation, eager for his lips to meet hers. But before she could savor the moment, ANI intruded, flooding her mind with a cascade of numbers. The digits danced, emblazoned, erased, re-written, re-calculated, revised, and repeated until every known variable was accounted for. Once again, Jade's calculations confirmed what her intuition had been telling her since she took on the assignment.

"It can't just be a coincidence," Jade mumbled.

"USS Endeavor to Dr. Cardea?" Aeron's voice sounded muffled and distant until he placed his fingers under her chin. Taking a deep breath, she looked into his eyes. The blue was reminiscent of the horizon where heaven and earth meet, and the sea and the sky become one.

"There you are." His voice held the sound of his smile, but his brow wrinkled in worry.

"I'm here," Jade whispered with a sigh of relief. Inching forward, she brushed her lips against his. Aeron responded, deepening the kiss with a gentle urgency, teasing her with the promise of more.

"Did I tell you about the stellar remnants?" Jade mumbled against his lips.

Aeron chuckled, pulling away. "Last week and again last night. In the middle of the night." He yawned. "Black holes, white dwarfs, neutron stars, and other cosmic remnants all along Stellar Cometra's path through space, right?"

"Yes. That's why it was so crucial to be here as it passes Lumina. Real-time data...." Jade yawned.

"Am I boring you?" Aeron quipped.

Jade blushed. "Oh, be quiet," she said, with a nudge to his ribs. "You know I haven't slept."

"And yet you are working another shift?" Aeron raised his

brow with feigned seriousness. "As your Captain, I should make you aware that CITADEL regulations stipulate maximum hours on shift, and I think it's safe to say you have exceeded your allotted time, as well as that of all the other crew members combined."

"I know." Jade whispered, looking down sheepishly.

Lifting her chin, Aeron lowered his voice, dropping all pretense. "Hey, you know I only bring it up because I worry about you. Just because you can survive and stay awake on infusions, doesn't make it good for you."

"True. A recent study proved that—"

"You need to take a nap." Aeron interjected with a chuckle.

Marveling at the way his eyes lit up when he smiled, Jane smiled. "Well yes, I do need a nap, but not right now."

"Then, shall we eat?" Aeron gestured to the other side of the room where he had set up a table complete with linen and candlelight. "Or shall we..." he let his voice trail off suggestively and began kissing her neck.

"But Stellar Cometra will...any moment," she stammered. But even as she spoke, she found herself tilting her head to allow him access.

"I'm aware," he whispered against her tender skin, feathering kisses to trace a path to her right earlobe. "There's nothing that can be done right now. You can't do more until you have the rest of the information. Besides, we're both supposed to be off duty," he murmured, sending shivers down her spine.

Despite the allure, Jade couldn't stop thinking about the proximity of the stellar remnants to the anomalies. There were now too many for it to be written off as mere coincidence.

"Something is blocking long range, um, sensors," Jade faltered, her lack of sleep making it hard to focus as his lips elicited goosebumps.

"You'll have them soon enough." Aeron's hot breath caressed her ear as he nibbled her earlobe.

Moaning softly, Jade shifted, giving him more room to work. "And the Counsel wants...the Counsel wants...we need answers."

Switching to the other side of her neck, he continued his ministrations. "The crew has it under control, and Asterios or one of the other bridge officers will brief us later. But right now, I'd prefer to be debriefed by you." She could hear the amusement in Aeron's voice as he resisted the urge to laugh at his own pun.

"The only data we have is from the archaic probes available before the establishment of CITADEL. I should double-check the—"

"You've double-checked already, twice, probably three times," he interrupted, an impish glint in his eye.

Jade blushed, holding up four fingers. Their eyes met at her fingertips, and they burst into laughter — a cathartic collision of exhaustion and relief that bordered on tears, yet brought a moment of pure, unadulterated bliss.

"Why do you put up with me when all I do is obsess about work?" The laughter died in Jade's throat. She had asked the question in jest, but something had struck a nerve, and she felt a knot form in the pit of her stomach.

"What do you mean? I love you," Aeron said, still catching

his breath. "You and your brilliant mind, even when you and ANI travel at lightspeed."

As Aeron spoke, Jade was struck by the sincerity in his voice. He truly loved her, just as she was. He always had. That realization gave her pause. Perhaps she did have a few minutes to spare.

No sooner had the thought crossed her mind than she felt her legs give out beneath her. The world around her started to fade into a blur, and Aeron became nothing but a fuzzy silhouette, then vanished.

"Jade!" As if watching from outside of herself, she saw Aeron catch her in midair and carry her to the two-person seat he had suggested earlier. Tenderly arranging her head on a decorative pillow, he slid his body under her outstretched feet, allowing her calves to rest on his thighs.

"How long has it been since you got some real sleep?" Aeron asked as Jade's eyes fluttered open. A pang of guilt rippled through her. Aeron's look of concern was unmistakable this time.

"I'm okay. I promise. I just need another energy infusion." With her eyes half-closed, she watched as he caressed her shin with his fingertips. Jade managed to gingerly tap a few commands onto her wrist display. Within seconds, newfound energy flooded her system.

"Don't get me wrong, I know your work is vital, but I'm worried about you." He flashed a smile, but he gazed at her with worry. "You know, the medtechs have all said infusions are not a substitute for real rest."

Before she could answer, a chime from her wrist drew Jade's

gaze. As the status bar turned green, she tapped her wrist cuff and grinned.

"I need to get back to work," she said, sitting up. "The download has the data we've been waiting for, and if I hurry, ANI and I can set up the interface for a live simulation." Jade's heart raced with excitement. With data from the unmanned probes at the edge of the known universe, she could finally prove her theory and move one step closer to solving the mystery of the spatial anomalies.

Standing, Jade continued, "I'll finish this up tonight, take a power nap, and then we can watch the passing of Stellar Cometra up close and personal in CyberScape."

"Can I get an ETA on that, Doctor Cardea?" Aeron smirked, raising an eyebrow.

"Tomorrow, I promise. Captain Custos." Jade returned his smirk, adding a little flair to the word 'Captain.'

"Tomorrow sounds intriguing, but isn't that what you said yesterday?" Aeron replied, his tone gentle but tinged with sadness.

Jade opened her mouth to speak but was interrupted by a familiar series of ascending notes signaling the delivery of ANI's preliminary analysis.

Aeron placed a hand on her arm. "Before you get back to ANI, take a look around. The view is incredible." He paused, as if considering his words carefully. "Just remember, tomorrow isn't guaranteed for any of us."

"Aeron...." The lump forming in her throat made her voice

nothing more than a whisper.

"I know this is important," he said softly. "Go save the universe, take a nap, and get some real nourishment — none of those infusions or capsules. Rest and food, captain's orders." Aeron's reassuring smile buoyed her spirits as he stood and wrapped his arms around her waist.

"Tomorrow, we'll revisit this in CyberScape," he said, leaning in to give her a tender kiss. "And this time, I'm holding you to it."

Now face to face, she wanted to tell him how much he meant to her, how much she appreciated him requesting this commission to be with her. She wanted to tell him that things would be different just as soon as she could prove her theory on Quantum Convergence. But before she could say anything, their world turned upside down.

Red lights flashed as the research vessel lost power and fell from orbit. Jade reached for her wrist display, bypassing the "Critical Alert" message and quickly delving into the ship's processor.

"Aeron, sensors detected a power surge from beyond the star," she said, her heart sinking. "And now Lumina's gravitational pull is increasing exponentially."

Aeron met her gaze, then tapped his communicator. "Asterios, status report."

Jade noticed the shift in his demeanor as he took on his role as Captain Custos, speaking over the alarms that echoed throughout the ship. Despite the sudden onset of a zero-gravity environment, he felt like a harness tethering her to safety.

"Quantum engines — offline. Propulsion engines — offline. Life support — offline. Shields — offline. Engineering—"

"What would it take to get us back online?" he asked, cutting off the report of his First Officer, Lieutenant Elara Asterios.

"I...don't know, Captain. This isn't supposed to happen. We have redundant systems, fail-safes. A malfunction of this scope is technically impossible." The lieutenant's confusion didn't escape Jade's notice. Given her training, if Asterios didn't understand what was happening, this had to be serious. She held her breath as the lieutenant continued, "We would need a space dock and a system-wide level one diagnostic to even begin."

Jade's heart plummeted, sending her thoughts into overdrive. Was it a coincidence or did this have something to do with her research or the data download? What if there was a deliberate reason behind these anomalies? Could someone be using them for nefarious purposes, even to the point of destroying a CITADEL ship? With the anomalies themselves posing a threat to the existence of all life in the universe, Jade couldn't ignore the possibility. She gestured to get Aeron's attention, pointing to her wrist for urgency.

His face tensed, but Aeron maintained his composure. "Lieutenant, Dr. Cardea's instruments picked up an energy pulse. Is it possible we're under attack?"

"Engineering confirmed the fluctuation, but without full power to our sensors, they can't say for certain," Asterios said. "But Captain, I wouldn't dismiss the possibility." She hesitated. "And with the shields inoperable...Captain, we are an easy target."

"Copy. Standby," Seemingly unphased, Captain Custos ended the transmission. Grabbing the lip of the door frame, he pulled himself to an upright position in front of the ANI-accessible control panel.

"Don't worry," he added, pulling up the ship's diagnostic on the workstation. "The Endeavor's emergency fusion cells can maintain a hospitable environment without active life support long enough to — his words faltered as their eyes met.

"We can figure this out," he added with a determined expression.

Jade's lips pressed into a thin line. "We have less time than you think."

Still hovering in the weightless environment, she extended her hand, allowing Aeron to pull her towards him. Anchoring himself to the workstation with his legs, he held her in place while her hands flew across the touch screen. As her brain interacted with her bio implants, complex calculations appeared and then seemed to solve themselves. The situation was graver than she had feared. "We aren't just drifting. We're accelerating at an exponential rate. Given Lumina's sudden increase in gravitational pull and our growing rate of descent, we have minutes, at best."

Without hesitation, the captain touched his wrist again, activating a channel to the bridge. "Asterios, Code Gray."

His order fell with a palpable finality that rendered everything else irrelevant.

"Copy." Lieutenant Asterios answered. The console chimed as the First Officer activated ship-wide communications.

"By order of Captain Custos, under Galactic Regulation 3825.33. Code Gray. Abandon ship." Jade could hear a subtle tremor in Elara's voice as ANI control panels across the ship lit up, detailing each step of the mandated self-destruct protocol.

As the transmission ended, Aeron's eyes met hers, and she understood. The ship was in danger and as Captain it was his duty to ensure the safe disposal of the vital and sensitive data stored in the ship's processor. Her worst fear had come to fruition. His duty as the commanding officer could cost him his life.

"You need to get to an escape pod." The urgency in his voice was a startling contrast to the self-assured captain who had spoken moments before.

"I won't leave you." Jade wrapped her arms around him, interlocking her fingers to brace for his objection. "Besides, you know as well as I do that with the exponential increase in gravitational pull, the escape pods are unlikely to break orbit." For a moment he looked like he might argue, but to her surprise, Aeron nodded. Maybe it was because he knew she was right, maybe it was because he couldn't bear to live his last moments without her, but either way, Jade was grateful that she didn't have to justify her decision to stay by his side.

With a deep breath, Jade nestled her head against his chest, feeling surprisingly calm despite the chaos around them. Aeron returned her embrace, fear and sorrow receded, leaving nothing but peace in their wake.

Captain Custos tapped his wrist, silencing the ship-wide alarm and, together, they watched as each step on the list turned gray, marking the crew's progress.

"Are you sure, Jade? There's still a chance you could make it." Aeron searched her eyes as if hoping for a change of heart.

Jade shook her head. "Not without you."

* * *

With flawless execution, every crew member fulfilled their final duties with speed and precision. Experiments were shut down, civilians escorted to their escape pods, and core emissions neutralized. Most importantly, the memory bank and all pertinent information were sent on an encrypted channel to Admiral Fidus, the head of CITADEL's defense.

Aeron's voice, amplified by the ship's speakers, resonated through the corridors. "Before we execute the final evacuation procedures, I want to express my gratitude to each of you. It has been an honor and privilege to lead this exceptional crew." He paused, tapping the command sequence into his cuff. His tone was somber yet resolute as he continued, "Initiating evacuation sequence now. Fly on the wings of Soteria."

With a nod to the ancient goddess of protection, Aeron and Jade watched as the escape pods launched one by one from the vessel.

Jade's thoughts slowed as she watched the departure of the pods on her display. In the absence of flashing red lights, the distant stars shimmered like diamonds against the velvet canvas of the cosmos. At the center, Lumina's mesmerizing dance of light and energy captivated her senses.

"Wow," she murmured.

Aeron's laughter echoed through the room as his hands deftly began the final phase of the protocol, wiping the ship's processor. "So, this is what it takes to pull you away from work?"

"Aeron! Wait! That's it!" Jade's voice rang out, grabbing his hand at the last moment, a surge of adrenaline rushing through her. Before them, the star grew larger as they approached.

"Shield failure imminent." The ship's processor issued the warning just as the normally transparent force field began to glow and rapidly turn red. Under enormous strain, the vessel shook violently.

"The Quantum Convergence Theory," Jade said, accessing her research and experimental interface. Using the ship's emergency power to link the prototype to the shield, she continued, "If we can align our quantum field with the white dwarf's gravitational pull, we can generate a portal." Biting her lip in anticipation, Jade initiated one final simulation.

Adrenaline turned into exhilaration as the status bar at the bottom of her screen turned green, validating Jade's theory and calculations. "I think I can port it to the escape pod control systems, too." With the interface working perfectly, there was no time for doubt. There was no time to double and triple check her calculations. It was now or never. Fingers poised over the control panel, she met Aeron's gaze. With his nod of approval, she pressed her finger to the screen.

The ship lurched forward, spinning around Jade in a dizzying blur as she struggled to stay conscious.

"Jade!" Aeron's voice sounded distant and distorted as time and space stretched, pulling her essence in every direction. Then everything faded to black.

* * *

They were dead. Jade was sure of it. Her theory had been a failure, the experiment a disaster. There was no tomorrow. Those were the first thoughts that crossed her mind as she became aware of the soft surface that caressed her skin.

Skin. She had skin. She had a body. She was safe and warm. Jade kept her eyes closed for a few more seconds, afraid of what she might see if she opened them. Then, just as she became aware of the sensation on her skin, her other senses began to take in the world around her.

That scent. She would know that fragrance anywhere. A captivating blend, with hints of woodiness and subtle spice, stirred her senses. Blinking her eyes open, Jade found herself gazing into the familiar depths of his ocean-blue eyes. A rush of affection flooded her heart.

Aeron, his features etched with worry, chuckled. "You're okay." He choked on his words, fear and desperation giving way to an unbelieving sigh. "You're okay."

"So are you." Her voice cracked. "And the crew?"

"All well and accounted for." Aeron grinned. "That was a hell of a calculation you cooked up. And, it looks like the universe finally found a way to give you a nap as a reward."

"How long have I been out?" Jade reached over her head, stretching.

"Thirty-eight hours, ten minutes, and some change." He recited the answer as though he'd been keeping track of every passing moment. "We're not entirely sure why. Your health diagnostic didn't show any abnormalities, so it's likely exhaustion. But I couldn't risk taking you to a medtech, not without risking possible cultural contamination."

"Where — when are we?" Jade sat up, eager for answers.

"Take it easy." Aeron put a gentle hand on her shoulder. "Exhaustion or not, until we know for sure, you need to take care." When she relaxed, he continued, "Interestingly enough, our coordinates haven't changed much. According to the ship's processor, the star date hasn't changed, and we are on Verdantis 9, but well, you'll see."

"Protocol—" She clasped his hand with hers, then tried to stand, but the world blurred as dizziness enveloped her.

"Protocol has been followed to the letter, each pod has been hidden, and I've had the crew transform the Endeavor into a cloaked observation blind." His eyes sparkled in a way that reminded her of their youth. "If you promise to be careful, I'll show you."

Jade nodded. Helping her stand, he guided her to the far wall. With a few taps of the control panel, the solid wall of the blind turned transparent. She knew nothing had changed for anyone who happened to be glancing in their direction, but now she and her fellow crewmates could see their surroundings. Beyond the cloak of their adapted research vessel, a proto-fusion society revealed itself.

Jade glanced at the sprawling valley below, where a labyrinth of pathways bustled with personal combustion engines. "Space travel?"

"No. Astro-exploration is rudimentary at best." He sighed. Then, as if determined to keep her spirits up, he gestured to a large open space in the corner of the room. "I've set up your usual workstation, but we can reconfigure the space however you want."

Jade looked at the area he had designed for her, feeling her heart lift. Aeron knew her too well. He understood that even while stranded in another universe, in a strange and ancient civilization, the scientist in her would have to collect data.

Immediately, her mind began to formulate a plan. Cultural observations of a primitive planet were usually conducted by a number of teams, and as the first representatives of CITADEL, their limited crew had significant responsibilities. Research had to be conducted remotely and, in the field, samples had to be collected, and everything had to be cataloged according to strict standards. The weight on her chest mounted as her mental to-do list grew.

"Don't worry, we'll get it done," he murmured, sweeping her hair behind her ear. At the sound of his voice, her anxiety dissipated.

"Let's not talk about work right now," Jade replied, chuckling at the comical expression that appeared on Aeron's face.

Grabbing his hand, she wrapped his arm around her shoulders and leaned into him. In the stillness, she could feel his heartbeat intermingle with hers. "I mean, look at this view."

As if on cue, rays of sunshine peaked over the horizon, bathing them with a soft golden light and painting the sky in hues of purple and pink. Below, the valley unfolded before them like a living tapestry. The land spread beneath them like a vibrant mosaic, revealing fields of interwoven vines and radiant clusters that added a splash of color to the canvas. The landscape, dotted with quaint dwellings, winding trails, and clusters of blooming orange flora, was reminiscent of the ancient societies they had studied at the academy. From their vantage point, they could see a population density in the distance coming to life as the day began.

"First things first, I need access to their communication systems." Jade took her place at her workstation with a grin.

"Excited?" Aeron smirked at her affectionately.

Jade nodded then continued. "Then I can configure the ANI interface on the Endeavor to receive and analyze the data on a global level." Her fingers flew across the display for a few seconds, then froze. "I'm in."

Aeron's eyes sparkled with pride. "Of course you are. You're brilliant."

She smiled. Using the holographic display projected above

her workstation, Jade accessed the visual and audio feeds from various sources.

Pulling up a camera on a picturesque boulevard, she zoomed in on a sign that arched over the street and froze the image. "According to ANI and the universal translator, it's a place called Temecula." Jade said softly, watching the vibrant street scene unfold before her. "It seems so full of life and energy."

"Not a bad place to be stranded," Aeron embraced her from behind. "It might be a nice place to stay awhile."

Jade turned to face him and as her lips met his, everything else faded away. This universe, or the next, it didn't matter as long as they were together.

Contributor Biographies

Veronika Childs

Veronika Childs is a versatile writer known for her evocative poetry and compelling children's books. Her poetry collection, *From Embers & Ash* delves into themes of heartache and healing, while her children's books, *The Power of Art: When My Feelings Can't Talk* and *The Power of Love: When Bad Things Happen* help young readers navigate complex emotions. Veronika also ventures into young adult fantasy with her captivating short story, "Within the Walls." Her diverse works reflect a deep empathy and a talent for storytelling across genres.

Mya Hill

I am Mya Hill. I have loved art since before I can remember. I have been painting since I was two, and I haven't stopped since. I do both digital and traditional art, and have always loved picking up a new medium.

Illustrating has been a fun, new opportunity and I hope to do more of it in the future.

MURRIETA CA
POST OFFICE

Community Corner

WHERE HAVE ALL THE COWBOYS GONE?

Story by Karen Robertson

Illustration by Mike Smith
Colored Pencil

Lost are the Days

A N ELDERLY COUPLE EXIT the church. The white-haired woman wears navy blue pants and a lightweight print jacket with blue and aqua patches of color. She walks tall and proud. Her husband is bent slightly and sports a cowboy hat, a tweed sports jacket, starched Wranglers, and cowboy boots. Arm-in-arm, they make their way across campus, dodging laughing children and the stampede of families headed for the parking lot. The last service before noon is always packed.

The woman guides their forward motion until a man, about twenty-five, wearing a red T-shirt and faded jeans with holes in the knees nearly knocks the couple off their feet. The old man frowns and notices the young man's baseball cap as he leans heavily on his wife.

"Oops! Sorry," says the younger man, as he grabs the old man's arm to steady him. He takes a brief look at the older man, grins and says, "Hey, I like your costume," and ambles off, waving to friends across the courtyard.

The old man doesn't hear, the comment, but his wife does, and she becomes incensed. Costume? Humph! Rather than get on the fight, she finds a place for her husband to sit down so she can correct what she feels is, either a misunderstanding or incredible ignorance.

"Rest here for a few minutes, Honey. I'll be back." She helps her husband get settled on a brick planter full of sweet-smelling flowers. Finding the man in the red shirt isn't difficult. He's standing with a small group, busy with his cell phone.

"Young man?" The woman saunters up to his side and taps him on the shoulder.

"Yes?" He turns slightly but does not look her in the eye.

"If you have a few minutes, I'd like to talk to you."

The young man looks around, as if there might be someone else he needs to talk to in the group. They are already occupied in conversation without him. Hesitantly, he turns his attention to the white-haired woman and sticks out his hand.

"Sure, I'm Frank," sounding less than enthusiastic. "I think I spoke to your husband a minute ago."

The woman takes his hand and gives it a firm shake.

"I'm his wife, Mrs. Sands, and I wanted to explain that your comment was quite an insult."

"Insult?" He cocks his head, as if he didn't hear her correctly.

"Yes, that's not a 'costume' my husband is wearing. That's what a real cowboy wears."

"Pardon me?" The young man replies with a shrug. "I have a cowboy hat, but I only wear it as a costume."

"Well, there you go. Two things set Mr. Sands apart from someone who wears a cowboy hat as a costume. His hat is sweat-stained and dirty around the crown from hard work. It's custom-made and cost $500. His name, Dusty Sands, is embossed in gold inside."

"Hmm. My hat is just a cheap one."

Her volume rises and she looks a bit agitated. "Yes, well, he'd know that at a glance. And another thing that sets him apart is that he knows when to take it off in respect. It drives him to distraction when men wear their hats, and baseball caps, inside the church or during the flag salute, national anthem, or even prayer."

"I see." He takes his cap off and runs his hand through his thick dark brown hair.

"Did you notice his boots?"

"Oh, yeah. I've got some pretty cool cowboy boots, too."

She reaches up and puts her hand gently on his forearm. "Not like his. He's wearing his Sunday-Go-To-Meetin' boots today. But his working boots have a spur ridge that keeps the spurs from slipping down over the heel when he's riding and roping."

"Roping? What does he rope?" His interest heightened.

"Cattle, of course. Back in the day, he worked on a cattle ranch in Arizona, when he attended college at the University of Arizona. His best friend's family had a ranch of fifty-six square miles. On the weekends and in the summers, he worked there. He had to learn to shoe his own horse, rope, brand, dehorn, and castrate cattle."

The young man's eyes widen, and his eyebrows rise. "That must have been hard work."

"He loved the work, but there were obstacles. Making friends with the Mexican workers was a problem. They just laughed at him, and he couldn't figure out why. He thought it was because he was fair-skinned, blue-eyed, with blond hair. He tried his high school Spanish on them, thinking that would bridge the gap. That really cracked 'em up. Turns out, Spanish taught and spoken with a New York accent is hilarious. In fact, even the English-speaking cowboys found his New York accent laughable and insisted he learn to speak like a cowboy. He said he struggled, and the western way to say "sauce" was the hardest word he ever had to learn. And they made him ask to pass the hot 'sauce' at every meal until he could say it without a New York accent."

Frank is stuck on how a New Yorker says "sauce." But a cowboy with a New York accent doesn't make sense.

"Let me tell you how unusual his life has been. Dusty was born in New York City and raised on Long Island."

"What?! What are the chances of becoming a cowboy on Long Island? I don't remember any cowboy movies in that area."

"Fate was on his side. There were two horses in Baldwin, New York, and the Sands family moved right next door to one of them. The owner had trained riders for the cavalry back in the 20's and 30's. Dusty and his brother begged him to teach them to ride, and he finally did."

"Huh? I thought the Cavalry was a thing of the past."

"Yep, and it still exists, but just for funerals, parades, or special events. Dusty grew up watching the rodeos televised from Madison Square Garden and dreamed of competing someday. In high school, Dusty worked summers at a dude ranch in upstate New York. On weekends, the employees put on a rodeo to entertain the guests. Dusty started riding bareback broncs and bulls."

"He really did go after his dreams."

"Not just rodeos. Later, he even worked at Belmont Park on the racetrack. He did anything he could to be around livestock."

Frank holds up a hand to stop her. "I have to ask. Is his name really Dusty?"

She smiles. "No, it's John. When he was a kid, he wanted to be a cowboy so badly, he told everyone that was his name."

"How did he come up with that one?"

"Dusty Sands was the name of a gunslinger back in the 1800s."

"Huh. It's a cool cowboy name, for sure. Were his parents into horses?"

"No way. His father was a structural engineer and designed the added metal work on top of the Empire State Building. You can imagine how happy he was about Dusty wanting to be a cowboy. In fact, his father fought his college decision. He wanted him to stay on the east side of the Mississippi. Dusty wanted a college with a rodeo team...and U of A accepted him."

"Rodeo team, eh? That's cool."

"It would have been, but he had some tough times there. For one thing, he had to keep his grades up to be on the rodeo team. First semester, he flunked out. He got a job operating heavy equipment in the copper mines until he could get back into school. Besides getting married and divorced, he struggled through college. He always says he crammed four years of college into six years. He was determined to please his dad."

"So, he didn't get to rodeo after all."

"Sure, he did. He went out on his own to compete in professional rodeos."

"No wonder he struggled. Going to school, operating heavy equipment, competing in rodeos, working on a cattle ranch. Whew." Frank wonders if this guy is for real.

"When Dusty graduated from college, he came to Murrieta and took a job breaking horses at Los Cerritos Ranch. Everyone around thought he grew up on a cattle ranch in Arizona."

"Did he tell them he was from New York?"

"Heck, no. By then, he worked and sounded like the cowboy

he always wanted to be."

"When was that?"

A string of motorcycles thunders by on the street. The old lady puts her hands to her ears and waits. When they've passed out of sight, she is assaulted by the smell of their exhaust. She fans herself with her church program until the odor subsides.

"Um. That was in 1969. Part of his job was exercising racehorses. From there, he took a job as a cowboy on what used to be the Vail Ranch. Kaiser Aetna had just purchased it and Louie Roripaugh was the boss."

"The Vail Headquarters is that tourist stop in Temecula by Kohl's on South 79. I've been there."

"Yep, that's where he lived when we met. His room had been the cook's quarters in years past. Every day he and another cowboy drove up on top of the Santa Rosas and tended 300 head of cattle. There's still a rock corral up there by the Old Adobe, where they would leave their horses at night."

"I've taken that hike and I remember that rock enclosure. I didn't realize it was meant to be a fence for horses."

"There was also a couple of windmills to pump water for the cows."

Frank wants to hurry the story along, but he's still curious about a few things.

"When did you come on the scene, Mrs. Sands?"

"I came to Murrieta in 1971 to teach school, when the population was only five hundred. Murrieta Elementary K-8 had five teachers and Temecula Elementary School had six. All the eighth-grade graduates from both schools went to high school in Lake Elsinore."

She hesitates and looks over to see that someone is talking with Mr. Sands. It's a young woman with blonde hair and a short green dress.

Frank zones out for a moment, hoping Mrs. Sands doesn't keep talking about school stuff.

"We met when Dusty walked into the laundromat at the trailer park on Ivy Street. Even though he lived in Temecula, that little laundromat was where the local cowboys came to wash their clothes. I had a washer and dryer, but I needed someone to hook them up for me." She gives a sly chuckle.

"Was it love at first sight?"

"I think so, because we made a date to go dancing at the Valley Center Inn, and he promised to hook up my washer and dryer. We've been agitating together ever since." She pokes Frank with her elbow, hoping he gets the joke.

"That's funny. I bet you've said that line before."

"Sure. He's a wonderful dancer and that sealed the deal. About a hundred days later, we got married on a hay wagon at Warner Stewart's ranch. Mrs. Stewart, Marj, was the manager of the Bank of America at the Plaza in Temecula."

"A hay wagon?"

"Yep. We didn't have any money, so we didn't send out invitations. I just put a 3x5 card on the bulletin board at the post office. It said, 'Dolly and Dusty are getting married on Saturday at 4:00. Y'all come! Bring food. It's a potluck.'" She stops and glances around again. Mr. Sands looks like he's captivated by the shapely young woman.

"So, when you met, was he still riding bulls?"

"Oh, no. But he roped at least twice a week. In fact, the day after our wedding, I sat at an arena all day while he roped steers." Mrs. Sands giggles. "There were lots of cowboys in the Temecula Valley back then. In fact, Temecula had a rodeo arena right where Armstrong Garden Center is now."

Frank notices that Mr. Sands is quite animated in his conversation with the girl.

"Should you be looking after Mr. Sands?"

"Oh, no. He looks like he's occupied." Undaunted, she continues. "Dusty was making $13.33 a day, seven days a week as a cowboy. I made around $24 a day as a teacher. We were poor as church mice. I like to say, I married him for his money, and I'm stickin' with him until he gets it!"

"That's funny."

"Did you notice Mr. Sands' belt buckle?"

Surprised by her sudden change of direction, he refocuses, "I did! None of my buckles are fancy like that one."

"He won it when he roped competitively. He'd still be doing it, but his last horse is getting old and Mr. Sands' knees...well, those bowed legs didn't accidentally get that way."

The young man is beginning to see Mr. Sands as quite a hero. "More than anything, I noticed the scars on his hands. I wondered about that."

"I can explain. The Vail Ranch job ran out and Dusty decided to start his own horseshoeing business. That's where the scars came from."

"Huh? I don't get it. How does that cause scars?" He wrinkles his forehead and looks genuinely interested.

Mrs. Sands takes a deep breath. Her feet are starting to hurt, and she wishes he'd just quit asking questions. But she's in "teacher mode" now and continues with gusto. "There are lots of steps to getting a horse shod. He would pull off the old shoes, clean out around the frog, trim the overgrown hoof, smooth it with a rasp, hammer the new shoe to the right shape, nail each shoe in place, clinch the nail ends that poke through the wall of the hoof, and rasp off the ends. Some horses are cooperative, but lots of times they lean or kick or pull away. If nails are still exposed during the process, they rip fingers and palms."

"Oh, ouch!" He grimaces and clenches his fists.

"If you think that's bad, you should see inside Dusty's boots. He's got one big toe that's been stomped on so many times, he's lost count of the new nails he's had to grow. Toenails, that is."

Still looking puzzled, "If Murrieta was so small, how did he make a living?"

She chuckled. "Horseshoers were in great demand. A dozen major horse ranches were located right here in Murrieta. Not many people, but lots of horses. Lots of racehorses were bred, trained, and rehabilitated in Murrieta. Dusty also shod horses at Rancho California Track and Training Center out on Highway 79. Later, the name was changed to Galway Downs. He used to stop at the big Fruit Stand on that road and bring home fresh produce." Mrs. Sands stops for a second and her eyes seem to be looking into the past again. She can almost smell the peaches and oranges he brought home.

Frank shifts from one foot to the other and wonders if Mrs. Sands is getting uncomfortable. He attempts to move the story forward. "He didn't work cattle anymore?"

"After his horseshoeing business grew, he started buying cows. We had our own small herd for over thirty years. The whole family would saddle up and we'd drive them down Jefferson Avenue from where we pastured them in Murrieta to where we vaccinated and doctored them, almost to Temecula."

Frank tries to imagine being confronted by a herd of cows coming down the road.

"Later we had them up on the Santa Rosas, but we don't anymore." She turns and waves her arm to indicate the mountains that form a barrier between the inland valley and the ocean. "The conservancy bought all the land we had leased and kicked us out. We had to move our cows wherever we could find fenced land with feed. With all the horse ranches selling out to developers in the 80's, it got tougher and tougher to find places. We once had a few cows right here where we're standing, on the church property."

"Huh. That's interesting." He looks down at the ground as if he expects to see some leftover manure there.

Mrs. Sands looks back and sees Mr. Sands laughing with the woman.

"You must have grown up with horses and cattle."

She chuckles as she conjures up a memory. "When I first met Dusty, he planned the most unusual date. It wasn't unusual for him, but it sure was for me. I grew up as a small-town banker's daughter raised in the San Joaquin Valley. All I ever saw in the country was crops: peaches, almonds, and grapes. Dusty took us to a corral with about fifty calves. There were several families involved, and he invited me to participate. A few men roped the calves from horseback. We women and some kids threw the calves down and held them while other men castrated, dehorned, and vaccinated. We were all filthy, tired, and bloody when we finished."

"Where was that?"

"It was at a farm on the corner of Winchester and 395, right where the Promenade Mall is now. I know it's hard to imagine. After our work was done, men, women, and children let off steam by playing a wild game of football in Dr. Hill's pasture full of cow pies. The smell of cow pies mixed with blood, sweat, and cow snot was atrocious."

They both laugh.

Frank's stomach turns. He's not sure if it is the gnawing hunger or the idea of cow pies mixed with blood, sweat and cow snot.

Mrs. Sands doesn't even notice.

"Mr. Sands still helps other ranchers work their cattle. One time, we did a branding at the end of Pujol Street at the old Slaughterhouse in Temecula."

She runs her fingers across her chin and seems deep in

thought. "There used to be a Playhouse or theater on that same street. I don't know if it's still there, but I acted in a play once."

"What else was there to do around here?"

"In 1977, we went to the first Tractor Race in Temecula. If I remember correctly, it was partly on Front Street and partly in the riverbed. It's been a long time ago." She gazes toward Temecula, as if she's visualizing the replay of the race and remembering the dust accumulating in her hair.

"Where was I? Oh yes, for a while, Mr. Sands played softball. We'd take the kids for burgers at The Swing Inn after every game. That was the only place to eat. The Long Branch Saloon was also located on Front Street, but I never went in there. It was usually populated by 'Cowboys and Indians.' I heard things got pretty rough in there at times."

She pauses. "I did go in there later when the saloon shut down and the building became a church. Churches are more of my liking than bars. I heard some motorcyclists came in one day to have beers and the pastor told them it wasn't a bar anymore. One of the guys replied, 'Well, is nothing sacred?' I always thought that was a funny story. Now, that building houses the 1909 eatery."

A few moments of silence. Frank thinks Mrs. Sands may have finally run out of gas.

Mrs. Sands wonders if this young man ever gets hungry because she is ravenous.

Frank looks at his watch and hears his stomach growl again, but he doesn't know how to end the conversation.

"I'm sorry if I insulted Mr. Sands by calling his clothes a costume."

She pats him on the arm. "That's okay. He's so deaf, I'm sure he didn't hear you. After all those years of banging on the anvil, his hearing is permanently damaged. It was me who got my knickers in a bind. He probably would have let it go. I'm always looking to set things right."

"I can tell you were a teacher."

"Sometimes, I'd model for Judy Moramarco who owned a dress shop named The Grange in the Plaza. I looked forward to those fashion shows. That was fun."

"Gosh, you two really have been here a long time and seen a lot of changes."

"I'm sorry I've taken up so much of your time." Mrs. Sands is ready to call it quits.

"I really learned a lot."

"Then the results are good. It's just that when you've worked as hard as Dusty did, it's sad to get old and be taken for granted. That's not even the end of his story. You know, I told you he wanted to be a fireman?"

"No, you didn't tell me that." Frank takes a deep breath and braces himself for more.

"Oh, that's the best part of the story."

The young man leans in. "You mean there's more?" Almost jokingly now.

"Oh my, yes!"

"Okay, now I'm beginning to wonder about you. First you tell me this New Yorker turns cowboy, horseshoer, and cattleman, and now you're going to tell me something else. I feel like I'm on a rollercoaster."

"Well, I told you he was unusual."

"Mrs. Sands, I don't want to leave you, but honestly, I'm about to starve. Would you and Mr. Sands let me treat you to lunch? Do you think he'd consider it?"

She looks at her watch. "Oh, my goodness. I had no idea I'd bent your ear for so long. It's a wonder Mr. Sands hasn't objected."

Mrs. Sands loops her arm inside Frank's, indicating that she wants to be escorted. He responds by bending his arm and putting his hand on her hand. They head to where Mr. Sands sits.

"Mr. Sands and I have an understanding. If I want to find him, I just look for the prettiest girl around and that's where he'll be. He attracts them like flies." She giggles.

"That's funny. You don't mind?"

"No, if he wants to find me, he just looks for the best-looking young man, and I'll be on his arm." She looks up at Frank with a coy smile. "We're both harmless."

As they approach, Frank takes notice of the attractive woman who's been chatting with Mr. Sands.

"Honey, this is Frank. I've been telling him about your history as a cowboy and cattleman. He was impressed by your hat, belt and boots, and wanted to hear your story." She winks at Frank.

Mr. Sands puts out his hand to shake. "Nice to meet you. This lovely girl is Nadene. I've been telling her about my career in the fire service."

"Fire service?" Frank shakes Mr. Sands' hand and acknowledges Nadene with a nod.

Mrs. Sands takes her husband's hand and urges him to get up. "Let's go. You can tell Frank more about that at lunch."

With a grunt, Mr. Sands gets to his feet, wobbles a bit, and slowly straightens up.

"Uh, Nadene, can you join us?" Frank asks.

She looks around and realizes they are the only ones left on the church campus.

"Thanks. I guess I could. That would be fun. I want to hear more about Mr. Sands' life."

"I guess I do, too." Frank herds the three toward the parking lot.

As they walk along, Nadene drops back next to Frank. "Did you know Mr. Sands became a full-time firefighter when he was forty-five years old and didn't retire until he was sixty-six?!"

Frank shakes his head. "This guy is a legend, I think. I'm glad Mrs. Sands told me his story. Seems there's more to tell."

Mrs. Sands overhears and slows. "Yes, Frank. And believe me, if you'd seen him in his firefighter uniform or turnouts, you would never have said, 'I like your costume.'"

They all laugh, even though Frank and Mrs. Sands are the only ones who know the joke.

The story of Dusty Sands is based on the true life of Barry Robertson, Karen's husband, who has lived in the valley over 50 years. She wanted to honor him, his amazing life, and the history of the Murrieta/Temecula Valley.

Contributor Biographies

Karen Robertson

Besides being a teacher and stand-up comic, Karen has written comedy, poetry, novels, memoirs, speeches, magazine articles, manuals, grants, newspaper columns, and a couple of plays. She has written her own eulogy because she wants people to laugh, rejoice, and celebrate a life she enjoyed living. To access her books and videos: www.SayItWithHumor.com.

Mike Smith

Mike was a boy in Minnesota who copied the comics found in the Sunday funnies. It was hard to find a private place in a house of nine children, but space was found on a white piece of paper and some colored pencils. Mike went west. Art-related jobs were Tech Illustrator, editorial cartooning, t-shirt design, but drawing cards for birthdays, Christmas, and holidays was always there. He finds watching and hearing people laugh while holding a card he created a most rewarding thing. It might even be kinda important. He has a wife and a dog.

THE JOURNEY

Story by M.K. Warren

Illustration by Clarissa Lee
Acrylic & Colored Pencil

R ORY CALVIN FERGUS SR. was dying, no doubt about it. His breathing had become shallow, his extremities were cold, and his seventy-year-old frame seemed to sink into his hospital bed.

The people of Sunnyside, Oregon, where Fergus Sr. had always called home, were waiting to start a celebration when he passed from this world. They all agreed Fergus Sr. thrived on being the meanest old man of all mean old men. Bitter and vocal, he spent his waking hours terrorizing all living things if they were unlucky enough to come near his double-wide trailer or make the mistake of getting in his way as he shuffled through life. After word spread that Fergus Sr. was near death, no one felt sad. No one except his only son, Bleb.

* * *

Bleb's real name was Rory Calvin Fergus Jr., but because of events on the day of his birth Fergus Sr. said the boy didn't deserve to carry his name and the child became Bleb. How a man could use a term that meant a small blister on the skin as a nickname for his newborn was beyond people's comprehension. They went along with it because it was easier than dealing with Fergus Sr.

Though small in stature with bright orange hair, people remembered Bleb's friendly personality after they had met him. Folks said Bleb's kindness balanced his father's bad-tempered behavior and if anything came up, they went straight to the younger Fergus.

Fergus Sr. had always been grumpy, but his personality went from bad to worse after January 14, 2000. He left the house as usual on that day. Fergus Sr. never missed work; his job being one of the few things that gave him joy. He was 'Behind the Eyes', as it was called, being Dusty Dog, the mascot for the Mud Puppies minor league baseball team. He had gained a following from fans with his crazy antics and daring feats. For the first time, at that afternoon's Mud Puppies vs Shark Horses game, there were to be mascot talent scouts in the stands. Fergus Sr. believed himself a shoo-in for the majors and the start of a dream career if he could pull off the performance he had been secretly working on for months, the Boiling Condiment Fountain of Doom. Fergus Sr. was just about to take the field during the seventh inning stretch when an unexpected phone call came. It gave him the news his son had arrived prematurely, and his wife had not long to live. Though reeling from shock, Fergus Sr. made the decision not to cancel his act and rush to his wife's side. Instead, he went out and attempted his most dangerous stunt. What happened next is remembered with horror by all who witnessed it. Rarely spoken of in mascot circles, the event is known as the 'Nacho Cheese' incident. After it, Rory Fergus Sr. would never work again. He blamed this tragedy and anything else he could think of on young Bleb.

Bleb accepted his role as scapegoat for his father. The young man felt if he took some of the venom his dad spewed, then other people would be spared. His son's compliance irritated Fergus Sr. and reinforced his idea that Bleb was worthless.

So, without his father's encouragement or help, Bleb made his way in the world. He tried different activities hoping to find one thing that would make Fergus Sr. notice, but it was no use. Not successful in sports or in school, the young man was continually ignored by his father. Bleb ended up dropping out of high school at sixteen and taking a seasonal part-time job at Enchanted Forest, a local amusement park.

As Bleb sat at his dying father's bedside, he felt a wave of regret. Not for himself, but for his dad.

"You've been so unhappy all these years, Papa," Bleb whispered, "I know I've always been a disappointment. I wish there was something I could do." He watched his father struggle to take another breath. The hospital had removed all the machines to prolong life at Fergus Sr.'s request. His end was near.

Suddenly a raspy voice came from the figure in the bed.

"Did you bring it?" The sick man was referring to his old Dusty Dog jersey from the Mud Puppy days. Bleb had spent hours trying to get the orange cheese stains out of the white fabric with no luck. He hoped his father wouldn't be able to see the blotches with his failing eyesight.

"Here it is." Bleb walked over and laid the shirt on his dad's skeletal frame. As Bleb adjusted one of the sleeves, he felt something in the upper pocket of the tunic. He pulled out an old business card and read the name 'Whitney Q. Ruzz, Dream Maker' out loud.

"What was that boy?" Fergus Sr. became restless.

"The card says Whitney Q. Ruzz, Dream Maker." Bleb turned the cardboard rectangle over. There was a note handwritten on the other side. "On the back it says: A New Life Awaits." Bleb felt a tingle run down his spine. He decided it must be from sitting for so long next to his father's bed.

"What?!" came from Fergus Sr. as a wail. He attempted to sit up. Bleb tried to keep his father still.

"Please, Papa, don't. Lie back. Try to calm yourself." Bleb was startled by the older man's sudden burst. He thought his dad near death. "Who is this Ruzz?"

Fergus Sr. appeared to sink deeper into the mattress. Any remaining color had drained from his gaunt face. But his cloudy eyes were strangely wide, and they tried to focus on Bleb's face.

"The Furrier," the old man hissed, "He would've trained me. If only I had known. Maybe I could have reinvented myself after the incident. Now it's too late...too late." Fergus Sr. faded, his eyes drooped. Suddenly he grasped Bleb's wrist. Long, unkempt fingernails dug into the boy's skin with surprising strength. "You must go to him."

"What? No. I can't."

"Yes, you've got to."

Bleb could feel his father's grip tightening.

"That card was for you Papa," Bleb said, "Not me."

"He'll take you on as a student, I know he will. The Furrier will make you a great mascot, even better than I could have been. Promise me you'll go and finally make something worthwhile of yourself, someone I could be proud of."

"I don't know. He won't know me."

"Just tell him you're my..." Fergus Sr. hesitated, then said the thing Bleb had been longing for his whole life. "Tell him you're my son."

Bleb didn't hear anything else after that. Only when a nurse came in and told him Fergus Sr. had passed did Bleb realize he had been holding his father's hand at the end.

* * *

Over the next two days Bleb made arrangements for his father's interment in the cemetery plot adjoining Bleb's mother,

Maria. When all was done, he took Ruzz's old business card to the library to see if he could find where The Furrier lived.

Sue, the reference librarian, was very helpful. She had always been kind. They managed to find a Whitney Quintus Ruzz in a city in Southern California neither had heard of called Temecula. The town's name sounded exotic. Bleb decided to take the chance that this was who he was looking for. Besides, Temecula appeared to be a nice place to visit, and Bleb had always wanted to go somewhere exotic. He made some copies of maps and then went to talk things over with his best friend, GP.

Mr. GP Jim had come into Bleb's life a year before. The gentle soul had been in a cardboard cereal box on the side of the road. Bleb had been picking up cans and bottles to recycle when he came across the abandoned pet. Though Fergus Sr. called GP a rat, he was actually an Abyssinian guinea pig with messy white and brown hair and dark eyes. Bleb and GP became fast friends. The rodent was a great listener and brought a Zen-like atmosphere to Bleb's life. He found himself eating better because of his companion's herbivore lifestyle and they both discovered a love of yoga. GP was a natural yogi and Bleb had thought about opening their sessions to others, but GP still needed some time to get over his shyness.

After a lengthy discussion about the trip and its purpose, GP agreed to accompany Bleb on the sixteen-hour drive. The next day Bleb removed the large container of coins his father had been collecting for years from the trailer's back bedroom. He would take the loose change to the One Stop Shop. He wasn't sure his dad would be happy helping with expenses for the journey, but it was too late to ask.

It took Bleb an hour to cash out $227.17 in change in the machine. He was a little surprised at the amount and decided to splurge on a new pair of cargo pants and a teal shirt with tiny swordfish on it. He wanted to fit in with people in southern California and the polo was the closest thing to tropical attire the store sold. Bleb also bought a plastic container without a lid for GP and a canvas belt to attach it to his passenger seat. When he brought the items plus a case of water and a twelve pack of 'Sick Soda' up to Alma's register, she gave him a questioning look. She was the last person in town that had known his mother and had always kept an eye on him.

"Going somewhere?" Alma said.

"Yes, GP and I are leaving tomorrow. We're headed south." Bleb decided to throw a bag of beef jerky on the counter from a display near the check-out line.

"Well, that's nice." Alma was missing her top front teeth, so she spit a little when she spoke. Bleb had heard she used to wrestle semi-professionally. "You going to Eugene or Medford," Alma continued.

"No, we're heading all the way to California, to a place called Temecula."

"Sounds exotic. Good thing you're buying that shirt. Cali, huh? Make sure you have your pocketknife. And if you're going to drive through a big city, keep your car doors locked."

"Thanks for the advice," Bleb said. He wondered where his

pocketknife even was. Alma finished ringing up his purchases and then she leaned closer to him.

"Oh, and don't wear red or blue."

"Why?"

"Gangs," Alma said. She enunciated the 's.' Bleb received a spray of saliva. He wiped his face with his sleeve as he loaded the items back into the cart.

* * *

That night Bleb packed his blue Toyota Tercel's hatchback with a sleeping bag, a first-aid kit, his new polo, and jumper cables. He put fresh clear packing tape on the front passenger side where the window should have been and secured GP's container to the seat. He also put his friend's favorite green camouflage fleece blanket in the box for comfort. Bleb liked to travel light so the cargo pants would act as his suitcase. He made sure he had a new toothbrush, toothpaste, lip balm, deodorant, and the recommended pocketknife ready to go on his nightstand. He also stuffed clean underwear and socks into a grocery bag.

Putting the business card along with the cash from his last paycheck into his wallet, Bleb surveyed the trailer he had grown up in with his dad. He had few personal items here. It was mostly filled with his dad's junk including framed pictures of famous mascots, *Perry Mason* videos, and stacks of *Reader's Digest*. There wasn't much to worry about anybody taking but, even so, he had arranged for his neighbor to look after the place.

He had promised the elderly man, Herman, he would bring back something with 'California' on it in exchange.

It was still dark and slightly cool when Bleb loaded drinks, the grocery bag, and some cassette tapes into the car the next morning. He started the engine and made sure the interior was warm before he carried GP to his container on the front passenger seat. They were both nervous and excited about their upcoming adventure. GP squeaked several times and popcorned with all four legs in anticipation, while Bleb searched his music collection for just the right song to start the trip.

"How about some ABBA, GP?" Bleb pulled out the band's greatest hits. After giving his approval by running in circles, the animal settled and listened to the opening piano of SOS as they pulled out of the trailer's driveway. Bleb opened a can of the highly caffeinated Sick Soda. He hadn't slept well and already needed a pick-me-up.

Traffic was light and the early part of the drive seemed to go smoothly. They made it through two different 70's tapes before stopping for the first time, just after Eugene. Parked at a rest stop on the other side of the city, Bleb and GP enjoyed a snack of carrots, lettuce, and apples. They received some funny looks when man and guinea pig ran around in the grass, but people kept their distance. The rest of the day continued the same way. The two paused every couple of hours to snack, stretch their legs, or fill the car up with gas. It felt nice not to be on any sort of schedule.

When it was starting to get dark at about the halfway point,

Bleb realized he had drunk five sodas and four waters. He needed a bathroom. They had passed Red Bluff about a half an hour before. The small cities north of Sacramento would be their only choice.

Bleb reluctantly pulled into a small gas station in a town called Artois. The place looked deserted, and this made Bleb uneasy about stopping. Tufts of grass grew out of a crack in the pavement. There were only two beat-up pumps. The building behind appeared to house a little store. The lights were on, but Bleb didn't see anyone inside. He was about to pull away when he noticed a new-looking restroom sign hanging above a door on the corner of the structure. He moved his car closer to the building and parked. Completely covering GP by tucking the blanket around him, Bleb noticed the guinea pig was sleeping on Bleb's wallet. He had taken it from his back pocket because sitting on it and driving the long distance had become uncomfortable. Bleb made sure his possession was hidden under the fabric as well.

The door to the bathroom was locked when Bleb tried the handle. He decided to ask in the store.

Bleb opened the glass door and scanned the inside of the market. Low metal shelves made up two rows, but the displays were practically empty. Alongside an old-fashioned cash register on a well-worn counter sat a hot dog warmer. It had wrinkled weenies rolling like logs under heat lamps. Also on the counter, were two large boiling pots. Steam made their lids and ladles bounce noisily. Bleb stepped inside.

"Hello?" Bleb called out but received no answer. He walked cautiously towards the counter. He was about to peek under the lid of one of the pots when he was startled by a voice behind him.

"What do you think you're doing?"

Bleb turned around. Standing next to the entrance were two large figures. Wearing shorts that were too big and tank tops that were too small, they had a striking resemblance, in both size and body hair, to gorillas. They gave off an aura of menace. Bleb put his hand in his pocket for his knife, but he could only find his toothbrush.

"Hi," Bleb said trying to keep his voice from shaking. "I just need to use the bathroom. Is there a key?"

"Is there a key?" one said, mockingly. The other person laughed. "You got to pay a fee, Mr. Oreegone. We don't give things away for free, unlike your hippie-ass state."

"Of course," Bleb said, "I'd be happy to." Then he remembered his wallet. "I need to get some money from the car." Bleb had made the decision that once outside he would jump into his vehicle and leave.

"Do you think he means this, Pee Wee?" the more gargantuan of the two said.

"I think he does, Cobb."

Bleb noticed that Cobb was holding a green camouflage blanket bundled up. Bleb recognized it as the one from his car. He could see the tip of his wallet sticking out, but GP was not visible. Bleb reached for the roll of material.

"Thank you for bringing that to me, Gentlemen," Bleb said.

"I can make a purchase now."

"Not so fast." Cobb pulled the fleece away before Bleb could take it. "I think we need to collect a little for our special tax."

"Yeah, you maybe should pay a visitor's fine too," Pee Wee said chuckling.

Cobb's tiny eyes suddenly widened, and he grinned unpleasantly. "Don't he look like a little clown with his pale skin and red hair?"

"He sure does," Pee Wee said, and he giggled. "He should perform for us."

"Yep." Cobb hugged the blanket to his chest, "if you want this back, you better impress us. We used to perform professionally. So, dance, tiny clown, dance!"

Bleb was horrified. He had no idea what to do.

"No, please," Bleb said. He could feel his stomach clench with fear for himself and GP. His mind whirled trying to think of a way to escape.

Suddenly there was movement in the bundle Cobb was holding.

"What the—" Cobb said as he looked into the rolled-up fleece. He abruptly cried out in pain from a nasty guinea pig bite to his nose. He threw the blanket into the air and clutched his bleeding snout. Simultaneously, Bleb grabbed one of the heated pots behind him and flung it at Pee Wee. It struck the furry man in the mid-section. Bright orange molten cheese splashed over his tiny top. He cried out, began flapping his hands, and ran in circles. Bleb, in an amazing feat, was able to catch the blanket, the wallet, and the guinea pig before they landed. He, the items, and GP ran out to the car and fled.

Bleb got back onto the I-5 freeway. He didn't stop for a long while. Traveling in silence, Bleb and GP were both wide awake.

When they reached Sacramento, Bleb went into a fast-food restaurant and used the restroom. He then bought himself a cheeseburger, fries, and yogurt parfait. He parked in a corner of the lot.

"I feel terrible about what happened earlier, GP," Bleb said before he took any bites of his meal. He didn't get any response from his friend. "I think you saved my life back there, buddy. I owe you." GP made several low grunts. This was his way of acknowledging. Bleb felt better. He gave GP the parfait and started eating.

Over the remaining eight hours their stops were less frequent. They listened to the audiobook of *Pride and Prejudice*. GP was a big Jane Austen fan. The story kept them entertained and most importantly, awake. The scenery went from large orchards and farmland to grassy hills and then finally the city. Bleb had been warned about Los Angeles traffic, but they went through early enough in the morning they missed most of it. It wasn't until they reached a place called Corona that they met morning commuters.

GP and Bleb finally reached their destination at about 8 am. It was already getting warm in Temecula as they took an exit from the freeway. They were both fascinated by the palm trees of all shapes and sizes. Bleb thought about cruising around to look at the sights, but it soon became evident they should find a place to take a nap. Bleb drove over a hill and found something that was familiar to him — a library. The parking lot came with a lovely view of some sports fields below. Finding a corner with some shade, Bleb leaned back his car seat. He was asleep within minutes.

* * *

It was almost 11:30 am before Bleb woke up. GP was still sleeping so Bleb grabbed his new shirt and went inside the library bathrooms to do a quick freshen up. When he came back, he saw that his friend was awake, so he took GP's blanket out and gave it several big shakes.

"There, now we are both ready for action," Bleb said. They each ate an apple slice that was slightly brown but still crunchy. "I hope this meeting goes okay. I don't think I have the stamina or the supplies to drive back to Oregon right away."

Checking the maps he had brought, Bleb realized they were very close to the neighborhood Ruzz lived in.

"Let's get this over with." Bleb put the car in gear and drove out of the parking lot slowly. His friend made some low-sounding squeaks. "I know, GP. I'm nervous too."

They pulled into a neighborhood called Rayo del Sol. The sun was already heating up the summer morning more than Bleb had expected. The Tercel's air conditioning couldn't keep up. All the houses were painted in shades of brown with white trim and large windows. Every lawn was green and neatly manicured. There were lots of varieties of flowering plants, splashes of bright pinks, oranges, and reds. Bleb found the display enchanting. He located the house number he was looking for and parked in front. There was a shiny light-blue sedan in the driveway.

Bleb unbuckled GP's box and carried it with him up to the front door. Two ceramic gnomes had cacti in pots on their backs on the front porch of the house. The mat next to the front door read 'Mi Casa Es Su Casa'. Bleb heard a sudden loud crash come from behind the fence to the backyard, followed by some yelling. It sounded like a man was angry at his pool equipment. Hoping he wasn't interrupting, Bleb rang the bell.

The door was opened by a small elderly lady. A blast of cool air hit Bleb. He savored it then looked at the woman in front of him. Her wavy white hair was teased to form a fluffy shell on her head. She wore a floral shirt with half sleeves and peach-colored slacks that only came to just below her knees. Bleb saw toenails covered with pastel orange polish poking out from high heel sandals. She smiled.

"May I help you, young man?" the woman said. Her tone was slightly high pitched but instantly pleasing to Bleb. He stumbled with his answer. He had forgotten to rehearse what he was going to say.

"Uh," was all that came out of him.

"Are you selling popcorn or something? I'll have to get my purse."

"No, ma'am," Bleb finally said.

"Are you okay?"

"Yes, ma'am. My name is Bleb; I mean Rory Fergus Jr. Rory Fergus Sr. is or was my dad." He said it so quickly he wasn't sure the lady had heard him. She took a moment before she answered.

"Should I know that name?"

"Are you Whitney Ruzz?" Bleb said.

"No, that's my husband. Why don't you and your...box come inside," the woman said with a natural sweetness that made Bleb feel welcomed. She took his arm and guided him in. "It's going to be another hot one today. I'll go get Whit. He's in the back trying to avoid calling a pool repairman. Be right back." Her shoes clicked on the pale marble floor as she walked off.

Bleb looked around the foyer, in awe. It was the most beautiful place he had ever been in. It felt magical and a tingle ran down Bleb's spine. Everything was shiny and white. There were high ceilings and clean furniture. On the walls hung real painted pictures of amazing scenery and flowers. The place smelled great too. There was a sweet scent like someone made cookies, but it wasn't strong so perhaps they had been baked a few hours before and a hint of cinnamon and sugar just lingered. Bleb tried to absorb it all. He suddenly had a longing to be part of this world. His fantasy was interrupted when an older man in khaki shorts, a teal swordfish polo, and flip-flops came over to Bleb. The man was slightly hunched, and his skinny tan legs were a little bowed, but he still walked with purpose.

"Hi there. Whitney Ruzz at your service," the man said and extended his hand for Bleb to shake. "What can I do you for? Nice

234

shirt, by the way."

The handshake was strong and confident, but not too firm. The older man's eyes were a deep blue, and his face was wrinkled in various spots like he smiled and laughed a great deal. "It's very nice to meet you, Mr. Fergus."

Bleb nodded in acknowledgment. "Are you The Furrier?" Bleb pulled his wallet out and found the old business card.

"I haven't been called that in a long time," Whitney said. He looked at the paper in Bleb's hand.

"Do you still train mascots?"

"No, I'm too old for the business." Whitney dropped his head with sadness. "Last two young men I tried to work with were so mean and malicious I had to send them back up to Northern Cal. After that, I decided there was no place for me these days."

"You don't help anymore," Bleb said realizing what Whitney had just said. "So, I came all this way...."

"It's a shame too." Whitney continued, "I really liked guiding people toward their dreams."

Bleb stopped listening. He suddenly felt very weary and stupid for traveling all this way chasing something his dad wanted.

"You look a little pale, fella," Whitney said to Bleb, "maybe you should come and sit down. I sense you've a tale to tell."

Over the next couple of hours Bleb, with the help of GP, told Mr. and Mrs. Ruzz his life story. They were great listeners and they fed Bleb several plates of nachos with extra cheese sauce, glasses of lemonade, and snickerdoodles. At the end Mrs. Ruzz, who had asked to be called Joan, wiped away tears. Whitney also seemed choked up, but he showed it by staying silent for a few moments after Bleb had finished.

"Rory? You don't mind if I call you that, do you son?" Whitney said as he came over and sat next to Bleb.

"No, sir. You can call me whatever you want," Bleb said, "I'm sorry I've talked for so long. I don't mean to burden you, or Mrs. Ruzz."

"Now, don't worry about that," Whitney said, "I want to help you — no, I feel compelled to help you. Don't you agree, Mother?" Joan nodded. "Why don't you stay with us for a while until we can get things figured out."

"But" Bleb said, "You hardly know me, and I can't pay you."

"Don't worry about that. I've always been a good judge of character. I do remember your father and I believe anyone who could have survived living with him deserves to be rewarded. I hope you will consider this offer. We have plenty of room since our boys went out on their own."

"And it would also be nice to have someone to help out," Joan added, "we're not getting any younger."

Bleb thought about their generous offer. He knew he didn't want to go back to Sunnyside anytime soon, there wasn't anything there for him.

"I can't make a decision until I talk with my friend GP," Bleb said, looking at the plastic tub. "This affects him too."

"Of course," Whitney said, "we'll give you some privacy." Joan and Whitney left Bleb sitting on the floor next to GP's box.

"What do you think?" Bleb patted GP's head. "It would be a big change, but I think I could be happy here. It's okay if you don't want to stay. I know how fond you are of hearing rain on the roof. I'm not sure how much of that they get."

GP was quiet for a while then he gently nibbled Bleb's hand.

"Okay, great. And I can always send you back to Oregon by overnight mail if you change your mind."

Instead of telling Mr. and Mrs. Ruzz right away, Bleb walked over and peered out the large French doors onto the patio. The backyard had a pool that was tiled and had small designs made of cut glass along the edges. Potted tropical plants and blooming flower boxes dotted the cement, and the sunshine made the water sparkle. His father's passing had given Bleb a chance for a new life. The idea of Temecula was a little scary, but it was also kind of thrilling. He had never lived anywhere exotic. Bleb decided that along with a different city he would change his identity as well. Bleb was gone, and Rory Calvin Fergus Jr. emerged.

Rory found the elderly couple in the kitchen.

"Mr. and Mrs. Ruzz, GP and I would like to accept your offer," Rory said, extending his hand to Whitney.

"Fantastic!" Whitney said, taking it, "Okay. Do you fellas have any ideas about what kind of careers you would like to pursue. No rush, but if you have any interests, I would like to know."

Rory smiled and looked over at the plastic container GP was sitting in.

"As a matter of fact, I do know GP has a desire to teach yoga. He just needs a little encouragement."

"All right, I can look into that," Whitney said, smiling. "What about you, Rory?"

Rory glanced out the kitchen window and sighed. "I have always dreamed of being a swimming pool repairman."

Contributor Biographies

M.K. Warren

M.K. Warren is a part-time author living in Southern California. She has been writing off and on all her life focusing on short stories and dramatic works. Since she was a teenager, M.K.'s skits, puppet shows, and short films have been produced by schools and clubs. Recently, she has focused on her fiction and plans to publish a collection of short stories in the coming year.

Clarissa Lee

Clarissa Lee is an arts educator who has spent her life making the arts more accessible to her community. She worked for the nonprofit organization Arts Education in Maryland Schools. She has championed the arts by serving as art and music docent for schools in Los Angeles, the Bay Area, and San Diego. Ms. Lee is currently a public-school arts educator, while also serving as Director of a local arts nonprofit.

Ms. Lee holds a Bachelor of Fine Arts from the Maryland Institute College of Art, a Diploma in Piano Performance with Distinction from the Royal Schools of Music, and a Master of Arts in Education, Secondary Teacher Education from University of Phoenix.

FAR FROM HERE

Story by Kristen Tregar

Illustration by Reggie DeMatos
Digital

"YEAH, I WORK IN my dad's company but it's not because he's my dad. Like, obviously I would have been a competitive applicant, although at this point, all these diversity hires are making it harder for people like me to find a job...."

Date #472 paused for a moment to take a swig of his Coors Light, and for the first time in a long time, Maggie felt something other than dismay. Relief, perhaps, for the brief silence in what had otherwise been a flood of sound emanating from #472. In that quiet moment, Maggie reflected on how wide the gap seemed to be between an online dating profile and the person those profiles represented. #472 seemed to have potential, seemed to share

Maggie's appreciation for travel, for wine, and for somewhat eclectic folk music. Instead, however, the individual Maggie encountered when she arrived for dinner at La Petite Abeille was seemingly only interested in the sound of his own voice.

#472's droning resumed and continued through the rest of the entrees. Maggie spent the time quietly imagining creative ways to leave immediately after dinner without ordering dessert. When the server stopped by their table and inquired whether or not they'd like coffee, Maggie jumped in before #472 had the chance to order anything, declined anything further, and swiftly handed her debit card to the waiter.

"This one is on me, so nice to have met you," she said, "but I'm afraid I must get home. I have the opening shift at the library tomorrow so it will be an early morning."

Before #472 could say a word, Maggie was out of her seat, had slid deftly into her wool coat, and wrapped her scarf around her neck. The waiter returned Maggie's card, flipped the card terminal for the input of a tip, and with a press of the screen and a quick signature, Maggie was on her way out into the frigid temperatures of a February evening in New York City.

Snowflakes were just beginning to fall, the harbingers of a full weekend of intermittent precipitation and bone-chilling dampness. The remains of the previous week's storm, pockmarked piles of salt-and-dirt encrusted snow, lined the sidewalks, narrowing the available space for pedestrians. Maggie avoided eye contact with the people around her as she wove her way towards 7th Avenue. She was tired. Yet another Friday

244

night had been spent in the company of someone who, rather than offering companionship, had made the tartness of Maggie's loneliness more apparent.

When she first arrived in New York City five years ago to study library science at Queens College, part of the allure had been the ability to balance proximity to new people from around the world with the possibility of retreat as a nameless, faceless member of the crowd. Her upbringing in a Vermont small town where everyone knew everyone else had implanted a seed of wanderlust and a fervent belief that, somewhere out there, she had a soulmate waiting for her. With so many people in New York, there had to be one whose angles and edges would align with her own in just the right way. But now, a graduate degree later, she still found herself largely alone. There were colleagues at work, of course, and friends from school, but Maggie had yet to find a companion who made her feel complete, with whom she could be entirely honest and authentic without fear of judgment or reprisals.

It was this last moment of reflection that brought Maggie to a slow stop at the corner of 7th Avenue. She closed her eyes and listened for a moment to the sounds of the winter city: an orchestra of voices drifting in and out, punctuated by occasional laughter; cars moving in fits and starts as the traffic lights changed; a barking dog in the distance; and underneath all of it, a peculiar silence that only seems to happen when it snows. The loneliness of that silence panged in Maggie's heart, breaking her out of her momentary reverie, and she found herself standing in the neon glow of "Madame Claire's Psychic Salon."

"Oh, why not...." she sighed. Surely, a tarot card reading couldn't fare worse than the multitude of dating apps Maggie had tried over the last few years.

She opened the door, accompanied by the sound of a ringing bell, and was immediately confronted with the competing aromas of sage and patchouli. The belligerent scents prompted the briefest of pauses before Maggie crossed the threshold into what could only be described as a room-sized Victorian curio cabinet.

To her left, a bright pink Chesterfield sat between two small round tables, each covered with a lace tablecloth and a vase full of dusty long dead flowers. Above the couch was a painting, which appeared to be a homemade attempt at recreating Guercino's "Et in Arcadia Ego." The proportions in the painting had been manipulated, making the skull almost twice as large as it had been in the original, while the two shepherds had been reduced in size such that they more closely resembled fairyfolk than men.

Meanwhile, the wall across from the entry door had been covered in a strange array of taxidermy. The usual deer and antelope heads found themselves in the company of a sleeping owl, a jackalope, a coyote wearing a party hat, something that appeared to be an attempt at a chupacabra, and finally, a plastic bass fish which would almost certainly start singing if the button at the base of its panel were pressed.

The creak of an old wooden floorboard drew Maggie's attention to her right. She turned and saw a small, wrinkled face with surprisingly vibrant green eyes peeping out from behind a purple velour curtain marking the entrance to the next room. For a long moment, Maggie looked into those eyes that seemed to gently search her face. "This must be Madame Claire," she thought. With only a nod, the little body behind the curtain turned abruptly, and with a wave, invited Maggie to follow.

In the room's center, a round table cloaked in a violet and indigo batik cloth sat, bearing the weight of an assortment of geodes, crystals, bundles of sage, and several decks of tarot cards. Madame Claire gestured to a wooden chair by the table before making her way to the opposite side and settling down on a stool. As Maggie sat, she noticed a number of candles burning on irregularly placed shelves all around the room. Wax dripped from several of them, resulting in small piles of white debris along the baseboards of the walls.

"I wondered when you'd arrive," Madame Claire began. "I was expecting you, of course."

Maggie resisted the urge to roll her eyes, certain that this was the standard opening for fortune tellers in general. She was already questioning the wisdom of delaying her return home by coming inside.

"Personally, I think I would have left the moment he ordered a Coors Light, but perhaps that's just me."

Now speechless, Maggie gaped at Madame Claire. That wasn't a detail that would have been easy to guess, and Maggie was confident she hadn't somehow offered any subtle clues since her arrival.

"I have your attention. Good. Listen closely. Give me your hands." Madame Claire reached across the table, laying her forearms with palms facing up. Her hands were callused and wrinkled. They had seen plenty, handled hot wax and extinguished candles. And yet, despite their roughness, Maggie could not resist their magnetism. Extending her hands across the table, she was surprised by the sudden firmness of the psychic's grip, which carried a degree of authority that seemed to exceed the rest of her body.

Madame Claire closed her eyes and began to hum, a hypnotic yet atonal melody. Maggie's mind began to wander and yet her thoughts lacked a destination or focus. The sound seemed to envelop her and she was shocked when, with no interruption in the music, the old woman began to speak.

"The one you seek is far from here. To end your solitude, you must go to the Valley of Horses. There, when you can travel no further, you will find the one who will complete you. Your soulmate will call to you when you arrive. Hurry! In seven days, your window of opportunity will close."

Having completed her pronouncement, Madame Claire released Maggie's hands, rose, and moved swiftly to the doorway.

"That's all I have for you, my dear. You must be on your way; time is of the essence. No, I'm not sure exactly where to find the Valley of Horses. And no, for you, there's no charge."

Again, Maggie found herself staring in frozen silence, her questions answered before she had the opportunity to speak them aloud. She mutely stood from her chair, nodded towards

Madame Claire, and then found her way once again onto the frigid street.

As she walked home, Maggie repeated Madame Claire's message over and over again, whispering the words to herself in an effort to etch them verbatim onto her mind. She arrived at the brownstone where her studio apartment sat on the fourth floor, knocking the mud and salt off her boots before climbing the stairs. The moonlight was streaming in through the skylight over her tiny kitchen as she came through the door and hung her coat. As if being operated by a remote control, Maggie executed the tasks of her evening routine, showering, getting into pajamas, and putting a handful of birdseed in a small bowl on the outdoor window ledge for the pigeons. When she finally climbed into bed, sleep came in a rush and a dreamless night overtook her.

The following morning found Maggie once again behind the circulation desk of the New York Public Library, where she'd spent much of the last few months helping patrons research a wide range of topics. The history of jazz in New York City, styles of ancient ceramics, works by Early Modern female playwrights — these were a few of the requests that had entertained Maggie of late, providing a welcome distraction. Today, though, there were no pending inquiries and Maggie was free to embark on a research project of her own.

Typing "Valley of Horses" into a search engine yielded nothing but references to Jean Auel's book of that title. Adding "map" and "location" to the search did not improve matters. Maggie tried adding continents and countries, but still, there was nothing. As the hours ticked by, her attempts to locate a place called the Valley of Horses failed one by one. The shadows across the library stacks were growing longer as the day dragged on, and Maggie was no closer to finding her destination. Finally, after resting her head in her hands for a few minutes while wracking her brain, Maggie decided to try a new tactic. She considered several options before translating "Valley of Horses" into Spanish, typing "Valle de los Caballos" as her cursor blinked impatiently. The search results appeared almost immediately on the screen and once again, there was little besides Spanish editions of Auel's text. But, as Maggie scrolled down the list, a single link stood out to her. It pointed to a real estate website offering properties for sale in "Valle de los Caballos Temecula, CA."

Immediately, Maggie fed those words back into the search engine and she was immediately greeted with pages and pages of hits, all pointing towards the same place. It appeared that the "Valle" was an area of Temecula characterized primarily by horse farms and wineries, beautiful weather, and hot air balloons. Websites for hotels, spas, and bed-and-breakfasts promised magnificent sunsets that lit up the surrounding mountains, dining options ranging from the usual chains to farm-to-table haute cuisine, friendly people, and boutique shopping. It sounded like a lovely place to spend a few days, even without the possibility of finding a soulmate. She thought back to her last vacation, now more than a year earlier, and decided that taking a few days to explore somewhere new could be just what she needed to recharge.

By closing time, Maggie had successfully requested time off and booked a flight from JFK to San Diego scheduled for the next morning. After a fitful night of sleep, she hopped on the A train and headed out to the airport, watching the snow drift down from slate-grey skies through the city grime smeared across the train windows. Despite the weather, her plane lifted off on time and with that, she was on her way to the West Coast. The roar of the jet engines did not prevent Maggie from settling into a somewhat uncomfortable but nevertheless deep sleep.

The jostle of the plane's wheels touching the tarmac in San Diego abruptly ended Maggie's nap. She blinked her eyes open and was startled by the brightness of the sun streaming in through the small window to her left. Slowly, she adjusted to the glare and noticed blue sky above, hills to the east dotted with residential properties, and glints of the ocean beyond the airport. Taxiing to the gate seemed to take forever, but finally, Maggie's turn came, she pulled her carry-on bag down from the overhead compartment and hustled to deplane. She'd reserved a car the night before and quickly made her way to the rental car desk adjacent to the baggage claim.

It was already closing on noon by the time Maggie had finished picking up her rental, a nondescript grey Toyota Corolla that smelled far newer than it looked. Living in New York City meant that there had been little need to drive and Maggie felt a bit rusty behind the wheel. She slowly edged out of the parking garage and onto the street, narrowly avoiding a collision with a large white pickup truck that seemed to be hurtling far faster than was advisable towards the onramp to the I-5. Settling into her lane, she turned on the radio and scanned through the stations, finally settling on one playing Joni Mitchell's "Big Yellow Taxi." The upbeat tempo seemed apt for Maggie's adventure into this new, surprising landscape.

Over the next hour and a half, Maggie made her way inland and onto the I-15. As she did, she marveled at her first exposure to Southern California. The contrast of the landscape to that of the East Coast could not have been more stark. The highway, alternately four or five lanes wide in a single direction, cut a path between hills covered in tenacious sage-green shrubs and early wildflowers that bloomed in wide orange and yellow swaths. Above these vanguards of early spring sat sprawling houses looking to the west, their palm and cypress tree-lined driveways climbing the hills at unnaturally steep angles. "Who would put a house there," mused Maggie, "and how do they get out in the snow?" She laughed to herself then, remembering that such snowfall would be unlikely in a place where the vegetation was already springing back to life in February.

Between the hills sat valleys of strip malls and newly built condominiums, biotech firms and box stores, car dealerships and fast-food drive-throughs. These indicators of habitation seemed suburban, and yet, interspersed with them were flower and tree farms and avocado groves, whose frequency increased as Maggie continued northward. She passed a series of towns she had never heard of, Escondido and Fallbrook, and smiled as she noticed signs for an exit off the highway for a place called "Rainbow." The hills that lined the highway were covered in enormous boulders, and Maggie wondered how often one of these sentries would lose its grip on the dry earth beneath it and tumble down onto the road she presently traveled. Abruptly, her forward progress slowed, and Maggie marveled at the number of cars required to create so much traffic across a full four lanes of highway. She inched her way past a border patrol station that seemed oddly out of place, and slowly rolled up to the crest of a hill, where she caught her first glimpse of the Temecula Valley.

Snow-capped mountains rose in the distance, marking a clear and glistening boundary against the cloudless blue sky. Below them, a wide, mostly flat plain cradled a bustling town. To her right, Maggie noted the well-tended greens of a golf course, beyond which lay a number of residential neighborhoods, distinct from each other only in the variety of roof materials and colors. A wide and busy commercial street stretched to the east, offering access to a hospital and an array of strip malls and box stores. To the left, a wide dirt path crept upwards through the rugged stone-covered hillsides, and Maggie was surprised to see a couple of intrepid hikers making use of the trail.

A passing car traveling southbound caught the midday sunlight and redirected the glare into Maggie's eyes. Unaccustomed to the brightness, particularly after months of New York's low-slung winter clouds, she squinted, wishing she had a pair of sunglasses. Just then, her GPS noted that she had half a mile before the exit that would lead towards the room she had booked at one of the local wineries. Conveniently, it seemed that her route would take her right past a national drugstore chain, which would give her an opportunity to both stretch her legs and remedy her need for eye protection. She took the exit and made a right turn onto southbound Route 79.

Maggie only needed to travel a half mile up the road before finding a drugstore. She parked, got out of the car, removed the sweatshirt she'd had on since leaving New York early that morning, closed her eyes and breathed in the air, warmed by the sun and yet cooled by the light breeze. The urge to just stay in that sunlit moment was almost insurmountable but she was shaken from her reverie by the sound of a motorcycle revving as it wove through the traffic on the nearby road. "Just as well," she thought to herself. "There's plenty of time. I'll be here all week."

It was a relief of sorts to walk into the drugstore and find that the layout was no different than the same chain store's locations on the East Coast. The only immediately perceivable distinction was the cashier who called out "Welcome in!" from behind the registers. Maggie glanced in his direction and waved hello, while feeling a little uncomfortable at having been noticed. An aisle bearing an expansive collection of sunscreens caught Maggie's attention, prompting her to realize she'd neglected to bring any. She paused briefly, selected a tube that promised a cruelty-free organic high SPF coconut-scented product, and continued on towards the rack of sunglasses at the other end of the aisle. Striking quickly, she grabbed a pair with polarized lenses and headed back towards the cashier.

"Did you find everything okay?" asked the young man who had greeted Maggie when she walked in.

"Um, yes, thanks," Maggie replied.

"Great! How's your day going?"

"Um…. Fine?" Maggie paused and suddenly felt that the silence after her answer was awkward, despite the cashier's question seeming a bit invasive. She wondered if this was a cultural divergence from New York and thought she'd try to reciprocate. "How about you?" she asked.

"Oh, it's good. My shift's almost over, which is great because I've been here since pretty early this morning. But I'm meeting a couple friends out in Oceanside later this afternoon to hit the waves, so that's cool. I'll have time to go home and get my wetsuit and everything, maybe even have time for a nap. Great choice on the sunscreen, by the way; that one's my favorite. It's waterproof and will totally last for a couple hours in the water. Did you want your receipt?"

It took Maggie a moment to recover from the flood of speech that she had just experienced. Even the friendliest regular patrons at the library in New York had not shared the details of their day with her, which made the level of specificity the cashier, a complete stranger, had given her seem all the more excessive. She mused to herself that Californians seemed to be as warm as the weather before responding "No, thanks…. Have a good day."

"You too," replied the cashier, offering Maggie a shaka as she picked up her items. Maggie had seen the "hang ten" gesture before in television series set in Hawaii or California, and she was surprised to learn that actual people did it too. As she got back into the car, she reflected on how out of place she felt. Should she have come, she wondered, or was this just some kind of fool's errand? And yet, she quickly remembered the delicious pleasure of the sun on her face and the ability to be outdoors without even a sweatshirt, and decided that it didn't matter whether or not she actually found who she was looking for. It was enough to be somewhere new, where the people were friendly, the sky was blue, and where unpaved land was close enough to civilization that you could easily find yourself amongst the wildflowers.

Maggie got back on the road and followed her GPS directions to the outskirts of town. On a corner at a crossroads, she saw a stone pillar with a metal plaque that marked the entry to the Valle de los Caballos. Immediately, her heart skipped a beat — she had arrived! Pausing at a stop sign, she repeated Madame Claire's words to her: "To end your solitude, you must go to the Valley of Horses. There, when you can travel no further, you will find the one who will complete you. Your soulmate will call to you when you arrive. Hurry! In seven days, your window of opportunity will close." It seemed like so much had happened since her encounter with Madame Claire and yet, if her augury was correct, only five days remained before the clock would run out.

Maggie turned right onto De Portola Road and was promptly greeted by lush green pastures and tidy white fencing. She passed a series of horse farms and, shortly thereafter, started to see vineyards nestled among the stables and bridle paths. A pair of riders were making their way along a dirt road to the south, and Maggie made a mental note to look into trail riding, a beloved travel activity, at some point. Shortly thereafter, Maggie made a right turn onto a narrow road, which ended in a cul-de-sac with driveways to the left and right leading to expansive homes, while straight ahead lay an elegant iron gate and a sign that welcomed visitors to "Special Providence Cellars."

Maggie made her way through the gate, continuing up the tree-lined driveway. Neat rows of vines spread out down the hillside beside the driveway, just beginning to put out leaves after their winter rest. Ahead lay a Tuscan-styled building with a gently sloping tile roof, natural cut-stone walls, and heavy wood doors with iron accents. On either side of the stairs leading to the front door, four cypress trees had been carefully trimmed into corkscrew topiaries. Maggie was immediately impressed by the sense of symmetry that had designed the property with such care and attention to detail. She followed a sign directing her to the parking area with an expansive view of the vineyard beyond. Taking her luggage, she made her way to the front door.

The spacious lobby boasted a striking curved wooden desk, tasteful paintings of Italian landscapes, and an impressive display of fresh flowers. As Maggie approached, an older grey-haired woman sporting a dark-blue silk dress and a variety of silver and turquoise jewelry stood and greeted her.

"You must be Maggie. Welcome in! You're our only guest this weekend — February is often a bit quiet for us."

"What a beautiful place you have here," Maggie replied.

"Why, thank you! It's been a real labor of love. My husband and I bought this property 30 years ago and we've been working on it bit by bit since then. He passed away just a couple years ago, so now it's me and my son that keep it going. You'll see him around too. He should be along shortly and he'll show you to your room."

"I couldn't help noticing the name of your winery. Is 'Special Providence' a reference to *Hamlet*?" asked Maggie.

"Yes! No one ever recognizes it! Back in the day, I taught Literature and the name is a reference to one of my favorite Shakespeare quotes — 'There is a special providence in the fall of a sparrow.'"

"Yes, mine too! I'm a librarian back in New York."

The sound of a door opening caught Maggie's attention and at that moment, time seemed to slow. Here she was, in the Valley of Horses at a winery at the end of a dead-end road, and the name of the place itself suggested that fate had a hand in what was happening. Another door opened and Maggie held her breath. In walked a tall, sandy-haired fellow with blue eyes, sporting jeans and a t-shirt. He walked over to the desk, reached behind it, picked up a key, turned to Maggie, grumbled a bit, and gestured for her to follow. To her dismay, Maggie realized that he held a Coors Light in his hand. Clearly, he was not the one. Without a word, he led Maggie to her room, handed her the key, and disappeared without a sound. Disappointed, Maggie unpacked her belongings.

As she stowed her empty luggage in the closet, Maggie felt

her stomach rumble and realized that she'd had nothing to eat for hours. She headed back to the car and thought she'd take a drive around the area, stopping when she saw somewhere that looked promising for a bite to eat. She made her way out towards De Portola Road and then found herself taking a back road, rather than turning onto the main street. She passed several stables, one of which had long-horned cattle resting in a large paddock.

Turning down a tree-lined street, Maggie felt a jerk and heard a loud thump. She limped her car over to the side of the road, turned off the ignition, got out and found a very flat tire, visibly punctured with a substantial nail. She sighed and pulled out her cellphone to call for assistance, only to find that she had no signal at all. Reflecting on how a day that had started with so much promise could deteriorate so significantly, Maggie made her way across the street to a horse farm bordered by white fencing.

She saw a young man walking out of the barn towards the driveway where she stood. He was on the shorter side, with a kind eye set in an otherwise somewhat unremarkable face. Clad in jeans, boots, and a t-shirt, he didn't look like an iconic cowboy, but instead presented as generally ordinary. Maggie called out "Excuse me" and caught his attention.

"Yeah? Can I help you?" he asked.

"I hope so — I just got a flat tire out there and my phone has no signal. Could you help me call for a tow?"

"Sure," he said, "but first, let me take care of this horse. She started fussing and calling out a minute ago, which is weird. She's never been one for this kind of drama. For the last few months, she's mostly just stood there sadly since her owners moved away and left her."

In that moment, Maggie became aware of a horse whinnying and she turned to look in the direction of the sound. In a paddock on the other side of the riding arena, a dark bay mare was staring at Maggie, calling out with what could only be described as urgency. As she watched, the horse leaned forward against the fence, shifting her weight back and forth, whinnying all the while. "Is she okay?" asked Maggie.

"I'm not sure. She's not usually like this." Maggie realized that she'd started walking alongside the young man, heading towards the paddock. As they approached, the mare quieted slightly, her whinny turning into a nicker.

While she'd never spent much time with horses, Maggie couldn't help but feel like the mare was trying to speak to her. "What's her name?" she asked.

"Well," the young man began, "we call her Farrah but she's an off-track Thoroughbred and her racing name was Far From Here. I looked up her record once using her tattoo number and she seems to have done fairly well."

"Her tattoo?" asked Maggie. "Yeah," he replied, "it's how they identify them on the track, although often at this point, they use a microchip instead. But if you ever wanted to look her up, her number is Q10473."

By this time, they'd made it to the fence and the mare had quieted, although her focus on Maggie never wavered. She had soft eyes that peeked out from behind a thick forelock, large ears that suggested intelligence and vigilance, and a fine bone structure with good muscling. Her coat, mane, and tail were perhaps a bit shabby, but despite her lack of experience, Maggie somehow knew that some time spent with a brush would bring out dapples and a bright shine. She reached out towards the mare, who gently pressed her cheek into Maggie's hand and closed her eyes. In that quiet moment of connection, Maggie realized that she'd found exactly who she'd been looking for.

Contributor Biographies

Kristen Tregar

Kristen Tregar is a dramaturg, director, and playwright. With John deLancie, she is the coauthor of *The Dover Play*, which premiered on Star Trek: The Cruise IV in 2020. She recently completed a new translation and adaptation of Eugene Ionesco's *Rhinoceros* from the original French, and has adapted Shakespeare's *Hamlet* and *Taming of the Shrew*. Kristen holds a PhD from the UC San Diego and UC Irvine joint program in Theater and Drama, a MA in Educational Theatre from NYU-Steinhardt, a MS in Forensic Science from CUNY — John Jay College, and a BA in Biology from Bryn Mawr College.

Reggie DeMatos

Reggie DeMatos is an emerging concept artist, animator, and illustrator. Reggie grew up in Massachusetts and has always had a love and fascination for horses. He moved with his family to Murrieta in 2021, wherein his family became the owners of their first two horses. Reggie enjoys studying the subtle nuances of his horses' behaviors, inspiring several animations and creations.

LEAD AND VENOM

Story by Monzer Farouk

Illustration by Bryant M. Nelson
Oils

Sheriffs and Outlaws

TWO BOYS PLAYFULLY CHASE one another outside of a large estate. One wears a homemade sheriff costume; the other wears an outlaw costume.

"Your best course of action would be to head inside and put that loot back where it belongs!" Sawyer, the sheriff boy, demands.

"You're no match for me! I'm better than you'll ever be!" Vincent, the outlaw boy, shouts.

An out-of-shape, rough looking man watches the boys as he

rocks on a chair, smoking a cigarette.

Vincent pushes Sawyer to the ground. Sawyer gets up and chases after him. Vincent stops in his tracks and punches Sawyer in the face.

"OW! Da — Westcott, he punched me!" Sawyer cries.

"I did not!" Vincent shouts.

"Agh, toughen up, boy." The man drunkenly brushes off Sawyer's complaint. He takes a drag from his cigarette, squinting into the distance to avoid eye contact with the boy.

Sawyer pouts. He notices his brother laughing at him. He looks to the man, his father, Westcott, who cracks a smirk.

In a fit of rage, Sawyer pushes his brother to the ground.

"HEY!" Westcott shouts, he takes one last drag from the cigarette and tosses it. "DON'T fuckin' put your hands on him, BOY!" He shoots up from his chair and darts towards Sawyer.

Sawyer stands his ground. "He started it!"

Westcott smacks the boy across the face, sending him to the ground. He continues to hit Sawyer as he's down.

Westcott walks over to Vincent. "Vinnie? You okay? Get up son." Westcott helps Vincent up and ignores the injured Sawyer.

Sawyer crawls away.

1906 – Present Day

Tuscan tan and smoky sienna sands radiate heat that is smoke thick. Wind blows over the landscape, sending clouds of dust skyward in rebuttal to the sun's blazing attack. The air is filled

266

with toxins pushed by the wind, creating a harsh environment for the eyes and for the creatures trying to survive in the barely existing western town of Temecula.

This place is void of prospering life. In corners of the town are traces of previous criminal activity — robbery, looting, and evidence of intense pursuit on horseback. Townsfolk roam the dirt streets, wearing rags of old cotton clothing. They are desperately trying to sell what little they have to get by. The people here live in fear of the Sutherland Gang — six criminals who single-handedly caused the downfall of this once thriving town.

Sheriff Sawyer returns to Temecula, again unsuccessful in his most recent attempt to capture the gang. He finds his way to the town stage, where a town meeting is being held. Most of the townsfolk are present and waiting for the Mayor. Sawyer approaches on his stallion, but stays about ten feet away from the crowd.

A man glances at the sheriff, then pointedly turns back to the crowd so as not to acknowledge him.

Mayor Westcott walks out on stage. He is an old man, dense from years of gluttony. The floorboards can barely handle Westcott's heavy weight. He reaches the stand; the sun's glare illuminates his round, gray face and peppery hair. To the crowd, Westcott looks like a formidable lead ball.

Westcott scans the audience and notices the sheriff. Sawyer raises a timid hand to dip his hat, but Westcott ignores him.

"It is with pride that I reintroduce our retired deputy

mayor, my amazing son, who has returned with a wonderful announcement after ten terribly long years away." Westcott announces. "Ladies and gentlemen, Mr. Vincent Westcott!" The townsfolk applaud as Vincent comes out on stage, beaming. He shakes his father's hand and straightens his suit as he steps up to the stand.

"People of Temecula, it's good to be back. However, I wish it was under better circumstances. As y'all know, this town is facing a decade-long crisis due to an outlaw rampage." Vincent looks to Sawyer, whose eye twitches in disbelief at the sight of Vincent's sudden return. "Which is why I've decided to take action. Temecula will receive a donation of $20,000 dollars from my investments to restore the town back to its rightful glory."

The townsfolk erupt in strong applause and celebration; the tired and old ignite with enlivening energy. All except Sawyer, who has moved up in the crowd to get a better look at his long-lost brother.

Nowhere to be found for ten years, and suddenly he's out for MY job? Sawyer grits his teeth.

"And uh...what makes you think you can just come back and act like you own the place, Christopher Columbus?" Sawyer bursts out, snickering at his own joke.

The cheering stops. They can't remember the last time the Sheriff spoke; the crowd gets quiet and awkward.

"HEY!" Westcott's thunderous voice claps. "Show some respect, BOY!" Westcott glares at Sawyer. Vincent clears his throat.

"I know I have been gone for quite some time now," Vincent announces to the audience, "but if it wasn't for Temecula, I never would have been able to build my automobile empire, which has grown like a wildfire in the last couple of years! I owe it to this here town and to my father." Vincent smiles at Westcott, who smiles back.

Appalled at the sight of his father's grin, Sawyer stares in disbelief. He hasn't seen any joy on Westcott's face in over a decade.

"So, it is my responsibility to ensure that my town is safe from any unlawful activity. And since this task seems to be beyond the capabilities of the current Sheriff..." A few people chuckle before Vincent continues, "...we need a talented investigation team to devise a plan to bring these criminals to justice!"

Before Sheriff Sawyer can even open his mouth, the townsfolk erupt in a raucous cheer for their new savior — Vincent Westcott.

Sawyer retires to his house, defeated.

Graveyard

The door creaks open and Sawyer lights a lantern. His house is empty, yet filled with dead memories. Framed photos hang on cramped walls — old photos of a younger Sheriff Sawyer and a joyful group of townsfolk celebrating the captures of outlaw gangs from years ago: The Brandy Bandits in 1886, DuFisk and Jones in 1888, Los Hijos De Degeneranos in 1890, Omar Spirit in 1891, and Johnny Hyde in 1895.

In each picture, Mayor Westcott wears the same dull, unimpressed look.

Sawyer walks along the wall and reaches the last frame — an empty one, with a broken glass and an unfulfilled caption: The Sutherland Gang capture, 18__.

Sawyer reflects on the photos, remembering the times he was revered as a hero. The empty, broken frame mocks him, resembling the shattered window in him that admits an infinite cold.

Sawyer feels Temecula is no longer a place he's welcome. He is an outcast, leading a frozen, lonely existence, fulfilling a worthless role in this community.

* * *

The sheriff storms into the mayor's quarters; his icy demeanor brings a chill to the previously warm atmosphere.

"Do you mind?" Westcott spits angrily.

Sawyer freezes, sensing he has barged into a private meeting between Westcott and Vincent.

"We can't accept your money," Sawyer says to Vincent, who looks offended.

"What was that?" Westcott shoots up from his seat, jumping to Vincent's defense.

"We don't need to hire anybody. I'll take care of it. I'll catch these scum myself. It's my jurisdiction and my job," Sawyer growls.

"Your job? You haven't made any arrests in over a decade. You haven't been fit for this job in a very long time, boy."

Sawyer, avoiding eye contact with his father, stares at Vincent.

"How can you just come back out of nowhere and take my fuckin' life away?!"

Vincent shrugs innocently. "I'm...just trying to help the town, Sawyer."

"Sheriff," Westcott marches up to him. "You've wasted a decade trying to catch these guys. You've come up empty handed every single time. You failed, boy." Westcott stands right over Sawyer; he blows smoke in the sheriff's face. "Vincent has a solution. So, unless you can make a $20,000 donation — you'll work the town-duty until we decide what to do with you."

"Please. Look, I know I've been out of the game for a while, but...."

Westcott stares blankly. "Get out."

Sawyer looks pained, he chokes. He leaves.

Town-Duty

Sawyer watches the clouds moving across the dark, dead sky, like spirits lingering in purgatory. The townsfolk are either in their beds or in the bars. Everyone is under something — under their covers or under the influence. Sawyer is at his post, sitting on horseback, slurping on scalding stew, unaware of its scarring burn. He draws deeply on the cheap whiskey from his flask. He is alone with his paranoid thoughts. He turns to the soup, allowing the steam to warm his face.

The sheriff scans the desolate town. Nightmarish screams waft through the air as strange creatures creep through the surrounding desert. The noises set every nerve in Sawyer's body on edge. Sawyer's stew appears to freeze over; the fat covering the top in a frozen layer forces him to stare into his own broken reflection. Ice forms around Sawyer's bony face and stringy hair. He hurls the container at the ground. The bowl shatters, splashing the soup on the cold ground and breaking the illusion.

The revving of an automobile engine grows. Sawyer glances over to see who's inside. Vincent. He doesn't notice as he passes Sawyer. The sheriff's gaze locks onto the vehicle as it drives behind the bank.

An idea creeps into his head.

* * *

Sawyer arrives at the Westcott estate, the place he was raised but could rarely call home. He shatters a window with his elbow, then turns the door handle from inside; Sawyer assumes Westcott's doors were locked as a safety measure, but he wonders if it was done to keep him from returning. The broken glass crunches under his boot as he enters. It's dark; it's ear-ringing quiet. He lights a lantern and takes a swig from his flask.

Making his way through the monolithic corridors, Sawyer reels under a familiar feeling — coldness — not a cold present on his skin, but one that seeps into the cracks of his fragmented spirit, locking every muscle, joint, and bone into a frozen prison. This familiar coldness has been around for as long as he can remember and tends to flare up like a blizzard every now and again.

Sawyer lives to escape the paralyzing cold from his dying inner being, even if it means immersing himself into a blistering fire.

Sawyer climbs the staircase. Each step creaks louder, unraveling his already frayed nerves. A locked door blocks his path, a door Sawyer has never seen behind. He unsheathes a knife from his boot; his breath hitches as he breaks the lock.

The door swings open, his pupils dilate as he enters the unfamiliar room. Sawyer takes in the furniture that decorates the office, the lavish paintings hanging on the walls, and the small, framed photos cramping every surface. The photos depict the two Westcott's running the town as a unit. In one prominent picture, a smiling Mayor Westcott stands proud with his arms wrapped around Deputy Mayor Vincent Westcott.

In some of the prints, Sawyer is faintly seen in the background, excluded.

One photo is different from the rest — Vincent and Westcott, shaking hands in what looks like a goodbye. A caption is written beneath the image: Deputy Mayor Vincent Westcott retires to pursue automobile business, 1895.

Sawyer glances at the images, then to the desk. He finds neat handwritten plans for the town's renovation: Vincent's outline to capture the Sutherland Gang and strip Sawyer's job away — to throw him out in the cold, to let him freeze to death.

A blizzard descends upon Sawyer's soul. He sets the lantern on the desk.

The sound of carriage wheels outside filters into the room.

Sawyer shoots up, his pupils constrict in fear. Westcott! He grabs the plans, then scans for an exit. He hears footsteps, followed by the sound of crunching glass.

"WHO'S IN HERE?!" Mayor Westcott's terrifying voice explodes down the corridors and up the staircase.

Suddenly sweating, Sawyer glances at his knife. It reflects a painting hanging on the wall behind him — a large portrait of an angelic young woman with eyes like a starry sky and a soft caramel smile. Sawyer sheathes his knife. Tears puddle in his eyes, but he presses on his pupils to snub them out. Without hesitation, he climbs on the icy window sill and dives.

Westcott bursts into his office and darts to his desk, the papers are gone. Noticing the curtains in a windy dance, he rushes to the window. Westcott grabs the warm window sill and scans the overpass; he sees nothing.

Sawyer hides behind a large oak tree, struggling to catch his breath without revealing his location. He watches carefully as Westcott looks out, fuming with rage, trying to find signs of movement. Finally, looking frustrated, the mayor seems to give up and disappears back into his office.

Sawyer, thinking himself in the clear, scurries away.

Dead Man

Sawyer paces around his house going over the stolen documents, his sense of paranoia growing by the moment. He's been up all night, hell bent and scheming; trying to figure out how to sabotage Westcott's plans.

A slow, heavy knock rattles the door.

Sawyer shoves the papers into his vest as he walks over and carelessly opens the door.

His father stands over him like the Titanic — pushing his way into the house; pushing Sawyer, the pathetic glacier, out of his way.

Westcott's look is debilitating, unsettling. He stares with the eyes of a madman.

"Where were you last night?"

"Uh...I was working the town-duty, at my post."

Westcott slams the door shut and the house shakes as if an earthquake has struck. Sawyer freezes, terrified to move.

"Terrible news. My estate was broken into." Westcott pauses. "Did you happen to see who it could've been?"

"Oh. Must've been one of the six, I was watching Sutherland all night." Sawyer twitches, his nerves shaken.

"Ahh...I see." Westcott shows theatrical sympathy. He drops his head; Sawyer's muddy boots catch his piercing glare. Westcott points at the sheriff's boots, noting the familiar, rusty-brown soil caked on his soles. "Must've been some chase. On foot, in the dead of night. Heh, aren't you exhausted?"

Sawyer trembles. "Well, yeah, you know how it gets." Sawyer hides one foot behind the other.

"Are you sure that's not mud from my backyard? It is the only place in Temecula with fresh dirt like that, after all."

Sawyer shrugs as he fumbles for a lie. Westcott's poker face hides a psychopathic rage.

Westcott tears the badge from Sawyer's vest, pulling Sawyer forward.

"You're fired." He growls, "You're lucky I'm not having you thrown behind bars."

"Dad, don't do thi—"

Westcott swings his hand across Sawyer's face, leaving a mark. Sawyer recoils from the slap.

"DON'T YOU DARE CALL ME THAT, BOY!" Westcott explodes. "There's no damn difference between you and those outlaws! Vincent could have taken care of this by now."

"Vincent. Your precious Vincent!" Sawyer's voice trembles in response. "You've always put him over me. Do you have any idea what that feels like?"

Westcott grabs Sawyer by his vest. "You're nothin' but poison to me, boy." Westcott yanks the papers from Sawyer's vest and shoves him back. "You're incapable of arresting a group of low-life criminals. Pathetic!" Westcott adjusts his tie and turns to walk out.

"Since when did catching bad guys matter to you?"

"What'd you say, boy?"

"You haven't shown the slightest bit of concern for a decade, and now that Vincent's back, you care all of a sudden?"

"Bite your tongue."

"Y'know, maybe if you cared, just a bit, maybe just enough to show up to take photos, or just enough to congratulate me — maybe I would've done something about...." Sawyer cuts himself off.

"What? You haven't been trying? You mean, you willingly put this town in danger?" Westcott steps closer. "Like you did to your family?" He pauses. "I guess old habits die hard, hmm?"

Suddenly, a lone bell rings repeatedly, an alarm warning the townsfolk of trouble. Westcott's attention diverts. Sawyer barely notices, still reeling from what Westcott implied.

"I can't believe you let this happen." Westcott says with disbelief and disgust. "You're sick."

Suddenly, the bells cut through Sawyer's anger and he sees an opportunity. He reaches out and struggles to retrieve his badge from Westcott. The mayor swats at him like a bear catching salmon. The two wrestle for a moment, before Sawyer grabs Westcott by his thick, fleshy neck.

"I'm NOT going to give YOU another reason to choose him over ME! I'll finish this, then you can have this WORTHLESS BADGE!" Sawyer snatches the badge and elbows Westcott's nose, leaving it running with blood.

Sawyer escapes.

"GET BACK HERE!" Westcott roars, "IF YOU LEAVE NOW, YOU'RE DEAD TO ME!"

Sawyer hops on his stallion and races away.

After ten years of being in control, the Sutherland Gang isn't afraid of Sheriff Sawyer — they enjoy the fight, and the chase that follows. On this Sunday morning, they've chosen to harass church-goers as they exit the chapel at the far end of town. Gang leader Lance Sutherland watches from a short distance away as his gang wreaks havoc on the townsfolk, having fun at the expense of the crowd.

Sutherland grows impatient waiting for Sawyer. He's had enough fun bullying the townsfolk.

He looks down the road; a dusty figure appears in the distance, racing with ferocity. Sutherland smiles at the sight of his decade-long rival. About damn time.

Sutherland whistles for his crew. "C'mon boys, the sheriff's in town!"

* * *

Sawyer races towards the confrontation and his chance at redemption. He sees Sutherland and his crew harassing the church-goers.

After this, Westcott will know never to doubt me again, even if it's the last thing I do.

Sawyer rides hell-bent towards the closest gangster at top speed. He draws his weapon and fires. His victim's crooked smile is extinguished as he hits the ground, dead. One down.

Sutherland looks bewildered, as if he wasn't expecting a fight.

"END OF THE LINE, SUTHERLAND!" Sawyer fires at Sutherland, grazing the side of his head.

Recoiling from the wound and appearing dismayed, Sutherland fires at Sawyer, winging him in the shoulder. Sawyer is knocked from his stallion. He jumps up as the rest of the gang closes in.

One of the outlaws, his chin as pointy as the knife he holds, flies at Sawyer. Sawyer jumps back so the blade only slices across his chest. Pointy lunges again, but Sawyer pulls his own blade and counters the attack. He plunges his weapon into Pointy's chest.

Sawyer sees another gang member draw his gun, his bony face contorted with rage. Sawyer, still holding onto the knife in Pointy's chest, uses it as a handle to turn the corpse to use as a shield. Bony empties his gun into the body, continuing to pull the trigger desperately after the last shot. Sawyer rips the knife from Pointy's body and flings it at Bony. The gunman falls to the ground with the knife handle protruding from his left eye.

Sawyer smiles, enjoying the most excitement he's had in years.

Taking cover behind the church walls, the two remaining crooks take aim at Sawyer. He draws both revolvers and screams as he fires lead in all directions. The two outlaws duck for cover.

Sawyer looks behind; Sutherland watches from a distance.

Sawyer's guns click as they empty, and he jumps behind the nearby desert boulders. Bullets chip the stone, flying in from Skinny and Curly.

With no rounds left, Sawyer unsheathes his knife and viciously charges the two outlaws. He tackles Curly to the ground, who twists his leg as he falls.

Skinny fires at Sawyer's back. Three bullets find their mark. Sawyer screams. Curly punches Sawyer off of him.

Sawyer lays on the ground, coughing. Sutherland watches from a distance as his two men walk up to finish the job. Curly's leg drags as they approach Sawyer.

Curly aims his gun at Sawyer's abdomen. Mustering the strength he's hidden, Sawyer kicks Curly's injured leg, sending him to the ground. The gun drops from Curly's hand. Sawyer rolls out of the way as Skinny aims and fires. Sawyer retrieves his knife and launches it at Skinny's thin neck, slicing the carotid. Four down.

Curly crawls towards the gun, Sawyer leaps for it. Wrestling for the weapon, Curly desperately crawls onto Sawyer like a roach, trying to grab the gun before it's too late. But Sawyer grabs him in a chokehold and manages to take Curly at gunpoint.

"STOP!" Sutherland commands, pointing a shotgun at Sawyer from forty feet away.

Sawyer tightly holds Curly in a headlock; he digs the gun into Curly's thick hair. He stares at Sutherland trying to intimidate him.

"We had a good thing going, Sheriff." Sutherland says in

disbelief.

Curly, struggling in the headlock, shouts. "What are you waiting for? Shoot this bast—"

Sawyer fires point blank into Curly's skull; the outlaw slumps to the ground. Sawyer turns his aim toward Sutherland. "I told you this was the end of the line, Lance."

"They did not have to die, Sheriff." Sutherland sighs. "We were just having a little fun."

"It's about time you got what you deserved." Sawyer struggles to stand up.

Sutherland seethes with anger, he fires his shotgun. Sawyer goes down, lying motionless on the ground. It falls silent.

Sutherland walks up to Sawyer, still aiming at him. He gets close and stares at the sheriff's body. He lowers his weapon.

Suddenly, a shot. Sutherland grasps his chest. He looks around to see where the shot came from. He notices Sawyer's injured hand, the smoking revolver firmly in its grip, pointing directly at him.

Sutherland gives a wry laugh and falls.

The two mortally wounded men take ragged breaths as they lay on the sizzling hot ground.

* * *

The horse treads slowly down the road, carrying two men that hover near death.

"I heard the stories about you. 'Sheriff Sawyer' — nobody

could stop you!" Sutherland rasps, tied up on the back of his own horse. "Not DuFisk, not Omar — you were a legend!" Blood bubbles in his throat as he cackles. "But after our first few chases, I thought they must've been crazy; I never believed them. Yet... today you mysteriously became that legend I heard about. You somehow proved them right. Just tell me, how was that possible?"

Sawyer rides with his mouth shut, saving his energy.

"ANSWER ME!" Sutherland's shouting echoes off the nearby hills repeating the question over and over.

Sawyer finally responds.

"I always loved playing Sheriffs and Outlaws. And I didn't want it to end...until I did."

* * *

Sawyer arrives at Westcott's quarters, where people are gathered awaiting news. The crowd parts as their sheriff arrives beaten, bloody, and on the brink of death.

Sawyer slides off the horse. He struggles to stay upright as he pulls Sutherland roughly to the ground and drags him through the crowd.

"I've got your outlaw," Sawyer announces. "Where's the camera?" he says bitterly.

Silence.

"You are the outlaw now," Mayor Westcott blankly states.

Sawyer stands as confident as ever, finally embracing himself.

282

"Do you think Vincent could've done this? No. Still, I'm nothing because you treat me like poison!" Sawyer chokes as tears run down his face. He strides angrily to Westcott. "And I'm the outlaw?" Sawyer points the revolver in Westcott's face, "WHERE IS VINCENT NOW?! WHERE IS HE?!"

Westcott firmly backhands Sawyer. "You make me sick. You're nothin' but a poison."

Stunned, Sawyer lowers his weapon and stares at his father.

"I am exactly what you say I am." Sawyer mounts the horse and races off without looking back.

* * *

Sawyer makes his way to the Westcott estate, he breaks the door in with a single kick. Entering the parlor, Sawyer splashes whiskey from his flask on the dry oak walls, the carpets, and the paintings. He grabs the desk lantern and shatters it on the floor. The room is set ablaze. Flames dance around his feet. Sawyer shuts his eyes and smiles.

"SAWYER!" Vincent screams. He charges through the flames, heading towards his brother. He pulls him from the burning building. Smoke curls from Sawyer's vest.

"Sawyer, get up! We need to get away from the—" Sawyer strikes Vincent in the mouth.

"GET OFF OF ME!" Sawyer rages. Vincent collapses on the front lawn of the burning family homestead. Sawyer jumps onto Vincent and hits him in his face over and over. He breaks

Vincent's nose and continues to pummel him.

The smoke and flames draw a crowd. One by one their attention falls on the fighting siblings. They watch as their ex-sheriff mauls the deputy mayor.

Vincent lays unconscious on the ground. Sawyer moves away to catch his breath, now shaky and rattling. He looks around, searching for his father.

Mayor Westcott shoves his way through the crowd. He viscerally trembles with fear at the sight of the towering flames. His fear magnifies tenfold as he watches Sawyer unsheathe his knife and hover over his precious son.

"I am what you say I am, father. This is on your shoulders," Sawyer says without remorse as he deliberately slashes Vincent's throat.

Westcott screams as if it were his own throat that was slit. He grips his neck, frozen, terrified to make a sound. Without thinking, Westcott shakily pulls out his gun and fires. Sawyer is hit in the chest. He coughs up blood and falls to the ground.

The townsfolk gasp as they witness their leaders turn primal. Westcott looks around dazed at the horrified faces. He runs to Sawyer.

Sawyer wheezes through torn lungs. "You got me," Sawyer laughs.

Westcott doesn't recognize his son in the man lying on the ground. Tears build at the corners of his eyes. "I'm sorry, Sawyer."

Delirious from the pain, Sawyer doesn't hear him.

Westcott walks over to Vincent. He lays there beaten, with

two black eyes, a broken nose and thick blood pouring from his throat. "V-vinnie, Vinnie, Vincent — please, get up Son," Westcott mutters. "Please...." Tears run down, leaving streaks through the soot on his face. The crowd surrounds the mayor and his precious, deceased son.

* * *

Sawyer can barely breathe, feeling the life drain from his broken, dying body. He listens to the fire crackling from the building behind him, his 'home.' He instinctively crawls towards it, leaving a trail of cold blood on the front lawn and into his home.

As he makes his way down the flame-engulfed corridors, the foundation begins to collapse. Wooden pieces fall from the ceiling, the wallpaper curling up. He watches as the photos burn and fall off the walls, their frames shattering onto the hot floor below. Sawyer turns to look where the door used to be. He watches as Westcott bursts into tears, cradling Vincent's body. Wooden pieces collapse in front of the doorway, trapping him inside.

Flames engulf Sawyer, immersing him in the blistering fire. Finally, there in the flames, the paralyzing blizzard deep within him is gone.

As Sawyer lays dying, the photo of his mother stands before him, and he remembers....

A young father and boy playfully chase one another outside of a large estate. The father wears a homemade sheriff costume; the boy wears an outlaw costume.

"If I were you, I'd head inside and put that loot back where it belongs, mister," the father demands.

"Sheriff, you best keep runnin' along now. It's not safe for you out here," the little boy responds.

The two stare each other down with their hands on their shiny metal cap guns. The boy rolls across the yard and shoots at his father's boot.

"Ah! You got my foot!" Westcott tumbles to the ground.

The boy rolls over and jumps on his father, grabbing him in a chokehold.

"Alright, alright, you got me, Sawyer!" Westcott laughs, massaging his stiff neck. "You're getting pretty good at that. Maybe one day you could be the sheriff."

"You think so?" The little boy beams.

A woman with wide, beautiful eyes and a soft smile comes out into the garden. "Boys! Soup is getting cold."

The two head inside.

"Hi Baby, have you caught any criminals?" she says, tickling his tummy as he walks into the home. She stands upright to give her husband a kiss.

"How's our little Vinny?" Westcott asks.

Hoarse wailing erupts from a tiny baby laying in a wooden

carriage.

"Ugh! You'd think he would've tired himself out by now. He's been crying all day!" She rushes over to tend to the baby.

"He's a fighter, just like his dad!" Westcott smiles.

Sawyer sneaks into the living room and finds his way to the gun rack. He opens the drawer and takes out a brand-new revolver.

"Wow…" Sawyer says in awe. "It's like I'm a real sheriff!" The boy aims it around. Westcott appears from behind and confiscates the weapon.

"Sawyer! You can't play with firearms. This is why you have toy guns!" Westcott lectures. He takes the weapon to the kitchen, away from Sawyer. The boy runs after him, jumping at his father's feet.

"I wanna try it again! Please!"

"Hush boy! Not now."

Sawyer jumps for the revolver, grazing it with his hand. Reacting as quick as possible, Westcott moves the weapon out of the way — behind himself, where he accidentally hits the trigger.

A shot rings out. Glass shatters. The lantern fades and the baby goes off like an alarm.

Westcott recoils at the sound of a body hitting the floor. His ears ringing, Westcott freezes. "BOY, GO…GO GET HELP!" His voice trembles; he doesn't want to look at the body. Westcott forces himself to turn, horrified at the sight of blood splattered on the walls and covering the dripping, crying infant.

Blood pools around Westcott's boots. He drops the gun and

falls to his knees.

"Mom?" Sawyer cries.

Westcott stares down at the body, shaking with horror. His soul shatters into a million pieces; a broken window that admits a paralyzing, infinite coldness.

"Is mom going to be okay?"

"You killed her," Westcott states blankly. "She's dead because of you."

Contributor Biographies

Monzer Farouk

Monzer Farouk is an Egyptian-American storyteller, writer, artist, and musician based in LA. He's been writing stories since he was 14 and working as an independent creative storyteller while working towards a bachelor degree in filmmaking. His biggest aspiration in life is to write and direct films of his own.

Bryant M. Nelson

Bryant M. Nelson has been painting and illustrating for the last 40 years. He specializes in portraits of cowboys and native Americans. He was trained by illustrator/painter legend, Richard Stergulz. Nelson has been awarded prizes in the Ralph Love Plein Air competition and his cowboy paintings were selected in a Temecula competition that were wrapped around a Temecula utility power structure. Bryant Nelson's website provides examples of his paintings at BryantMNelson.com.

BIRTH OF A BLUE HERON

Story by Jeff Waddleton

"Birth of a Blue Heron"
Illustration by Kathryn Otoshi
Watercolor, pencil, gouache

THINGS ALWAYS HAPPEN AS they should. A mixture of harmony and tension, the natural world exists in perpetual equilibrium. Over time, sandy reefs beneath the ocean waves are leveled by swirling currents, and granite monoliths atop mountain peaks are flattened by fierce storms. All objects eventually find their rightful place — some through quiet perseverance, some through violent alteration. It takes time. But in the end, balance persists.

It is a beautiful thing.

* * *

Mallory Durwood was stuck. Parked in place, she was unable to maneuver. There was nowhere to go and no way out. Fate had dropped her here, and over the course of time, nudged her outside the order of things. Movement was inevitable.

All around her, drivers in work trucks and carpool vans anxiously revved their engines, attempting to induce a push through the intersection. But school traffic took precedence. Parents in sleek electric cars hummed past with their brilliant progeny strapped in the back. In every vehicle, occupants sat glued like brightly colored origami in shadow boxes — kaleidoscopic snapshots of tiny, idyllic lives.

From the front seat of her tan Buick Skylark, Mallory watched as they passed, her eyes darting from one to the next. A visitor in a curious gallery, she studied each occupant like a strange piece of art behind glass — peculiar, perplexing, and as abstract as a painting made by a flock of wild geese. Mallory tried, but she couldn't relate to any of them. She felt disconnected, out of focus, and misaligned. And her arms were itchy.

"Who are those people?" a voice croaked from the back seat. It was Mother, accompanying Mallory on today's journey, stuck in limbo.

Mallory didn't answer. She rolled up the cuffs on her gray sweater and scratched at her wrists.

Mother's gaze hardened as she squinted through the dirty window. "Children!" she declared with disgust. Tapping on the glass and redirecting her attention to the front seat, she raised her voice, "Are those...children?"

A small group of high school students shuffled past on the sidewalk, wearing colorful sneakers. They jostled each other and giggled.

"They're teenagers, Mother," said Mallory, eyes lifting from her dry skin to the rearview mirror.

"What do they think they're doing?" Mother's eyes drifted back to the teens, suspicious.

"It looks like they're walking to school."

"Well...," Mother shook her head in what appeared to be equal measures of shock and disgust. "They're going to freeze to death." Her sentiment lingered in the air like damp smoke from a freshly extinguished fire.

"They'll be fine," Mallory said, adding instinctively, "they're young." She couldn't help but notice the words tasted bitter as they left her mouth.

Mother's attention snapped back to the front seat. "Oh, you're some kind of doctor, now?"

"No, Mother," Mallory relented.

"Um-hmm. I didn't think so." Mother clicked her tongue.

"Still," Mallory continued, "I'm pretty sure those kids will be okay. You can relax."

Mother's eyes narrowed as she adjusted the stained beige blanket across her lap. "You sure know a lot about kids for someone who's never had any," she said. A cunning snake, Mother's tongue could deliver just enough venom to disable, but not kill.

Mallory drew a reactive breath to mount her defense but thought better of it. She didn't have the energy and wouldn't win anyway. Exhaling, she went back to idly scratching her wrists.

It was January 5th — a day Mallory might have chosen to spend at home had she looked closely enough at the calendar. But she was off kilter today. After a night of fitful sleep and disturbing dreams of being consumed by flames, she had woken to a strange hotness in her joints, and an eczema that had quickly crept up her arms past her elbows.

To combat her anxiety, Mallory attributed the condition to unseasonably dry weather, even though it had been relatively wet of late. Comfortable with her self-diagnosis, though, she held fast to her scheduled plans — today's outing. She scratched her arms again until skin flaked onto her slacks.

Meanwhile, in the intersection, movement in front of them had slowed to a crawl. From their respective roosts, agitated parents in designer apparel began to teach their offspring how to not tolerate others. The lesson expanded, and soon, several drivers exchanged crude hand gestures like peacocks posturing in the road.

Slumped in her seat, Mallory's eyes fixed on puffy white clouds meandering across the sky. Tumbling through a sea of bright cerulean blue, their playful nature soothed her pensive mood. Nebulous shapes morphed from owls to angels to giant white sailplanes, adrift on the wind in the morning sunshine. A lukewarm breeze from the car's air vents kissed her cheeks like the puckered lips of a cumulus capybara. With both hands loosely gripping the naugahyde steering wheel, Mallory floated.

In such moments, whenever Mallory felt stuck, her consciousness tended to slip free of conventional bonds. Instead of focusing on responsibilities and duty, she would drift away to places she had only seen in the brightly colored pages of her favorite travel magazines. With the slightest provocation, she could disengage from the present and take flight. This was not the result of being birdbrained or flippant. It was simply how she managed to survive.

Caught in the company of clouds, Mallory drifted. A thousand miles north, she sailed over summertime vistas of the Oregon coastline, waves crashing majestically into the craggy rocks. Of course, she had never been there in real life, but the snapshots were indelibly printed in her memory from *Coastline Vacationeer* and *Modern Traipser Monthly*. Mallory didn't need first-hand experience to taste the salt air and hear the winsome call of seabirds in the harbor. She didn't need open eyes to envision golden beams of sunlight peeking through overcast skies and washing the ocean mist in a warm yellow hue.

A raspy voice dragged her back to the front seat of the car.

"Why aren't we moving? Did you break the car?" Perched in the back on a nest of blankets and overcoats, Mother brooded. She was in a foul mood.

"There's traffic, Mother," Mallory replied. "We can't move."

"Went the wrong way, I guess, like always," Mother grumbled, her eyes surveying what little she could see over the windowsill.

Mallory took a breath.

Apparently aching for a fight, Mother tried again. "I wish I could get a better driver," she proclaimed, rolling her eyes.

"I'm not your driver." Mallory glared at Mother through the rearview mirror. "I'm your daughter."

"Well, you're no use as either," Mother muttered.

Biting her tongue, Mallory shifted her attention from the mirror back to the traffic blocking the road. There were no other routes to their destination, and she could have easily mounted a defense on that point alone. But Mallory knew better than to challenge an angry mongoose to a battle of logic.

The shadow of a passing hawk flashed across the windshield. Catching a glimpse of it slicing through the breeze, Mallory found herself wondering how it would feel to escape the chaos and chase up towards the sun. Rising on the morning current, the majestic creature dipped and turned, then disappeared over a ridge. Mallory waited, but it didn't return.

"Riddled with mites," Mother declared from the backseat, having noticed Mallory's gaze out the window. "All birds are, you know." Her face scrunched, exposing yellowed teeth. "Mites and...little worms," she added, gleefully sharpening her teeth on Mallory's flights of fancy. Idly rubbing her withered fingers together, Mother's expression gradually settled into a disgruntled glare.

Wings clipped, Mallory's fantasy vanished, and she dropped like a stone from the sky, back to the intersection where the decades-old traffic signal overhead burned a steady, unrelenting red.

Traffic had swollen to a state of total gridlock. Backed up in every direction, it would be that way for a while. The intersection, constructed years back to handle half the number of vehicles currently competing for space, was a cautionary tale of the need for optimistic forward thinking. In its absence, Mallory was trapped.

It was a familiar phenomenon for her — the color red regularly occurred in random settings. But it never led to the kind of unfettered, frivolous passion that she deeply craved. For Mallory, the color red didn't enhance the seductive cut of a party dress during a night out on the town. It never preceded the smooth velvet of a finely aged cabernet on the patio of a boutique winery. Not once had it gleamed in the candy-gloss coating of a vintage Italian convertible carelessly racing along a coastline highway.

No, the color red arrived regularly in but one variety for Mallory Durwood. Red was the color of STOP — the color that came to symbolize her life.

As a matter of fact, Mallory had heard the word "stop" so many times that she had forever abandoned trying to "go." From her earliest memories, attempts to spread her wings and fly were thwarted. It was not her prerogative to dream, she was reminded. It was not her right to be selfish. Her place was at home, and that's where she would stay. Eventually, the sting of "stop" had dulled to a muted numbness.

Under the hypnotic influence of the red light, Mallory sat motionless. She wasn't going anywhere. Caught in the confined space of the car, she felt like a caged bird, while Mother, a circling predator, probed for weakness.

A car ride with Mother was a risky affair, and something Mallory would never undertake on a whim. She had loaded up the Buick to fulfill doctor's orders — at least, that was the general concept. The physicians who oversaw their health had conferred and determined that Mallory and Mother both needed anxiety relief. More specifically, they prescribed fresh air, sunshine, and time spent enjoying nature. It was a treatment conceived to combat a deteriorating situation between the two — a directive whose true origin lay deeper in the intricate folds of the cosmos than anyone could have fathomed. The doctors, in their crisp white coats, smugly seemed to think they were right when they warned of an impending catastrophic medical event. Turns out, they were. But at the time, there was no way for them to know how accurate their prediction had been.

Nevertheless, mandate in hand, and with no authority to object, Mallory initiated the trek from their modest home in the suburban heart of Temecula to the Duck Pond, a midtown landmark. Because it was centrally located, with ample parking, colorful waterfowl, and proximity to a major-chain drug store just in case, it fit the bill perfectly. The only wrinkle in their plan was the high school traffic — exacerbated by the regular flood of last-minute motorists. Caught in that bottleneck, with Mother stirring in the back, Mallory felt the temperature rising.

Ironically, Mother saw it differently. "It's freezing in here," she hissed. "I'm going to catch pneumonia." She wheezed pitifully for emphasis and tugged down on the corners of her taupe beanie. After a heavy pause, she continued, "I know you're trying to kill me."

"No, I'm not, Mother," Mallory said, with measured restraint. "The heater is on. But you know it's broken, so it doesn't work that well. It's blowing as hot as it can."

"You're blowing pretty hot," Mother challenged.

Eyes closed, Mallory sighed, "You're going to be fine, Mother."

"Well...," Mother nodded dismissively as she glared out the dirty window, "we'll see,...Doctor."

Unusually diminutive for a woman born and bred on the gritty fringes of the Ozark Mountains, Mother appeared sickly and feeble by any estimation. Standing all of four feet, ten inches tall, she might have weighed 85 pounds, soaking wet. Of her frailty, she had the doctors thoroughly convinced. But under her weakened and wrinkled exterior lurked an angry and stubborn Missouri mule. Mallory had dodged its petulance for years.

Treading a tightrope, Mallory's daily duty was to stave off the dark shadows of death and shepherd Mother safely to one more tomorrow, all while trying not to get kicked in the teeth in the process. For her part, Mother regularly claimed that without constant scrutiny, her delicate constitution would surely collapse, and the Grim Reaper would lustily rap his scythe upon her door. Because Mallory's disposition couldn't bear the guilt of sending her own flesh and blood into the great dark abyss through sloppy inattentiveness, she bought into the propaganda. Shortly after her brothers left the nest and while still in elementary school, she embraced the job as Mother's caretaker. She had maintained her vigilance at the post, day in and day out, for most of her 58 years. It was what it was — Mother became Mallory's purpose.

Of course, as is sometimes the case, the unbearable responsibilities brought Mallory no satisfaction, comfort, or salary. A perennial victim of obligation, she had long ago accepted that her role was to give selflessly, her only recompense, the knowledge of keeping her dear mother on this side of the mortal veil.

At the end of the day, all the hard work paid off. Mother had remained alive for 95 years — a surprisingly long time for the bag of bees she'd been her whole life. Certainly, far longer than anyone would have guessed, given the dire prognostications, mostly from Mother herself. But Mother's longevity didn't speak to the level of care she received from her youngest child. No, Mother's unprecedented endurance highlighted the singular pillar of her many less-than-desirable character traits. The secret to Mother's longevity was her professional-level, Grade-A, master proficiency in the subtle art of hypochondria, while at the same time remaining fit as a fiddle, strong as a horse, and mean as a badger in a burlap sack. Whether actually at death's door or not, Mother persisted. As did Mallory's sacrifice.

Meanwhile, somewhere in the lofty, well-lit office suites on the gleaming third floor of City Hall, a well-dressed person of lesser importance received a telephone call. That conversation was transcribed and forwarded to someone of equal fashion sense and greater importance, who rewrote and re-forwarded it to the sparkly secretary of the good-looking mayor, who filtered it to a social media intern. Its contents concerned the traffic jam in front of the high school. Soon, a glib post appeared on a lesser-known app that somehow caught the attention of a conscientious sheriff's deputy riding a well-polished department motorcycle. Out of an abundance of boredom, and because he had a few minutes to kill before shift change, he decided to swing by and take a look at the situation on his way back to the station. Equilibrium in motion.

* * *

Mother watched as a chubby boy passed the car wearing a tight purple t-shirt with the phrase "How do you want me now?" emblazoned in bright orange letters on the front. His hair unbrushed and his shorts rumpled, he looked like he had just rolled out from under a bush.

Mother pointed as he walked by, mouth agape, but appeared unable to form a verbal barb that could exceed the damage his wardrobe choices had already inflicted upon him. Seemingly mystified, she remained silent.

Mallory watched Mother's reaction in the rearview mirror, bracing for another round of toxicity. When it didn't come, she took a breath, and scratched her arms again. She didn't notice that she'd drawn blood.

Never lost for words for too long, Mother recovered. "Rueben would have never gotten us stuck," she quipped, gesturing loosely towards the traffic.

"Rueben's not here, Mother," Mallory replied.

"Well...." When Mother didn't have a direct attack calculated, she liked to use ellipses like warning shots — a quick three across the bow would express her general disagreement.

Rueben was Mallory's oldest brother, and in all fairness to him, he couldn't have been there. Despite Mother's continual prayers, he was seven years deceased, and not likely to return. That didn't stop her from inserting him into any circumstance for comparative purposes. Mother regularly expressed that Rueben had no equal. It was no secret — dead or alive — he was her favorite.

Both of Mallory's brothers had died heroically doing the things men do. As legend had it, first-born Rueben had gone down captaining the ship in a high-seas storm off the coast of Morocco, heroically attempting to save the crew of a capsized hospital tender. Younger brother, Weiland, had been shamelessly gunned down by surly goons after successfully leading the federal prosecution of a top-level Chicago crime boss.

Their histories were robust, no question, but not remotely accurate. Rather, they materialized as an amalgam of Mother's cable television consumption. The truth of the matter was that Rueben, a robust connoisseur of budget supermarket steaks, died on his couch of complications from gout. And Weiland, a life-long medical skeptic and hoarder, stepped on a nail in his junk-filled garage and eventually succumbed to tetanus.

The boys had been the fire in Mother's eyes every day they drew breath, and if her memory of their histories diverged from fact on a few technical details, it was of little consequence to anyone. By Mother's recollection, they were perfect, and in their absence, they achieved sainthood.

To her earlier assertion, however, it didn't matter a hill of beans if either of the brothers had been present, divine or not. Traffic was traffic, and there was, quite literally, no way around it. Besides, destiny was in the driver's seat. Both Mother and Mallory were being ferried to a weigh station where taxes and penalties would be assessed. There was a balance due to be reconciled.

"I'm getting nauseous," Mother declared. "Your driving is atrocious."

"We haven't moved in fifteen minutes," Mallory deadpanned.

Mother gagged.

"Okay," Mallory replied. "Just don't throw up. We're almost out of here." She looked around anxiously.

Just then, a valiant sheriff's deputy rolled up to the intersection on a shiny BMW motorcycle and immediately set about directing traffic. Cars began to jockey for position.

A man in a bright orange work truck broke loose from the congestion and sped by in the opposite direction. As he passed, he angrily flicked a cigarette butt out his window. It tumbled through the air and kissed the center of Mallory's windshield, leaving an ashy imprint of its spent body on the glass. In it,

Mallory recognized the outline of a dove.

Soon, cars lurched forward and began making their way across the intersection. Little by little, traffic cleared, and Mallory and Mother were on their way to their destination.

* * *

The morning air was brisk across the moist grass surrounding the Duck Pond. Despite being located in the middle of town, the park was strangely serene. Various waterfowl bobbed delicately across the water, traveling in small groups looking for bugs. Aside from occasional vehicles passing by outside the fenced property, there weren't a lot of people around.

The goal was to honor the doctors' orders, take in the sights and sounds of the park, enjoy a few minutes of fresh air, and get back to the house in time for Mother to binge on reruns of her favorite 1960s variety show on PBS.

Mallory rolled Mother across the lawn in her wheelchair to sit near the edge of the water next to the Japanese garden. A patch of sunlight there dried the dew on the grass and sparkled off the tiny waves in the water. It also kept the chill at bay — mostly.

"I'm frozen. Where's my other blanket?" Mother croaked. "You left it in the car on purpose."

"No, Mother," Mallory assured her. "I just forgot it. You'll be fine."

"I know what you're doing," Mother accused. "But I won't let you kill me."

"Not trying to, Mother."

"Uh-huh. Well …," The cold air had hindered Mother's insult quotient, so she opted for more ellipses. She would take any victory, large or small.

Mallory obediently trudged back to the Buick to retrieve the blanket. An honest mistake, she had set it aside while transferring Mother into her wheelchair. She found it in the back seat.

Turning it over in her hands, she marveled that the threads still held together after so many years. Stained and dirty, it smelled of muscle ointment and mildew. This same blanket had shielded Mother from deadly chills for decades, regardless of ambient temperature.

Alone, Mallory lingered at the car. She was seldom separated from Mother, and the opportunity left her with a few moments to herself. She sat down in the front seat and took a long, deep breath. The mid-morning sunshine felt warm where it peeked through the windshield and fell on her face. The sky was a fresh, robin's egg blue.

Feeling suddenly defiant, Mallory pulled out her phone and opened her music app. Scrolling, she picked her favorite artist, Christopher Cross, and selected his best track. The lush sound of strings filled the car, followed by the gentle arpeggio of an electric guitar. A familiar, relaxed tenor voice began singing about a mystical, nautical journey.

Mallory closed her eyes and gently swayed to the hypnotic rhythm. Magically, she found herself transported by the soothing sounds that enveloped her.

This, of course, was a transgression Mother would never tolerate. Rock-n-roll music? Debauchery of the devil. But, right now, Mother wasn't there to render judgment. So Mallory turned up the volume and indulged.

Eyes closed and deep in the embrace of the song's pulsating refrain, Mallory enthusiastically drummed along on the steering wheel, losing herself. The melody built, the song crescendoed, and before she knew it, a sound escaped Mallory's lips akin to the melancholy cry of a lonesome seagull.

A few spaces over, a man who had just arrived looked at Mallory and raised his eyebrows.

Humiliated, she immediately stopped the song and exited the car. A painful tingling was spreading down her limbs. Away from Mother long enough, it was time to get back.

Quickly crossing the parking lot, Mallory nervously scratched down the length of her arms and across the backs of her hands. The rash had spread and was becoming increasingly more irritated. Frantically rubbing the skin as it flaked off in large, snowflake-like particles, she was alarmed to notice blood on the backs of her knuckles.

Returning through the red wooden gates at the edge of the park, Mallory came upon a curious sight. During her brief absence, while Mother sat alone by the water's edge grumbling to herself, a small group of ducks, only three or four initially, had gathered.

Mallory hesitated just inside the gates. "They're probably expecting bread," she mumbled. "They clearly don't know who they're dealing with."

The birds meandered at first, grazing on the lawn and cautiously eyeballing Mother. They murmured as they moved, uttering strange sounds. From where Mallory stood, she swore they were saying, "Mama."

It soon became clear the ducks weren't interested in food. As Mallory watched, they became agitated, slowly circling Mother's wheelchair, shaking their tail feathers and clicking their bills. An additional pair sped across the water and joined their comrades. More appeared to follow.

Concerned by their strange behavior, Mallory rushed down the slope, calling out, "Hey! Go away. Shoo!"

But the birds didn't listen. Emboldened by their increasing numbers, they nipped at Mother's slippered feet and aggressively circled just out of her reach. In retaliation, Mother kicked as best she could and swung her fists about her calves, attempting to keep them at bay. But the flailing only drew more attention to her plight. Soon, birds from the far side of the pond hastily made their way across the water to join. By now, a group of more than three dozen — ducks, geese, gulls, coots, widgeons, and a large double-crested cormorant — had joined the fray, angrily pecking and pulling at Mother's toes. More were closing in.

For her part, Mother howled and swung wildly with her feet and arms. But the struggle quickly depleted her reserves, leaving her exhausted and defenseless.

Transpiring so quickly, Mallory didn't have a chance to react. By the time she made it across the slick grass to the pond's edge, Mother had been encircled by a teeming conglomeration of frenetic attackers screeching, nipping at, and harassing their prey.

"Help!" Mother wheezed from within the tumult, increasingly desperate. "Help your Mother!"

In shock, Mallory was frozen in place outside the melee, her eyes darting from one bird to another.

Meanwhile, the tiny, feathered beasts set upon Mother like a pack of rabid hyenas, their numbers now increased to four dozen or more. The largest aggressors landed in her lap, mercilessly tearing at her face and arms.

"They're killing me!" Mother squawked, hysterical. "Help me, useless child!" Droplets of blood appeared across her face and ran down her neck as the birds dug further in.

Above them, outside the restaurant that served breakfast to tourists, a small crowd of people had formed along the balcony overlooking the water.

"Please, someone help us!" Mallory pleaded to anyone within earshot, circling the fray. She was trying to keep her eyes on Mother as the number of attackers swelled.

But her efforts were futile. No help was coming. A few observers nonchalantly filmed the assault with their phones, while most stood idly by, watching curiously from a safe distance. A young boy at the edge of the crowd held a red baseball cap in his hands with the slogan *National Bird Day Is a Hoot!* embroidered on the front. Mesmerized, he ran his fingers over the stitching as the action unfolded.

With Mother now lost inside the swarming knot of flapping wings and clacking beaks, Mallory hopelessly engaged the attackers. But the birds weren't having it. For every one she kicked aside or dragged off, two took their place. The entire avian population of the park had coalesced into a singular angry mob, completely obscuring Mother. Mallory found herself chest deep in a swarming mass of demented, feathery demons. Deep within the throng, Mother had fallen silent.

"Mother!" Mallory screamed. "Mother! Can you hear me?" But the only sound was that of tearing fabric and scratching toenails, and the clack of beaks against the metal wheelchair frame. "For God's sake, somebody please help us!" she shrieked.

Summoning all her strength, Mallory surged into the center of the pack, pushing aside birds caked in mud and splatters of blood, deranged and delirious. But in her attempt to rescue Mother, she angered the mob, and it turned against her. Without warning, the pack's energy shifted, and Mallory's efforts turned from offensive to defensive as the birds began a new assault.

Nipping first at her kneecaps and thighs, then slicing at her midsection, they snapped and slashed with their sharp beaks. The smaller ones kept Mallory off-balance by clawing her face and eyes, while the larger ones with their longer reach, stabbed and ripped at Mallory's clothing, shredding off long pieces of fabric. Backpedaling, Mallory stumbled on a loose patch of soil and fell, engulfed in a feathery frenzy. The icy rush of the muddy ground chilled her exposed torso and soaked into her hair. Bird after bird, pecking and biting, maniacally tore into her, causing her skin to rip open and bleed.

Trampled and battered under the crush of attackers, Mallory lost her bearings as the birds slashed at her body. Piece by piece, they were rending her apart. Pain snaked through her skin like burning fuses as deep lacerations opened on her arms, torso, and legs. Searing flames licked at her core while strips of muscle and tendon were ripped from her bones.

Her corporeal state had begun to disintegrate, and in the place of what used to be, wet, sticky feathers emerged. A dark ache permeated her being as, from within every inch of her eviscerated body, foreign cells suddenly began to replicate. Scaly legs stretched from her abdomen and feathered limbs expanded from her torso, dripping with a muculent residue. Her fragile frame elongated and extended. The crazed assailants ravenously picked at the last remaining bits of her human flesh.

And as suddenly as it started, the attack ceased.

The birds calmed and quickly receded from her lithe, slender form, re-entering the water to cleanse themselves. From her prone position, she could see Mother's empty wheelchair and bloody blankets strewn across the wet grass. Mother herself was gone.

She slowly rose and extended her tender new limbs to either side. Stretched out, they shone majestically in the warm morning sun, revealing breathtakingly vibrant hues of blue, gray, white, and splashes of gold. She reached out as far as she could, and her individual feathers ruffled in the breeze, drying off and sending a tingle through her body. Oscillating gently forward and back, she could feel her wings as they channeled the breeze beneath her frame, making her buoyant and weightless.

Instinctively, she hopped gently off the ground and flapped. And as she did, her wings caught the air, and she rose. Continuing to pulse her new limbs gracefully, she traveled higher and farther, the harsh captivity of the city dropping away below her.

She curled her toes and brought her thin gray legs back against her elegant silver body, and catching the current, ascended towards the clouds. A dip and a turn, and she escaped, chasing up towards the sun.

Contributor Biographies

Jeff Waddleton

Jeff Waddleton has worked in broadcast radio as a comedy writer and on-air personality, been a commercial scriptwriter, hosted three different podcasts, published a collection of short stories and poems, worked as a story consultant and content editor for novelists and screenwriters, adapted classic works for radio and stage, and mentored numerous writers in their pursuit of creative genius. He is a writing instructor for the City of Temecula Community Services Department, teaching "Creative Writing for Adults," "Teen Screenwriting," the "Writers Critique Group," and the "Memoir Writers Workshop." He currently serves as the President of **Temecula Valley Writers and Illustrators**.

Kathryn Otoshi

Kathryn Otoshi is a multi-award-winning author/illustrator and speaker best known for her number/color book series, *Zero*, *One*, and *Two*. Her latest character-building books, *Lunch Every Day* and *Calling the Wind*, all relate to finding healing and hope during challenging times. She goes to schools across the country to encourage students to develop strong character assets, and helps educators find creative methods to engage their children through art, reading and the power of literature. "Birth of a Blue Heron" has special meaning for Kathryn, who is currently caregiving for her parents in Temecula.

WRITTEN TOGETHER

Story by Erin Kane Spock

Illustration by NamNya
Digital

Jennifer, November 2004

D EAR DIARY... DO PEOPLE actually write that?

My name is Jennifer Colton. I am a thirty-seven-year-old single mom. I am a graphic designer and have my own business. I live in Oceanside, California. What else? I'm a Virgo and my favorite food is pizza. I'm a divorcée. That word has so many stereotypes pinned to it that I just can't see it applying to me, but who knows?

So, I started this journal project with Olivia, and now I have to do it. I have NEVER been good at journaling (even though I told Olivia that I love it). I've started a few times and then stopped caring. I don't think I can let that happen this time. I think it's important that I make this something special we do together.

Olivia was not happy about going to see Brock this weekend for a fake Thanksgiving. I think she was scared about meeting Britney. I don't blame her. The woman is only twenty-two. Funny, now that I think about it, but that's how old I was when I met Brock and moved in with him. Well, I must have aged out some time ago (even though I still look damn good). Perhaps I'm too old for a man with the maturity of a twelve-year old. Dammit. This journal is not supposed to be about my problems; it's supposed to be about me and Olivia.

We've been driving north on the I-15 from Oceanside to San Bernardino once a month for the past six months now. Today I had to get off the freeway for gas in Temecula (the middle of nowhere). Olivia woke up when I stopped the car and started whining for McNuggets. Fine. The guy at the gas station told me there was a McDonalds across the freeway...but I turned the wrong way. Happy accidents! The little street was so cute. There were shops that were not chain stores. Antiques, a garden place, and a little diner that had a big sign about cinnamon rolls.

I parked on the street right in front of a sign that said Pennypickles Something-or-other. Olvia thought it was a pickle place and wanted to go there (only because I didn't). I decided we'd walk by and Olivia's eyes lit up. No food. No pickles. It was an interactive child's science museum. I have never seen her so happy. Nuggets forgotten.

Hey, I've written a lot so far! Maybe journaling doesn't suck.

Anyway, we stayed there for almost two hours before I got too hungry to continue. We did buy these journals (a brilliant move on my part...maybe) and decided we would both write in them about our visit, and promised we'd come back.

Those cinnamon rolls were awesome. Olivia didn't even complain.

It's nice that Brock wants to have some sort of Thanksgiving with his daughter. It's not like he'd be welcome at my family's celebration. He's been in charge of the turkey ever since we got together. I wonder who will do the turkey this year. I don't care. I don't even like turkey.

Olivia, November 2004

Mommy bought me this journal and says I have to write in it about this thing we did. She said she loves writing in journals as well. I've never had a diary before. I might like it. I don't know. My name is Olivia and I am 8 and I like My Little Pony and my favorite pony is Rainbow Dash although Pinky Pie is also great. I like soccer and my friends. I really, really want a phone. This is a cool book that we got at a science place. I thought we were going to McDonalds and I was mad cuz I wanted nuggets. Instead we went to this museum that was cool and then had a big sin men roll at a place with motorcycles. There were no pickles.

Now I'm at Daddy's house with that lady that wants me to call her Mamma Britney but I won't. She wants me to help her make pies.

I don't think I like writing in journals and this is dumb.

Mommy said we should write about science stuff from Pennypickles so I will. There was a really cool experiment with a magnet that made a cake float. It wasn't a real cake but Mommy said that wasn't the point. The lady there also put soap in the microwave and it got really big. It was about the air in the soap getting hot and getting bigger. I think I'll show Daddy about that. He might like it. Britney has lots of soaps.

Jennifer, January 2005

I brought Olivia north today for the January visit. We did stop at Pennypickles. What a crazy name. The story is that it's the laboratory and home of Professor Phineas T. Pennypickle and his mouse, Beaker. So cute.

I'm journaling right now because I promised Olivia I would. I see that last month I mentioned Thanksgiving. Olivia got two Thanksgivings this year — one with Brock and Britney and one with me and her grandparents, aunt, and cousins. Her Aunt Julie, my sister, went through a divorce three years ago and I never really paid attention to the details. She didn't really share. Turns out she dealt with some major depression when I thought she was just being whiney. I guess I'm an asshole.

Am I allowed to swear in my journal? I say yes. It's my journal. Does Olivia swear? She's only eight, so that probably won't start for a couple of years. Right now, "stupid" is a bad word and she corrects me when she hears me lapse. If she does start to swear, it will be Brock's fault. He did have some particularly foul favorite curse words.

We got to skip the Christmas visit last month because Brock and his child bride were taking a Caribbean cruise.

Let me repeat that: He. Skipped. Christmas. With. His. Daughter. Who does that?

He'll bring her home again on Sunday. He better not be late this time. She needs to actually sleep at night before school on Monday. He's an asshole. Yes, I'm definitely going to swear here. Call it therapy.

Olivia, January 2005

I think Mommy forgot about these journals until I asked her about it. She said she would do it tonight so that we'll be doing them together even though we're not together. I don't like it here. Nothing's wrong with Daddy's new house, but he keeps calling it home and saying it's my new home and it's not. Britney (I will not call her Mommy Britney. Gross) decorated my room and it's all pink and full of Angelina Ballerina and that stuff's for babies and I'm waaaaaay too old for that. When I get home, I'm going to see if Mommy will help me decorate my real room again.

The science museum was fun again. I saw new things. Mommy sat with me on the time travel chair and pretended we were really going back a long time and we imagined what the place looked like before the museum was built, then before cowboys, and before people. It was really cool. I like when Mommy plays imagination with me.

She seems sad whenever she has to drive me to Daddy's. I'm sad too, but I don't want her to know because she'll be sadder.

Jennifer, March 2005

Driving up to Temecula no longer feels like a chore. This week, Olivia showed me a picture she'd drawn of both of us in that time-travel chair. My baby girl is so creative. Honestly, I have nothing to do with all the amazing stories that she comes up with; I just let her tell them.

We pretend time-traveled again, but this time it was just to when the street running through Old Town Temecula was new. The woman who runs the museum told us both about the ranchos and the back-and-forth fight for land. Olivia got excited because we had become part of the history. We still drive through Temecula every month (except when Brock cancels — did I mention he canceled again? I need a stronger word than 'asshole' that I can say without feeling trashy). I was worried he would cancel this month too. She misses her Daddy even though he's a...dick? Dickwad? Bastard? I'll find something better. Anyway, if he'd canceled, I still planned to bring her up to Temecula. We have a standing date at Pennypickles. When we're there, Olivia doesn't seem angry. She chooses to hold my hand. It's a special place.

Olivia turns nine next month. She wants to have her birthday party here, but Britney wants to host her party. With whom? She had no friends in San Bernardino. She goes to school in Oceanside and all her friends are there.

Olivia, March, 2005

Mommy said I can have my birthday party at Pennypickles! The old lady there said they do birthday parties and Mommy said she'd check into it. Britney wants to have a party for me, but I said no. And Daddy said I hurt Britney's feelings, but I said it's my birthday and I'm almost nine. Plus Britney treats me like a baby and always wants to do my hair. Yuck.

I wonder when that road next to Pennypickles was built. I wonder if it was a dirt road or always hard. Did people ride their horses on it?

Jennifer, April 2005

Today I packed the van full of fourth grade girls and drove to Temecula. The drive has never seemed so long before. Olivia really likes this CD from Kidz Bop. Seriously, I would rather listen to the old Backyardigan's songs. That said, Olivia and her friends had a good time singing along...they were so, so loud.

But that is not the main part of this story. We had the party at Pennypickles...Brock and Britney came. Britney brought her mom. Her mom brought her large poodle. The important thing was that the girls had a good time. Britney wore bubblegum pink, five-inch platform stiletto heels. Britney's mom wore an identical pair. The dog, a male named Brewster that she hires out to stud, matched the color exactly. A bright-pink male poodle with some serious balls and a lion cut. The sweet boy was straight from someone's acid trip. The people in rustic, Old Town Temecula probably thought they were hallucinating when confronted by

Old Britney, Young Britney, and pink Brewster doing their best to strut along the roughhewn boards of the sidewalk. I don't wish any harm on anyone, but they had it coming. I don't know who fell first, but I looked back and there was a pile of pink and a cacophony of shrieking and barking. Poor Brewster.

Meeting Britney's mom explained so much about her. She was set up to be shallow. An ornament. Her job was to catch a man who could support her. And she did. But now what? What comes next for Britney now that the goal has been achieved? She isn't prepared to mother anyone. Looking at her mom is like seeing into the future. I wonder if she's scared.

Who knew I'd have empathy for Britney?

I decided to stay the night here in Temecula since Brock took Olivia home with him and another parent drove the girl bus south. I did a wine tasting, followed by a fantastic early dinner under a pergola covered in vines. Baked brie with honey and walnuts with the recommended white pairing. Amazing.

I wonder if Olivia will journal tonight.

I think I'll check out the room service menu for dessert.

Olivia, April 2005

It's my birthday! I'm 9 years old, which means I'm practically 10 already. 9 is so much older than 8 and that's why Daddy and Britney got me a phone. Mommy will be MAD!!! Britney says I don't have to tell her but that would be lying to Mommy. Mommy said she'll never lie to me, so I can't lie to her. Do you think she will take it away? She might. I hope not. It's not her business anyway. Mommy Britney gave it to me (Mommy hates it when I call Britney that so I do it sometimes when she's being mean).

My best friend Shelly gave me a cool make-up kit. I could tell Mommy didn't like that. She gave Shelly's mom the same smile she gives Britney. Britney said she'll help me do my makeup. That might be cool. I don't know.

I hope Mommy is writing in her journal too. I like my room here now, it's pretty even though it's pink. Pink isn't that bad. It matches Brewster.

Jennifer, June 2005

I just dropped Olivia off with Brock. I won't see her for two months. He's taking her for the summer and they're going on a camping vacation. He bought a huge RV — of course he did. They're going to drive all the way to Yellowstone Park. I wonder what Britney will think of camping.

We did stop at Pennypickles on the way to Brock's. We didn't stop the last time because Olivia was in a pissy mood, and I said she didn't deserve to stop. She is also mad at me because I left the parental controls on her phone. She says she's really going to miss her friends and I don't understand what it's like.

She wasn't the only one in a mood, and yes, I'm the jerk. I shouldn't let my impatience hurt our traditions. We should have stopped at Pennypickles.

Random thought: Olivia will get her period in the not-too-distant future. Imagine the mood swings in our home when we both are dealing with that? Damn.

I won't see her all summer. It's fine. I'm fine. I'll have a great summer and spend time doing adult things. Like...I don't know, sleeping on weekends, maybe? Watch a lot of cooking shows? I have no idea what I'll be doing. I work from home, but now my home will feel empty.

Jennifer, July 2005

Olivia is not home yet. It's been a month and I felt like I was doing something wrong by not journaling. The very act of doing this makes me feel more connected to Olivia.

She's called me a few times along the trip using her cell phone. I HATE that Brock got her a phone. She's too young. But it's nice that she's been able to call me whenever she wants. I haven't called her, but I do send texts pretty regularly. I want her to know I'm still here when she needs me.

In her last call she told me that she and Brock were camping, but Britney decided to stay in a hotel until they're ready to come back. I guess Britney was not a happy camper. She probably was upset that she couldn't wear fabulous heels in the wilderness.

I miss Olivia so much.

Olivia, August 2005

Dad and Britney broke up. I'm not gonna miss her because she was annoying, but I'm sorry that she was so sad. Dad acted like it didn't even matter. Is that how he felt when Mom told him to leave? I never thought about it before. I know she made the right choice because Dad going on dates with Britney was so rude. Did Dad get another girlfriend again? Maybe that's why Britney left?

Dad will take me home in a couple days and I am glad. I hope my friends miss me. Mommy said she'll take me back-to-school shopping.

Oh, I went camping with Daddy this summer. It was fun sometimes. I liked the RV and I saw some bison, but sometimes Daddy and Britney would fight and I could hear everything. I also think (sooooo gross) that they did it. You know, "it."

Jennifer, August 2006

Olivia is ten. Our journaling somehow tapered off after last summer. Brock started coming down to Oceanside to see Olvia...sometimes. He says he's very busy with his job. I think he's probably got a new girlfriend and doesn't want us to know. I don't really care either way, but I think Olivia will. She became attached to Britney. I know she's young, but she notices things and asks thoughtful questions. She started asking me about her dad, and why we got divorced. I told her I'd never lie to her, but there are some things she shouldn't know about her father. I don't want to villainize him. Well, I do, but that's not fair to her. I did tell her the basics about him falling out of love with me and falling in love with Britney. I think that was the nicest way to say it. She asked if I still loved him and that was a harder question. Thank God for therapy. I realize that I loved what we had and the memories of some of those times, but I didn't love him anymore. He's just a sad man and I am 100% sure he has a new girlfriend who is just as young as Britney.

Olivia and I plan to go to Temecula next month even if it's not on the way to Brock's.

Olivia, September 2006

Pennypickles has changed a little since we were here last. I found Beaker again today, but it wasn't as exciting as I remember. Maybe it's because I'm 10 and in 5th grade.

Mom and I walked around the old-fashioned looking street. There were some cowboys pretending to shoot each other. It was a little scary, but cool. There was also an outside shop for garden stuff and Mom and I picked out a cool big pot to put on our patio. She says I can choose whatever I want to plant there, but it's made for strawberries. I will totally plant strawberries.

We also looked at some really pretty houses. They're called model homes. There was this one that had a room that was decorated to look like the ocean. If I lived far away from the ocean, like at Dad's, I would want an ocean room. Mommy said we were just looking at decorations and not planning on buying a house, but I don't know. I think I might like a new house with just me and Mom. I think our house makes her sad. And it would be fun to get a brand-new room that I can decorate. And maybe I'd make some new friends. Shelly has been being mean to me. A lot of people have divorced parents. Mommy said that it's nothing to be embarrassed about. Just because Shelly's parents are still married doesn't make her any better. Shelly doesn't understand anything. I thought she was my friend, but she says stuff to make me feel bad on purpose. Mom said that's not how a friend should act.

If we moved to Temecula, we'd be close to the spaghetti restaurant and Pennypickles, so that would be cool. I wouldn't miss Shelly at all.

Jennifer, September 2006

Yes, we went to Pennypickles and Olivia had fun. We also saw a Wild West show and did some shopping. The big news is that I'm thinking of moving us to Temecula. Houses are so much cheaper there than in Oceanside and I want to downsize anyway. It's just Olivia and me in a five-bedroom house. Brock and I bought a big house because we were going to have more kids, but NOPE. I got the house in the divorce, so it's all mine and paid for. My agent quoted some ridiculous market values, so I can buy a new home and still have a lot left over. Still, it's just a thought. I don't want to worry Olivia. I know moving can be stressful.

Jennifer, April 2008

I see that I haven't written here for almost two years. Sorry, journal.

It's funny, but now that we live in Temecula, we don't go into Old Town Temecula nearly as much as when we were just passing through. We've lived here just over a year and I'm glad we bought when we did, before prices spiked. Olivia turns 12 this month and wants to have her party at Pennypickles again. This will be with a different group of friends. Unfortunately, the space apart didn't allow the forever friendships of a 12-year-old to thrive. While Olivia misses her old friends, I'm not sad to see the back of Shelly. That girl was just plain mean. I blame her parents. Anyway, the birthday plan is a science workshop at Pennypickles followed by a science themed tea party at home in our garden. This only works because it's April. Any later in the year and it would be too hot to do something outside.

Honestly, the only thing I miss about Oceanside is the climate. Temecula, in summer, is the temperature of the sun. Yes, that's a little hyperbolic, but not much.

The house was a new build, so it had no landscaping. Olivia and I got to decide on everything and both of us love it. It's something that brought us together as much as Pennypickles did. We planted an olive tree sapling and designed the yard around it. They say that the Temecula Valley mirrors Tuscany, so I went with a Mediterranean style. I love seeing how the edges are smoothing out and the design is becoming more organic as the garden matures. Oooh, that sounds like a metaphor for something.

That brings me to another point: I love writing. This science journaling project led me to journal more seriously, which led to blogging, which led to writing. I've started taking classes about creative writing from the City of Temecula.

Olivia, August 2012

Oh my gosh, I just found this journal! I haven't written in it for six years. I guess I suck. It was cute to see what I wrote back when I was little. I'd forgotten about the camping trip with Dad. And Britney! I haven't thought about her for a long time. Dad has had a couple girlfriends since then. He got married about a year ago to Ginnie Le. She's super cute and I love her aesthetic, but I feel like a giant next to her (she says she's 5' 1" but I think she's shorter). I'm fourteen now and starting high school in a few days. I'm also 5' 10". My dad says that's good because I can play volleyball, but sometimes I just feel...I don't know. Ginormous. I know I'm not, that it's fine. I'm fine. My dad is tall, so it makes sense that I would be too. My mom is average, so I guess it was a toss-up. Genetics are interesting.

I still have my ocean themed room. I do have new friends. Sometimes I wonder about Shelly. She was my best friend and I still get sad about what we said to each other. I wonder why? I hope she's...I don't know. I hope she knows how she made me feel. I hope she feels bad about it.

Anyway, I do play volleyball, but I'm also part of the marching band in high school (Go Pumas!). I played trumpet in middle school. My mom said the world needs more girls on trumpet, because usually the trumpet are boys and "cocky assholes." I could not believe she said that. She was drinking a glass of wine at the time though. And who says that I won't be a cocky asshole?

Mom's fine. Actually, she's really good. She still has her graphic design business online, but she also works part time at a winery. I think that she likes one of the guys there. He definitely likes her. I met him once there and he totally tried to be cool so I would like him. It was so extra. What if they dated? She should date...but then would they do it? How gross would that be?

Maybe if Mom dated, she'd leave me alone. She wants to know everything about my life and it's none of her business. I'm old enough to make my own decisions. She says she can't trust me because of the piercing. Everyone has a pierced nose now. It's not a big deal. She took away my phone for a month and that wasn't fair. It's my phone. She said she pays the bills, so it's her phone. Whatever. She can be such a bitch sometimes. Mom handed me a book and told me that I could read if I was bored. It's a really good book, but I'm not going to tell her that.

So, anyways, I already have my outfit picked out for the first day of school. I will roll up the shorts when I leave, and Mom will never find out. She has some strict rules, and my friends will make fun of me if I show up in old lady shorts. I've already been at the school a lot for Band camp. Band has been so much work, but it feels so awesome when everyone plays their part and it comes together. I love it. High school will be great.

Olivia, December 2015

I wrote here a few years ago and mentioned that Mom liked a guy. They're dating! His name is Fernando and he's way old. She's 49. He's 52. I guess that's no big deal when you're old, but 52! He also has kids and they're already grown up. He's even a grandpa.

I'm a senior in high school. I can't believe that I graduate in just a few months! I think I want to be a teacher. Science, maybe. I don't know. But I've done a lot of tutoring at the Boys and Girls

Club of Temecula and it feels like I'm doing something that matters. Sometimes I think it might be the closest thing those kids have to home. I don't know. But, yeah, teaching.

I just reread what I wrote about my mom being a bitch. That is still true sometimes. But I know that I can be one too, so our relationship takes a lot of forgiveness.

Jennifer, December 2015

Olivia told me she wrote in her Pennypickles journal the other day, so I thought I'd find mine. I started this eleven years ago when Olivia still held my hand and called me Mommy. I miss that. I don't miss all the back-and-forth custody crap. I haven't seen Brock in a couple years and that is fine with me. Olivia has driven herself the last few times. He's divorced again. Olivia says that he still thinks he's a young stud, but he's got to realize that young women only see him as an old pervert. I should stage an intervention to help him accept his age as a fact that fancy cars can't fix. He needs to own himself.

Speaking of owning myself...I stopped being such a coward and decided to finally go out with Fernando. We'd been sort of flirting for a couple years. He asked me out before, but I felt weird about dating while Olivia still lived at home. She's the one who pointed out that she's graduating. She's almost eighteen. Plus, he's raised children himself and is a new grandfather. His kids are pretty healthy, well-adjusted adults. I'm sure he made some parenting mistakes that a therapist could examine, but there are no red flags. I wonder what I've done that will put Olivia into therapy eventually. So far, she seems pretty amazing. I'm so lucky. I think things turned out the right way. I mean, imagine if I were still married to Brock. Think of all the life that wouldn't have happened. I wouldn't change anything.

Jennifer, June 2020

I haven't written here in almost five years. This will probably be my last entry in this journal. As it is, it barely fits. Since this was always a magical place to work out my thoughts, I figured I would try one more time. Fernando asked me to marry him. Marriage seems silly when you're my age (53). Besides, we've been living together for over a year, so there's no point really. Is there? I haven't told Olivia yet because I haven't given Fernando an answer yet. I think we should keep on as it is. But maybe it would be nice to make those promises.

Olivia, April 2024

Wow! I can't believe It's been 9 years since I last wrote in this journal. What has happened? Ummm....

1. I went to college and graduated and got my teaching credential. I teach middle school Life Science. It's great if you can get past the kids' fake (or unfortunately, real) apathy.

2. Mom married Fernando in 2020. They had a small, social-distancing wedding. Mom looked fabulous. I was her maid of honor. She did not make me wear a dress. I'm just not a dress person.

3. I'm seeing someone. We actually have known each other

since we were kids, but our lives went in different directions. Our first real date was at a farmer's market and we both bought journals. She suggested we write in it about the time we spend together. That was a major green flag.

Today is my 28th birthday and I spent it at Pennypickles with my two step-nieces (Fernando's grandkids). We all drew hearts on our hands with highlighters for the black-light. They loved it. Later tonight, my dad will be joining me and Shelly for dinner at Goat and Vine.

I don't know what else to write here. This hasn't been a science journal for a long time. It was a good way for me and my mom to be connected during a time when life was in a state of flux. I'm glad we did this. Having Pennypickles was special. It's still special. Temecula has become home, not just a stop along the way. My mom is happy. I am happy. That's all that matters.

Contributor Biographies

Erin Kane Spock

Erin Kane Spock writes Elizabethan era historical romance with a focus on a woman's agency to choose her own happiness. Her favorite thing about the romance genre is that it inspires hope and optimism. Erin and her husband have two college-age daughters and a large pitbull who thinks she's a lap dog. Erin recently received the rights back for her two traditionally published novels, *Courtly Pleasures* and *Courtly Scandals*, and has jumped into the world of independent publishing. Find out more about Erin's fun and funny, sweet and sexy historical romances on her website erinkanespock.com.

NamNya

It really just took doodling a smiley face at three years of age, to then illustrating fantasy creatures, anime characters and comics. When how-to-draw books from libraries or scholastics catalogs weren't enough, take every art class possible. Including Bigfoot. After attempting college, NamNya earned an Associate in Graphic Design. Then proceeded with some jobs that always involved art.

Despite adulting and always craving for something good to eat, NamNya would typically spend their off time reading comics and watching anime. Not much to say, they just want to live a quiet chill life to draw for fun.

Acknowledgments

(Yes, I'm copying this verbatim from Book 1, as they're being released simultaneously. Psst: buy Book 1, too! —Ed.)

We sometimes speak of a large, crazy project as a "labor of love." While the focus is, appropriately, on the passion that drives it, there should also be a spotlight on the amount of time and effort — the labor — that they require.

Many people have poured that time and effort into this book. Without them, it simply would not exist.

Stacia Deutsch and Felicia Horton, co-founders of **Temecula Valley Writers and Illustrators**: thank you for the vision in establishing this marvelous, new, non-profit haven for Southern California creatives.

Jeff Waddleton, whose boundless enthusiasm for stories and art permeates everything he does. His manic 2 a.m. texts starting with, "And what if we...," always lead to ever-bigger and amazing projects.

Tony "Bigfoot" Moramarco: his dedication to this Valley and delight in teaching art has added such a vast dimension to this book.

Our editing crew performed miracles. Enormous puddles of gratitude go out to Lori Carson, Veronika Childs, Stacia Deutsch,

Rebecca Farnbach, Jennifer Moramarco, Erin Spock, Kristen Tregar, Jeff Waddleton, and John Waddleton for their able assistance.

Shoutouts to the City of Temecula, Coffee Bean Tea & Leaf, Better Buzz, and The Batter Up Bakery for places to gather and brainstorm.

Thank you to the Roripaugh Family Foundation and to Big Giant Media, Inc.!

We are eternally grateful to Rebecca Farnbach, who made a substantial, designated gift towards funding this anthology.

I thank my lucky stars every day for my wife, Sacha Hope.

— Trond E. Hildahl, Editor

Thank you...

...for reading *Stay Awhile Longer: More Scenes from Temecula Valley.*

We sincerely hope you enjoyed the stunning artwork and astonishing stories! If you did, **please consider leaving a review on the site you purchased it from.** Reviews are the lifeblood of authors and illustrators; you might be surprised how much extra attention it garners for our contributors.

Speaking of those creatives, please follow them on their social media handles to see what they are up to next.

Thanks again!

Temecula Valley Writers and Illustrators

"Creativity in Community"

Stay Awhile Longer: More Scenes from Temecula Valley is the second volume from the **TVWI** imprint. Authors and illustrators paired up with a theme of "Stay Awhile," taking you from historic landmarks to the far future, centered in the beautiful Temecula Valley region of Southern California.

Anthologies are available at any e-tailer or may be ordered through your favorite brick-and-mortar location. Connect with us on social media **@tvwicreatives**.

Also Available from TVWI Publishing:

Where did it all begin? Seventeen stories and poems with stunning artwork grace *Stay Awhile: Scenes from Temecula Valley*, the first volume of this collection. There's magic, murder, love and redemption brewing in the Valley!

**Stay Awhile: Scenes from Temecula Valley
TVWI Book 1: Illustrated Short Stories**

Order online or visit **temeculavalleywi.com**